KENTUCKY
Keepers

Published by Barbour Publishing, Inc., P.O. Box 719, Uhrichsville, Ohio 44683, www.barbourbooks.com

Our mission is to publish and distribute inspirational products offering exceptional value and biblical encouragement to the masses.

 Member of the
Evangelical Christian
Publishers Association

Printed in the United States of America.
5 4 3 2 1

INTRODUCTION

Hook, Line, and Sinker by Lynn A. Coleman
Travis Wells's curiosity is piqued when Ruby Townsend hires him a second time to build an addition to her home. Ruby's bitter divorce had her keeping men at arm's length, but since her ex-husband's death, she feels free to investigate her feelings toward Travis. Will Travis allow his new faith to catch, and will he hook, line, and sink Ruby into his life forever?

Reeling Her In by Jennifer Johnson
Barbara Elliott enjoys a life of meticulous order as state barber inspector. Time frames and details are the least of laid-back barber and fisherman Kenneth Marsh's worries—that includes inspections at his shop. After several heated encounters, the two are paired together on a pretournament fishing trip at Canyon Lake. Ken finds himself falling for the Barbie-doll look-alike, but has he waited too long to reel in his greatest catch?

Lured by Love by Gail Sattler
When men start coming into Nicole Quinn's craft shop to buy materials to make fishing flies, she is totally unprepared. In desperation, she teams up with Vic Thompson to run a fly-tying course. Soon their hearts start to become as tied together as the intricate flies. But before they make a decision on permanently "tying the knot" that will join them together forever, can Nicole first tie her heart to God?

Idle Hours by Kathleen Y'Bar
Former editor Lia Stephanos h
her frazzled health. When L
mother's depression by openin
Joe Corbin's soon-to-be-vacan
place they want to spend their

KENTUCKY *Keepers*

FOUR FUN-FILLED FISHING TOURNAMENTS
LEAD TO ROMANTIC CATCHES

Lynn A. Coleman

Jennifer Johnson

Gail Sattler

Kathleen Y'Barbo

BARBOUR
PUBLISHING

Hook, Line, and Sinker

by Lynn A. Coleman

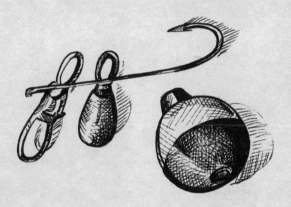

Dedication

I'd like to dedicate this book to my husband, Paul.
While he has a tough time catching fish
and even swinging a hammer well,
he's the strongest man of God I know.
I love you and appreciate your ministry so much.
God bless you, my beloved, my friend.

"Do not worry about what to say or how to say it.
At that time you will be given what to say,
for it will not be you speaking,
but the Spirit of your Father speaking through you."

MATTHEW 10:19–20

Chapter 1

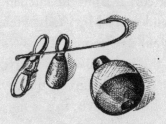

Ruby Townsend. When he heard her voice on his answering machine, Travis couldn't stop the grin that spread across his face. Especially when she said she wanted to talk to him about doing another construction project for her. There were a couple of perks that came with working on Ruby's house, and fishing off her dock was one of them. What could suit a man better than ending a hard day's work with an hour or two of fishing?

He grabbed his tackle box and pole, then hopped into his truck and headed over to the small house on Canyon Lake. Fifteen minutes later, he knocked on the cornflower blue front door that sported one of the nicest spring wreaths he'd ever seen. A smile creased his cheeks as Ruby stood there looking like a million bucks. Her short brown hair bounced when she moved, and her hazel eyes sparkled with life. "Hi! You left a message?"

Ruby smiled. "You could have called."

"Yeah, I suppose so, but with that lake behind you— well, you know I love working here."

"Come in. Bryce!" she hollered.

Husband? She's married? He glanced down at her left hand, third finger. No ring.

"Yeah, Mom." A young boy, perhaps eight, poked his head around the corner from the kitchen.

"Come in and meet Mr. Wells. He's the man who's going to build your new room."

Tentatively the boy walked in. "Bryce, this is Travis Wells." Ruby placed her hands on the boy's shoulders. He stood up to her chest. "Travis, this is my son, Bryce."

"Hello." Travis extended his hand.

Bryce reached out and gave him a wimpy handshake. Ruby bent down and spoke softly into Bryce's ear. "Go get your drawings."

"Okay." He ran off.

A son? I didn't even know she was married. Of course, we never talked about anything but business. It's odd she hadn't mentioned a son. And where was he last summer? And where's her husband? Or was there a husband?

As if in answer to the questions swirling through his mind, Ruby placed her hand on his forearm and whispered, "Bryce's father died about a year ago. I've been in a custody battle with his grandparents, and the courts have finally settled in my favor. He needs his own space. He needs to feel I want him." Her eyes pleaded for some understanding.

"Gotcha. What exactly do you have in mind for the renovations?"

"Sit down, Travis. Bryce is bringing his plans, and I'll add to them."

Travis let out a nervous chuckle.

"He's quite good."

Bryce returned. His hands shook as he placed his drawings in front of Travis. "Tell me what you have in mind, Bryce." Travis hoped that by allowing the boy to explain his plans he'd relax.

Ruby sat down on the chair opposite Travis, and Bryce knelt down beside the table. "Mom said I could design my own room. I know I don't have portions right, and some things might have to change because of supporting beams." Travis raised an eyebrow, and Bryce continued. "Mom said my drawing is pretty good. Mom told me about supporting beams and stuff like that. I'll redo the plans if you need me to."

"Perhaps you can help me draw up the real blueprints."

"Awesome. Mom, can I?"

"Sure. But let's finish showing Mr. Wells what we have so far."

"All right."

A constant stream of chatter describing the ultimate boy's room came at Travis. For the most part, everything was doable. Bryce didn't have unreal expectations, just a few costly ones. And Travis had to admit, the child had an eye for drawing.

"Now show him the room I want," Ruby encouraged her son.

It was hard to believe she'd ever been separated from him. How could grandparents fight a custody battle with the parent? The boy seemed perfectly content with his mother.

Bryce pointed out the simple design Ruby wanted for

the adjoining room. It appeared to be more of a study, and she wanted bookshelves covering two of the walls. *Who could have that many books?* Travis wondered.

"I'm picturing the addition adjacent to the north side of the house, but I'd like you to add a hallway or something so Bryce doesn't have to go through my room to get to his. What do you think?" Ruby asked.

"Sounds very doable." Travis took a moment to direct his thoughts back to the eight-year-old's artwork. "I can draw up the plans." Bryce looked down at his feet. The smile that had been there now turned into a frown. "Then I'll have Bryce go over them."

The blond head bobbed up, and the boy's face beamed.

Ruby's soft lips smiled. Travis looked back down at the boy's sketches. "Do you want a basement under these rooms?"

"I'm not sure. I certainly could use the additional space, but I'd hate to see it flood in the spring when the lake is full."

"Good point, although we could ensure against that—with some additional expense. What about an attic?"

Ruby placed her thumb on her chin and first finger on her nose. He'd seen this gesture before, a hundred times, while working for her last summer. "Can you match the exterior to the existing house?"

"Of course."

"Then an attic would be nice. Put the figures together, then get back with me."

Travis knew his cue and stood up. "I'll do that. Thanks for calling me back. Can I. . ." He pointed toward the lake.

Ruby chuckled. "Naturally."

Bryce bobbed his head back and forth between them like a trout trying to get off a hook.

"Fishing?" Travis offered.

The boy knitted his pale eyebrows.

"Perhaps Mr. Wells can show you how to fish," Ruby suggested. Bryce looked as if he couldn't care less.

For boys growing up on Canyon Lake, fishing was a rite of passage. No boy past three hadn't been out on the lake with a pole in his hand at least once. It was hard to believe Bryce had never been. The child must have grown up in the city. Ruby certainly wasn't from around here. "I'd be honored to teach him if he'd like to learn."

"No, thank you," Bryce mumbled.

"Suit yourself." He turned to Ruby. His palms dampened. She was a fine-looking woman. "I'll get right on this and call you when the plans are ready."

"God bless you, and thanks."

"You're welcome." Travis flopped his baseball cap back on his head and started back to his truck. *I can't believe the boy has no interest in fishing, and with such a wonderful fishing spot in his own backyard. What's the sense of that?*

Ruby called Bryce to dinner. They sat in silence until she got up the nerve to ask, "What do you think of Mr. Wells?"

"He's all right." He forked the mashed potatoes.

"I think he was rather impressed with your drawings."

Bryce brightened.

"You did a wonderful job on them."

"Thanks."

"Are you looking forward to visiting your grandparents this weekend?" As much as Ruby hated Bryce going to her former in-laws, she didn't want to take away their visitation rights, even though Bryce came home confused after every visit. She could only imagine the stories he was being told about her. Silently she prayed that Bryce would see the truth.

"Sort of. Mom, why did you divorce Dad?"

"I didn't." Ruby pressed the creases out of the napkin on her lap, then made eye contact with her son. "Bryce, you're old enough to know the truth. But remember, as much as your daddy had problems, he always loved you."

Bryce nodded.

Ruby went on to explain in the simplest terms what had happened between Gil and herself—how he fell out of love and into the arms of another woman. How he divorced her and married Dory. And, as tenderly as possible, she reminded him that Dory had killed his father. "Your daddy had a problem keeping his word. I loved your daddy very much. But I admit I drifted from him after you were born."

Tears fell down Bryce's cheeks. "Why'd she kill him, Mom?"

"I honestly don't know." Oh, she knew the rumors that Gil was having an affair. But rumors and fact weren't always the same thing. Gil and his family had money. Gil never learned to be responsible for his own actions. He'd lied to the court to get custody of Bryce—not because he loved the child more, but because he didn't want her to have Bryce. Gil's self-centered heart had more to do with their problems than anything she ever did or didn't do, but Bryce didn't need to know all those details. Gil was dead. Bryce still had contact with his grandparents. She wouldn't paint an uglier picture of the matter than she absolutely had to. And Gil's lies had made it hard to fight her former in-laws for custody. Thankfully they didn't know her other identity, or her career could have ended and she wouldn't have been able to support Bryce. Money was the least of her problems. Her books were selling well. Demands for R. J. Mack mysteries were high, and she had the next two novels already done.

"How'd school go today?" Ruby cut off a small piece of steak.

"All right." Bryce slumped in his chair.

"Make any friends?"

"Sort of."

"I know it's different than the private academy you went to before. . . ."

"It's an okay school, Mom. I know you can't afford to send me back."

How could she admit she could afford it but that she just didn't want him out of her presence? She'd fought too long and hard to have him with her. She wasn't about to let him out of her sight for nine months out of the year to attend an academy. "I'm glad you don't mind being here."

"It's all right, just different."

"Yeah." Ruby swallowed the lump in her throat and

hoped it wasn't a hunk of steak.

"At least I don't have to wear a tie every day." Bryce jumped out of his seat, grabbed his dirty dishes, and dumped them in the sink. "I'm going to my room, Mom."

"Okay. Do you want to watch a movie tonight?"

"Sure, whatever." She watched him drag his stockinged feet across the hardwood floors. He seemed so lost. Ruby's heart ached for her son. Had the academy taught him to be a loner? A brother would help. Of course, that would mean a husband, and by the time a new baby came on the scene, the children could be a decade or more apart. No, a new brother wasn't the answer. Not that she had any prospects in the husband department. Not that she even wanted to think about getting married again.

Suddenly an image of Travis flashed before her mind's eye. The memory of his handsome grin and wild, wavy hair made her smile. She shook her head and carried her own plate to the sink. Nope, she wouldn't entertain that thought. The man wasn't even a Christian; she felt fairly sure of that. Perhaps she could ask him what church he attended. She rinsed the dishes and placed them in the dishwasher, wiped her hands on a dish towel, and stared out at the lake. *Perhaps not,* she sighed.

Travis pulled into Joe's Bait and Tackle parking lot. He'd ordered some new flies for the fishing tournament coming up in a few months. He wanted to test them before the event to see if they were all they claimed to be. Generally he preferred to make his own flies. But every now and again, something new caught his fancy, as these had done in the latest fishing magazine. Not to mention, Joe passed his name on to many of the newcomers in town. *Spending time in the store is good for business, his and mine,* Travis reasoned.

"Hey, Joe, how's it going?"

"Not bad, not bad. How about for yourself? I heard you were fishing off Ruby Townsend's dock this afternoon."

A nervous chuckle passed through his lips. It wasn't like he didn't know about small-town gossip. But it still struck a man odd to hear what he'd been doing just an hour before. "Yup, she's asked me to bid on an addition."

"Is that so? Must be needing more room with her boy living here year-round with her."

The fact that Ruby had a child didn't seem to be news to anyone but himself. "I'm worried about that kid. He doesn't have any interest in fishing."

Joe slapped his jean-clad knee. "Now that's a real shame. Whatcha goin' to do about it?"

"Not much. Not my problem." Travis deflected Joe's gaze and looked over the jars of various baits. Truth of the matter was, he'd been hoping to get together with Ruby. For some reason, she fascinated him in a way no other woman had in a very long time. And there was something about Bryce. Travis had a desire to reach out to the boy.

He focused more intently on the array of jars full of strange-looking bait in neon and other funky colors. He pulled up a jar with neon red balls inside. The label read STEELHEAD EGG CLUSTERS. "This any good?"

"Never used 'em. The salesman said they were selling

well, so I bought some. You know city folk, and with the tournament coming, I figured I could sell most of them."

Travis placed the jar back on the shelf. "I'll stick with the flies."

"Tell ya what: I'll give you a jar, and you can tell me if they're worth anything."

Travis let out a chuckle. "Price is right. But I'd like to come home with a fish for supper. The label claims they have extra scent."

"Can't force ya to take it—just thought you'd be willing to try something new."

Joe had him there; he'd try anything once. "All right, I'll take the neon pink ones."

With his purchase of new thread and hooks and his free gift of neon bait, he headed out to his truck. Across the street, in front of the florist, Ruby strolled into the shop with a floral arrangement. *That's odd. Don't most folks take flowers out of the store, not bring them in? Unless she's unhappy with the arrangement,* he mused. He'd never been one to know one flower from another, let alone now how to arrange them. He didn't object to flowers, so long as they were on the side of the road or in other people's yards. His own yard—well, dandelions had their own unique appeal.

Admittedly the flowers paled in comparison to her. Travis coughed. He needed to do more fishing and get his mind off his newest client. On the other hand, the image of her in his mind might need to be worked out with hard labor. *There's a stack of wood that needs splitting,* Travis thought as he drove down the road to his home.

He could feel the tug of a smile lifting the right corner of his mouth. The woman was pleasant on the eyes. The next three months could prove quite enjoyable.

Chapter 2

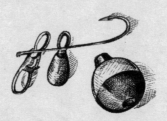

Ruby's gaze spanned the side yard. In the distance, one of the fingers of Canyon Lake reached into the horizon. Below her window, Travis manhandled a concrete block in each hand. His biceps bulged in all the right places. Ruby sighed. Her attraction to Travis grew every day, and it wasn't just his looks but how he went out of his way to speak to Bryce and include him in the building process.

A flash of red caught her attention. Standing in the shadow of the lilac bushes, Bryce was spying on Travis. Ruby leaned back in her office chair and watched. Getting the boy out of the house and away from his video games had proved to be a tough task. Travis seemed oblivious to her son's fascination, or did he? He brought a bucket of cement, or mud as he called it, over to the corner of the foundation where he'd previously set some blocks. He lifted the trowel and raised it slightly in the air, as if examining it. Ruby chuckled. Travis's exaggerated moves proved, once again, he was mindful of Bryce.

Easing out from behind a lilac bush, Bryce shuffled

his feet closer toward Travis.

"Wanna help?" Travis asked without turning around.

Bryce didn't answer but moved in for a closer view.

"It's not too difficult, but you need to keep everything level. If you don't, well, the Leaning Tower of Pisa might be straighter."

Bryce smiled but refused to say a word. *What happened to him?* Ruby wondered. *He's so fearful of meeting others.* She silently prayed Bryce hadn't been abused. The fact that his father was killed by his stepmother had to have taken a toll, as well as the long legal battle for custody. Her heart clenched in her chest.

Bryce inched closer to Travis over the next thirty minutes. Travis continued to build the foundation for the addition. Ruby knew she should be working, but at the moment she couldn't care less how the federal system worked regarding the blackmail of judges. Nor could she concentrate on the character development of the rookie FBI agent in the proposal she was developing. Unfortunately, with every attempt, the poor man looked like Travis. Not that Travis wasn't pleasing to the eyes, but she'd always been careful not to let her personal life and those close to her appear on the pages of her novels.

She supposed since she'd won custody of Bryce it no longer mattered, but she still didn't trust her ex-in-laws. On some strange level, they blamed her for Gil's death. She had no idea what kind of lies Gil told his parents and didn't even want to try to address them, unless the lies were problems between her and Bryce. She'd been so tempted to tell Bryce what she did for a living, but he hadn't asked. He just assumed she stayed home and played on her computer the way he played his video games. One day she'd have to tell him, but she wanted him to ask, show some interest in her, in something besides those silly video games.

"Here." Travis's voice brought her out of her musings. He was handing Bryce some sort of tool. "Roll it along here." Travis held Bryce's hand and showed him how to move the tool back and forth, then let Bryce do it by himself. "That's it, wonderful job," Travis encouraged.

The smile on Bryce's face equaled her own. *Dear Lord, thank You. Please help me with my attraction to Travis. I can't get involved with a man who doesn't know You.* Memories of Gil and their relationship were too real and too painful to disobey God's Word and get involved with a man who didn't believe. *Help me be cautious, Lord. Protect me from responding out of my attraction to him—not just the physical attraction, but his mannerisms, the way he does things, his integrity. I need Your help to hold my feelings in check.*

With a great deal of effort, Ruby refocused on her work. She reached for the research she'd been working on regarding the FBI's investigation in the allegations of Scientology's blackmail of judges. It was an old case but one worthy of examination for understanding both sides of an investigation.

Ruby closed the file and connected her computer to the Internet. Searching for blackmail cases took much longer than anticipated, even with a cable modem. After an hour, Ruby clicked off her computer and glanced out at Travis and Bryce. Bryce now had a trowel in his hand and was putting the cement on the top of one block as Travis instructed him through the process. Travis placed a level on top of the block and pointed to the various glass tubes. Bryce's eagerness and determination warmed her heart.

Travis needed to be rewarded for his kindness to her son. She ran to the kitchen and pulled another rib eye steak from the freezer. Living away from major towns, Ruby had learned to pack the freezer and overstock the cupboards. Once a month she made a day of traveling to the city and loading up on supplies. The grocery store in town offered a well-rounded selection for the towns-people's needs, but Ruby still needed that city connection once a month. To go into a place where no one knew her, to buy and select whatever she wanted and know that the local gossips wouldn't know what she was eating for dinner that night held genuine appeal.

"Cautious" could well be her middle name, instead of Jean. She'd even changed how people referred to her when she moved to Verde Point. She was no longer Ruby Jean, just Ruby.

Ruby exited through the back door off the kitchen and rounded the house to the construction area. She watched as Travis and Bryce continued working together.

"Travis?"

He dusted off his hands and walked over to her. "What's up?"

He smelled of cement dust and sweat. "I took a steak out of the freezer, and I'm wondering if you'd like to join us for dinner tonight." *What harm could there be in inviting him to dinner?*

His roguish grin revealed a man-sized dimple. "I'd love to. What time were you planning?"

"Five."

He rubbed the back of his neck with his handkerchief and sighed. "Five is fine."

She could tell it wasn't fine. He had other plans but weighed his options and decided on dinner with her. *Hmm, fine,* she thought to herself. "Great. I'll see you in an hour."

Unbelievable, Travis thought as he rounded the corner to the job site. He'd planned to fish tonight, but he wanted to get to know Ruby. Ever since she'd called three weeks ago, a day, an hour hadn't passed without him having a thought, question, or image of Ruby come to mind. *Face it, Wells, you're interested if you'd give up an hour of fishing just to spend time with a lady.*

"It's just business," he mumbled as he walked back to the foundation.

"What'd Mom want?" Bryce asked, eyeing the sight of the level and tapping the block just so to adjust it to level. The kid sure learned fast.

"She invited me to dinner tonight."

"Cool. We're cooking on the grill. Mom's making steak with potatoes au gratin and corn on the cob."

"Yum." Travis's belly grumbled. "Does she cook well?"

"She's all right. I don't like it when she makes those fancy lunches my grandparents loved. They're rich. They like to make food no one can pronounce. Mom thinks I like 'em, so I don't tell her. They're a lot of work. You have to. . ." Bryce rambled on as Travis's thoughts traveled.

If Bryce's grandparents were rich, that could explain how a woman who doesn't work pays her bills. The estimate for the addition had come in at a hundred thousand. He tried to keep the costs down, but the various items she wanted inevitably increased the cost. Granted, it would be quality and would last a lifetime with the proper care. He'd wondered how she could pay for it. Now he knew. He also wondered if she'd ever worked a day in her life. She never appeared to be snobbish about wealth. In fact, she'd been conservative in the first renovations he'd done on the place. What had changed?

On the other hand, the first job he'd done for her was to renovate the porch into an office, which included wiring and surge protectors for her computer equipment. She hid it well, and when he walked into the room, it appeared to be a sitting room. But he knew what equipment she had in there. Maybe she worked from home and had some online business or did online trading. Personally he still didn't trust the Internet, although he'd finally given in and opened an account on eBay to bid on some tools he wanted. He lost the bid. Someone outbid him several times before the bidding closed. Since then, he hadn't tried again. It was easier to go to the hardware store and order what he needed. You paid more in the end, he knew, but it was worth it.

"Mr. Travis?" Bryce called him back from his thoughts.

"Yes?" *What had the boy been saying? Ah, yes, his mother's cooking.*

"Why do you like fishing?"

He'd been fishing every night after the job and knew the boy had been watching him. "Wow, that's a tough question. I guess there's a thrill in just feeling that tug on the line and fighting to pull him in, but I also like the peace of sitting by the water."

"Is it hard?"

"No—takes some practice, but it's not hard."

"How come you throw them back?"

Travis chuckled. "Well, I live by myself, and I can't eat all the fish I catch. I release the ones I won't eat. I use a hook that doesn't have a barb on it."

The boy scrunched up his nose.

Pulling out his carpenter's pencil, he drew a hook on the cement block. "Most hooks have a barb, a small point that comes away from the hook to help catch it on the fish. It helps you not lose the fish. When I'm fishing the lake, and I'm just wanting to fish but not catch them for eating, I use a hook without the barb. It makes a clean hole on the fish's mouth, and the fish heals real quick."

"Oh."

"Would you like me to teach you how to fish?"

"Nah, I was just wondering."

He glanced at his watch. He had an hour before dinner. "I appreciate your help, but I'll need to get back to work and finish up this row so it can set up over the weekend. You're welcome to watch."

Bryce nodded.

Travis hated stopping the conversation. *But a man has to do what a man has to do.* And having a shadow would delay the work. It had been fine to encourage the boy ear-lier, but if Travis didn't keep his schedule, he'd fall behind on the job, then fall behind on the other jobs he was working around this one. He'd been thankful for Ruby's job. It would set him up for the lulls during the winter months.

Bryce sat on his haunches and continued to watch.

Travis finished off the row of concrete blocks, then cleaned up the job site. Sometime between washing the cement mixer and the bucket of tools, Bryce had left. Travis took off his shirt, hosed off his arms, then grabbed the clean T-shirt he kept in the cab of his truck. He'd picked up that trick after having to run into town covered with cement, paint, sawdust, or sweat all over him.

Don't need to get Ruby's house covered with cement. He tried to convince himself that was the only reason he'd taken the effort to "clean up" for dinner.

Travis climbed the front steps two at a time, then reached to knock on the front door. Bryce opened it before he made contact. "Mom says to come to the patio; we're eating on the deck tonight."

He found himself standing a little taller. He'd built that deck during the first renovations. "Sounds great."

"I'm cooking the steaks," Bryce offered.

He'd never met an eight-year-old who could cook. *Maybe I should have gone fishing.* They made their way through the small house and out to the deck. Ruby stood by the grill looking good enough to. . . Travis shook the thought away. She was a client, a good-paying client. He didn't want to jeopardize his business because of his growing attraction to Ruby. "Thanks for the invite." Travis placed his hands on Bryce's shoulders. "This boy learns quickly. Did you see him working on the foundation with me?" Neutral subjects were best.

A slow, developing smile rose on Ruby's lips. Slow enough that he wondered if he'd made a mistake encouraging the boy to work with him.

"Yes. He loves building things. Just like his grandpa." She turned her gaze to her son. "Ready to cook those steaks, Bugman?"

"Yup. Take a seat by the table, Mr. Wells. Mom and I will fix this up in no time."

Travis found a seat in the shade and sat down. Ruby was excellent with her son, the way she helped but gave him the impression he was doing more than he was.

"How do you like your steak, Mr. Wells?" Bryce asked.

"Rare to medium rare."

Bryce nodded. Ruby smiled. That smile could motivate a man to raise a roof in a day. Travis let out a slow, deep sigh.

A flash of metal swung over Bryce's head. Ruby let out the most horrific scream he'd ever heard.

Chapter 3

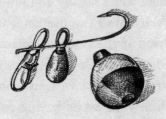

Ruby examined the tender, pink scar on her cheek. It had been a month since the accident. The doctor had said the sun would worsen the scar, so she'd been stuck inside for the better part of the month. Bryce still felt horrible, and Travis didn't feel much better. He'd reacted quickly, calling the paramedics who drove her to the county hospital. The spatula had cut through to the cheekbone and burned the skin around the wound. Bryce's fear of bees had caused him to swing wildly at an insect, not realizing how close she'd been.

Ruby glanced out the window. The shell of the addition and the roof were up. The doors and windows were in place. Most of the time Travis worked alone, although on occasion he'd hire some guys to help, like the day they put on the roof. Bryce sat side by side with Travis down on the dock and actually had a fishing pole in his hands. She placed the wide-brimmed hat over her head and headed down to the lake.

"How's the fishing?" she asked, trying to be nonchalant, and leaned against one of the pilings that held up the dock.

"Wonderful," Travis said.

"Okay," Bryce answered at the same time as Travis.

Okay was big stuff coming from her son. "Would you like me to purchase some fishing equipment for you?"

"Nah, Mr. Wells says I can use his."

Ruby wondered if there was a video game for fishing, then immediately shook off the thought, reminding herself she was trying to get him away from the computer. "You two have fun. Will we be having fish tonight?" she asked.

"Nope, throwing them all back tonight. But I'm noting their size. The annual fishing tournament is coming up, and I'm trying to decide which hole will produce a winning fish this year."

"You do this every year?" Ruby knew the man loved to fish, but she didn't realize he took the annual Canyon Lake Fishing Tournament so seriously. Then again, there wasn't much for entertainment or social activity in this community, and fishing was big business and definitely a boon for the town.

"You betcha. I've won a couple of times." He winked.

Ruby chuckled. "All right then, how about steaks on the grill?"

Travis's and Bryce's countenances fell a notch.

"Bryce, you have to forgive yourself; it's time. Besides, I like how you cook the steaks on the grill." Ruby folded her arms across her chest for emphasis.

"Sounds like a plan, buddy. Your mom's right; the best thing for a man to do is to get back on his feet and pull himself up out of the lake if he falls in."

Bryce nibbled his lower lip. "All right, Mom. I'll be careful."

"I know you will, Bugman." She turned to Travis and asked, "Would you like to join us?"

"Thank ya, ma'am. I'd be honored." Travis grinned.

Ma'am. When did he start calling me ma'am? I'm not that much older than Travis, am I? she wondered. Ruby wagged her head and walked back up to the house. *Just how old does he think I am?*

Inside the house, she took a closer look at her hair. Had the gray moved in overnight? At thirty-two, she still had a few good years left. Seeing no offending hairs, she had to wonder if he used "ma'am" as a way of teaching Bryce how to respect his elders. She'd heard more than one parent correct their children if they failed to use that term of respect.

For the past seven weeks, she'd had too many fancy ideas flying in her head about Travis and a possible life with him. Unfortunately she still didn't know if he believed in the Lord, and she'd been too afraid to ask. Tonight she would ask. No sense keeping hope alive if there were none. And if he didn't have a relationship with Jesus, she should be sharing the gospel with him.

"Wonderful job, Bryce." Bryce smiled at Travis's praise.

Ruby patted him on the back. "Thank you. I know how hard it was for you to cook tonight."

"It's all right, Mom. Me and Mr. Wells—"

"Mr. Wells and I," she corrected.

"Mr. Wells and I were talking down at the lake."

Ruby wanted to know what Mr. Wells had said down at the lake. Whatever it was, Bryce had done well and stood with confidence at the grill.

"Mom, are you going to get married again?"

Ruby could feel the heat rise on her face. "If the Lord provides the right man."

"Mom." Bryce stood up and put his hands on his hips. "Even God expects us to do some things."

"True, but a spouse has to be just the right one for you."

For a moment, confusion fell over his face. Then he slowly lifted his head and nodded. "You mean, like Dad and Dory."

"Right," she sighed.

Bryce took his dishes into the kitchen and didn't return.

"What was that all about?" she drilled Travis.

He raised his hands in surrender. "It wasn't me. Sorry. What was that about his father and Dory?"

"It's a long story, but suffice it to say, my ex divorced me to marry the girl he was having an affair with. About a year and a half into their marriage, they had a terrible argument and Dory killed Gil."

"Ouch. So that's what has the kid so timid."

"That, and the fact that he's been apart from his parents for three years. He's been living at an academy. But don't get me started."

Travis nodded.

"What about you?"

"Never married; never found the right one."

"Oh." Ruby held off asking if he was saved, afraid he might think she had put Bryce up to asking the question. "What are you looking for in a spouse?"

"Tough question. I'm not sure, but a good sense of humor. . .and I'm not expecting God to find her for me."

Ouch. It had been as she suspected; he didn't believe in the Lord.

"Don't get me wrong. Christianity is great for those who need it, but I haven't found a need for it."

"I suppose you could think that Christianity is a crutch for some, but a relationship with God is more than that. On the other hand, I don't know how I would have survived the past three years without being close to God."

"Like I said, I ain't against it—it's just not for me. I went to church when I was a kid, know all the Bible stories, but—" he paused "—as I got older it just didn't matter. I suppose it was fun going to church when I was a kid, but you outgrow that stuff when you become a man."

Ruby wanted to ask what "becoming a man" was to Travis but thought she'd better let that drop. "I'm not one to force another, but if you're ever curious by what I mean by a relationship with God, feel free to ask."

"Thanks, I might just do that." He stood and picked up his empty plate. He headed toward the back door and the kitchen, then turned back to her. "I suppose you wouldn't be interested in going out sometime with a sinner?"

"As a friend, I wouldn't have a problem. If you're thinking of something more, then no, not at this time."

Travis knew he shouldn't have asked the question. He'd been around enough to know that people who were serious about their Christian faith avoided being "unequally yoked." The problem came in that he couldn't stop thinking about Ruby. He stopped by Joe's on his way home.

"Evening, Joe."

"How's it going at Ruby Townsend's?"

"Fine. I'm about to start finishing the interior." Travis placed his purchases on the counter and glanced over at the beginner reels and rods. *Bryce could use a rod and reel,* he mused. Then he thought better of it. No sense developing the relationship when it couldn't go any further.

"Anything else?"

"Nope, thanks."

Joe slowly rang up the order, one item at a time. Just like fishing, Joe took his time. "You know, I've been meaning to ask you a question."

"What's that?" Travis discarded the paper and plastic wrappers that covered his new tackle.

"You know the tournament is coming up."

"Sure do. Wouldn't miss it."

"Three o five."

Travis reached for his wallet and pulled out the exact change.

Joe shuffled his feet, then fixed his gaze on Travis. "Would ya mind givin' me a hand this year?"

Joe had been running the tournament for as long as Travis could remember. "How can I help?"

Joe reached down below the counter. "All these need to be mailed. It's all printed, but writing out six hundred addresses takes a lot out of a man." Travis nodded. *Where's the exit? Time for a hasty retreat.*

"I know you have a computer, and, well, I was wondering if you. . ."

Travis nodded once again.

"Wonderful, thanks."

Travis stifled a groan. He'd shaken his head in agreement without really wanting to say yes. *There goes a few hours of fishing at least.*

"Ruby has a computer," he blurted out.

"Think she'd give ya a hand?"

It was a given—he'd just volunteered to help. "I can ask."

"Wonderful. And since you all are getting Ruby to help, would ya mind handlin' the registrations as they come in? I'm just thinkin' it all being on a computer would be a time-saver."

For you. "You're right, it would be." Travis debated with himself about whether he should call Ruby and have that talk she offered. They obviously couldn't have a relationship unless he changed his mind about God. "Hey, Joe, what do you think about God?"

"He ain't bothered with me, so I ain't bothered with Him. Well, maybe once, when my sister passed. Why'd ya ask?"

"No reason. Just curious."

Joe chuckled. "I wasn't born yesterday. I know Ms. Ruby is a churchgoer. Ya thinkin' of going to catch a female fish and start a school of your own?"

"You're an old man, Joe. Give a guy a break."

Joe chuckled and waved him off. "Thank ya for the help. I'm beholdin'."

You have no idea. Travis went out to his truck. He flipped open his cell phone and dialed Ruby's number.

"Hello?"

"Ruby, I need your help. I just stepped into the swamp, and I'm sinkin' fast."

"What are you talking about?"

"Answer me one question first." He eased his truck out on the main road and headed toward Ruby's.

"All right," she said in a hesitant voice.

"How fast can you type?"

Ruby rubbed the back of her neck. The hands on the old grandfather clock were perilously close to both hitting the top center, number twelve. "I think we should call it a night."

Travis yawned and glanced at his wrist. "You're right. Thanks for all your help. I never would have gotten this much done in three days, let alone three hours. You are fast."

"I'll remember not to admit that again to anyone who asks. I still can't believe Joe's been writing these by hand every year."

Not only had they been typing in a database to print off labels, but they had also been redesigning the previous year's flyer. Ruby had found several misspelled words and had corrected the sentence structure. Now they were ready to print the flyer on her laser printer. Thankfully she had purchased some colored paper for a fan mailing of her own she'd been hoping to get out in the next couple of weeks. Ordering new paper wouldn't be a problem.

"These look 100 percent better. I suppose some folks might be wondering if something happened to Joe. Especially when they see me handling the registration. I'm glad you have two computers."

"Three, but the older one I gave to Bryce."

"What do you do with all this equipment?" he asked.

Ruby placed her hands over her face and yawned. She hadn't intended to be so obvious, but once it began, she couldn't contain it.

"I'm sorry," Travis apologized. "We can socialize some other time. I've taken too much of your time tonight."

Ruby went to the laptop Travis had been working on and inserted her USB memory drive to transfer his work to hers. "Give me a minute to blend the two databases."

He watched with fascination. Then his eye caught her newest novel on the pile of today's mail. Ruby stiffened.

"Hey, you like R. J. Mack? He's my favorite." He pulled the advance copy the publisher had sent her. "Don't recall this title. I thought I'd read all of his work."

"I'll let you borrow it after I'm done." He didn't need to know she'd already read it a half dozen times, not to mention written it.

"Thanks, but I'll order one. I like having my own copies."

"It won't be out for a couple of months. That's an un-edited proof copy."

"So, you review books?"

"Sometimes," she admitted. Of course, the reviews were now endorsements of other authors' works.

He laid the copy back down on the pile. "Do you enjoy R. J. Mack's novels?"

"Yes," she confessed, needing to change the subject before admitting the full truth. At this time, she still wasn't ready to surface. She'd grown fond of her privacy. She and Lia, her editor, had been discussing this very issue when she'd come down from New York last weekend. The custody trials were over, but Ruby didn't trust her ex-in-laws; they had plenty of time and money to burn to try to reopen the case. Her lawyer had warned her that the material she had in her house on perfect crimes, poisons, and other methods of study regarding serial killers would not go well for her in court. Even if she proved she was R. J. Mack the mystery writer, they would question her parenting environment with those kinds of materials in the house for a young boy to see. It wouldn't matter that they were kept in her bookshelves that closed in the front.

Ruby sighed. She definitely would have to deal with this soon.

"Cool. Well, I won't keep you up any longer. Thanks again for the help. And thanks for letting me come into your home."

"You're always welcome, Travis." Her heart ached. She continually fought off her interest and desires to get to know him, but little by little he was becoming a large part of her day, until she couldn't imagine life without him.

She escorted him to the front door. " 'Night."

"Good night, Ruby. Thanks." He moved swiftly and brushed her cheek with a featherlight kiss. Ruby felt the warmth from the tip of her toes to the top of her head.

She stepped back inside and silently closed the door. She watched until he opened the door of his truck; then she switched off the front-porch light. "Lord, get that man saved." After she worked her way through the house, shutting off lights, and was in the sanctuary of her own room, she fell on her knees and prayed for God's grace, strength, and peace concerning Mr. Travis Wells.

The old country song of the devil wearing blue jeans swam through her mind. Travis was temptation with a capital *T*.

Chapter 4

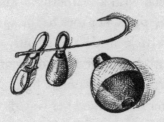

Travis raced to Ruby's house. He'd overslept and was afraid he'd be late for a meeting with the building inspector to have the plumbling and electrical approved so that he could move on to the next phase and close in the walls.

Bill Turner stood on the front porch with Ruby. The lilt of her laughter tickled Travis's ears. *Man, do I enjoy that sound.* Bill's laughter joined Ruby's, and a surge of jealousy and a need to protect her welled up inside Travis.

"Overslept?" Bill asked.

"Afraid so. Come on, the addition is over here."

"Just a minute." Bill turned his attention back to Ruby. "So, will you come?"

"Yes, I'd like that." Ruby glanced in Travis's direction. Travis felt his blood pressure rise. *She wouldn't go out with me, but she'll go out with Bill? Humph.*

"Great, don't forget to bring your Black Forest cake. I love that."

"All right, talk with you later, Bill. Good morning, Travis."

"Good morning." He'd forgotten to say hello to Ruby when he drove up. They weren't even dating, and yet he a felt protectiveness for her. This was crazy. Then it dawned on him. Bill was single; maybe they were dating. He hadn't thought of that when he asked Ruby out. They'd never talked about each other's personal lives. He'd never seen anyone coming or going, but then again he left the job in the evening if he wasn't fishing off her dock.

Bill placed a hand on Travis's shoulder. "I trust you're doing right by Ruby on this job."

"Of course I am. You know me. I don't cheat the customer."

"I know, and I suppose I shouldn't have said anything, but Ruby is a special friend."

"How do you know her?"

"We attend the same church."

Travis's heart sank deep in his gut. "You go to church?" He hadn't meant to speak, but the words blurted out before he could stop them.

"Have been for a year. After the wife left, I started drinking kinda heavily and, well, I wasn't doing so good. Then my brother challenged me to try God instead of booze. I've been going ever since."

Bill did look healthier than he had in years. Travis wanted to ask if he and Ruby were dating but didn't feel he had the right.

"So, whatcha got for me today?" Bill asked. They made simple work of going over the various points of interest to the inspector. "The woman likes to have a lot of power."

"For her electronics. She's got a fancy computer system up there."

"Ah, that's the reason for the extra surge protection. Nice thought."

"Thanks."

"Everything appears to be in order." Bill scribbled on the clipboard, then tore off a carbon of the form he'd filled out.

Travis reached for the proffered form. "Thanks. Sorry I was late."

"No problem. Ruby told me what the two of you were up to last night. Glad to hear you're helping Joe out."

"Are you registering?"

"Does a fish have gills?"

Travis chuckled.

"Send me a couple of those flyers, and I'll post them up at the county buildings."

"Excellent. I appreciate it."

"Hey, brings in some revenue, not to mention a lot of fun." Bill wrote a brief note to himself on the remaining papers on the clipboard. "Well, you're good to go. Gotta run." He took a few paces toward the exit, then turned back and said, "You know, you might wanna check out God, too. What can it hurt?"

Travis let out a nervous chuckle. "I'll consider it."

"No problem. As for me, I'm not too crazy about the heat if I don't get right with God."

Travis shook his head. "You actually believe in a real place called hell?"

"Yup, see it as God's grace; just imagine how it would be to be sitting in His presence day and night for year after year when you can't stand or even hate God."

"I don't hate God. I'm just not inclined to believe I need Him."

"I see—so, your life's pretty perfect right now."

"Yup. Work's going well. I fish whenever I want. Not much else a man needs."

"Travis, I've been there. Thought all of my life was in control; then Beth left me, and my whole world collapsed. It took me awhile to see that Beth left me because I left her first. I was so wrapped up in my wants, my needs, my desires I hardly gave her the time of day. I can't blame her for seeking out what I didn't give her as a husband. I know you aren't married, and as far as I know, there's no one special in your life. But the world is a pretty boring place when all you think about is yourself. Just give it some thought and think about why God created those fish you love to catch so much."

Travis nodded. He didn't want to be rude to the man. After all, he never said he hated God. He lifted the inspection form. "Thanks."

"You're welcome. Have a nice day."

Travis leaned against a four-by-four support beam and kicked an eightpenny nail toward the swept-up pile of debris. *Right, I've been told I'm going to hell, and he wants me to have a nice day.*

Ruby had seen little of Travis since the night they set up the database for the fishing tournament. He'd been there to work, but he hadn't come in to socialize. He didn't even stay to fish off her dock at night. She couldn't help wondering if her refusal to go out with him had created this huge gap in their relationship.

Bryce was away for the weekend with his grandparents. The old fears and doubts resurfaced. She had found it extremely hard to let Bryce visit them. And she still had the lingering doubt of whether or not the ex-in-laws would return her son.

The social was at Bill's tonight, and she didn't want to go. She peeked out the front window, and Travis's truck sat in her driveway.

She hurried out of the house and rounded the building, entering the addition from the gray steel door Travis had installed. "Travis, are you in here?"

"In Bryce's room. What can I do for you?" He walked toward her with his tool belt slung around his hips.

Ruby closed her eyes. She shouldn't be so attracted to this man, she cautioned herself. "I was wondering if you'd like to go to Bill's party with me."

"As in a date?" Travis grinned.

"No, as in a friend going with another friend."

Travis closed the gap between them. "Ruby, I like you. I like you a lot. I don't want to be just friends."

Ruby took in a deep breath and let it out slowly. "Travis, we need to talk."

"The God thing?"

"That, and other stuff."

"Okay, shoot." Travis crossed his arms and leaned back against the studs.

"The God thing, as you put it, is important to me. But beyond that, I've lived life with a man who didn't believe as I did, and it's not easy. There were many days that were horrible. I'm not saying we didn't have good times and some fun, but we never connected on a real deep level. Perhaps that's why he had affairs. I really don't know and try not to think about that. But I know a relationship where two people don't see eye to eye on some of their basic beliefs is doomed for trouble."

He relaxed and let his arms fall to his side. "I'm sorry you were hurt, but I'm not that man."

"No, you're not, but—"

"Ruby, I would never step out on the woman I loved."

God, help me. I . . . "Travis, I would like to be friends with you. If you can't just be friends, I understand."

After a long pause, Travis stood up and placed his hands on her shoulders. He closed his eyes and leaned his forehead down. Ruby feared he would try to kiss her. He opened his deep chocolate brown eyes. "I want your friendship. I'd love to go with you to Bill's. You two aren't. . . ?"

"Bill and me? No, never."

Travis smiled and nodded. "Are you upset about Bryce visiting his grandparents?"

"Yes, and I didn't want to be alone, even at Bill's tonight."

"Is this a church thing?" Travis asked, releasing her and taking a step back.

"I suppose it is in one sense. We meet regularly for Bible study, but tonight is just a social. Can I ask you something?"

"Sure."

"Did anything ever happen to cause you to have problems with God and church?"

"Nah. Just wasn't a big deal in our house. I mean, we went to Sunday school on occasion when we were kids, but it just didn't seem necessary. Can I ask you something?"

"Tit for tat, huh? Go ahead. What do you want to know?"

"What do you do for income? I mean, you don't go to work. Your ex-in-laws seem wealthy. Are you just rich or something?"

Ruby laughed. "I'm not rich. Well, maybe by some people's standards, but I'm a writer. I work from the house, no need to go in the office to write. I e-mail most of my manuscripts in."

"A writer—interesting. Have I read any of your work?"

More than you know. "More than likely. I started out writing magazine articles. But now I— Travis, I use a pen name because of the custody battle with my ex-in-laws and the possible lawsuits. So, forgive me if I don't tell you who I am. Soon, I hope to be able to reveal it, but not yet." She'd almost confessed she was his favorite author, R. J. Mack. She didn't like keeping secrets, but her lawyers still encouraged caution. "Long before anything happened to my ex, I wrote a story that was almost played out in my life. The lawyers feel my ex-in-laws could try to sue me over that. They wouldn't win because it's all documented, but they have enough money to keep me in court for years. Once they've adjusted to their loss in the court case and see that I'm not going to keep them from seeing their grandson, I plan to reveal who I am."

"Wow. How do you deal with the stress? You don't fish."

Ruby let out a nervous chuckle. "I don't always do well. But mostly I pray and the Lord brings me through."

"Fishing helps."

"I'm sure it does. Just never had an interest."

Travis wiggled his eyebrows. "I'll tell you what—you try fishing, and I'll try your God stuff."

Ruby shook her head in disbelief. "You're impossible."

"But wildly handsome and appealing." He flashed a smile that could knock her off her feet if she wasn't careful.

"Deal." She reached out her hand and offered to shake on it.

He took her hand and gave it a hearty shake. "Deal. Do we have time to fish before we need to be at Bill's?"

"I don't want to smell like fish."

Travis let out a rumble of laughter that came from deep down. "You won't. You never could. You always smell wonderful."

I can't believe I agreed to go to church. No, offered to go to church, just to spend more time with a woman. Ruby wasn't like any other woman he'd known. And he'd known his share. And it wasn't like he hadn't been considering Bill's statement for the past week. A man could do worse than to go to church. What could it hurt? "Sunday-morning fishing," he grumbled to himself as he hoisted his toolbox into the back end of the truck.

Ruby's hazel green eyes lit with desire, he could see it. He could feel it coming from her. She liked him, but the boundaries were clear. The only question was, was he man enough to respect them and not go over those lines? It would take a tremendous amount of willpower. He saw the fear in her expressive eyes when they spoke about Bryce going to his grandparents. The more Travis heard about these people, the more he wondered about the wisdom of Ruby sending Bryce off for a visit.

"God, if You're up there, You best reveal Yourself to me, cause Ruby deserves to have a man who is her equal, not an old carpenter who could tear her down. I reckon a man shouldn't come to You for the sake of a woman, but I don't have any other reason at the moment. I suppose Bill's right in saying I've been living for myself, but who else is there? I still don't see the logic in what he was saying. I'll give You this: You did a mighty fine job in creating this place." Travis prayed for the first time in his life. Oh sure, he prayed over some meals, had said amen once or twice on the rare occasions when he did attend church as a child, and mumbled along when they said the Lord's Prayer, but never had he just talked to God. Or like Ruby said, had a relationship with God. Was that even possible?

"Travis," Ruby called, "the sky looks threatening. Are we still going fishing?"

He glanced up at the horizon. The wind blew in from the northwest. He scanned that direction. "I think we have enough time to get an hour in."

"Okay, I'll be ready in ten."

The question was, would he? With his tools safely put away, he reached for his fishing pole and his old one that he'd been letting Bryce use. He'd planned on giving it to the boy, but at present, Bryce didn't show too much interest in the sport. Travis felt he enjoyed the companionship more than the actual fishing, although he did finally get the boy to put a worm on his hook.

He dusted off his jeans and headed down to the dock. Five minutes later, he watched Ruby, dressed in a gunny-sack, or some other ugly contraption, walking toward him. "What are you dressed for?"

"Fishing." She stopped. "Why, what's wrong?"

Upon closer inspection he found her to be wearing an old army poncho. "Expecting a monsoon?"

"Hey, I never commented about those T-shirts."

"What's wrong with my T-shirts?"

Ruby's face flushed. Travis looked at his torso. His well-defined abs and pecs looked pretty good, if he did say so himself. "I don't get it."

Ruby chuckled. "Maybe I'll tell you one day."

"Whatever. Come on. Time is a-wasting."

"So what are we fishing for?"

"Large mouth bass."

"Do they bite?" Ruby asked.

"No. You've never been fishing?"

"Deep-sea fishing off the coast of Key West. But I was on a boat, and the deckhands took care of baiting the hook; we just sat there and watched our poles until they bent over. It was fun. I wrestled in a twenty-pound dolphin. The fish, not the porpoise," she amended.

"Key West." Travis whistled. "I've never been there. Haven't been much of anywhere except here. Have you traveled a lot?"

He fixed her hook and handed her the pole.

"A bit. Not as much as I'd like. I've kept a low profile for the past three years, and before that I was married to Gil. He didn't care for traveling either."

"Hey now, I didn't say I didn't want to travel. Just that I haven't."

"Really? Where would you like to go?"

"Cancùn, Mexico. I had some friends go there for their honeymoon. They said it was beautiful."

"It is."

"Deep-sea fishing off Key West sounds like fun. Perhaps I'll give that a try."

"If you decide to go there, let me know. I have some friends who have a time-share down there, and we— Well, I could ask them to let you use the place."

"Ruby, it's okay. I like you, too. It's not a crime to think of each other in the future, is it? I mean, things could change between us, couldn't they?"

"How do I swing—cast this?"

Obvious deflection. A friendship with Ruby is going to be tough. We've been talking for about five minutes, and— boom—we're thinking future. "Ground rules."

"Okay."

He hadn't meant to say that. "First thing. . ." He went on to explain the various parts of the reel, how they worked, and how to cast the line. Ruby was a natural. She did a fine cast after her third attempt.

After an hour, Ruby glanced at her wristwatch. "We should get ready. I'll need to change."

Travis laughed. "I agree." He was going to add that she wouldn't attract a man in that getup, but she already had. Even in the most ridiculous costume he'd ever seen her in, she looked positively beautiful.

"Is there going to be food at this party? Is this a BYOB?"

"Nope, I've made enough for both our shares. And I've put a half dozen soft drinks in the cooler." Ruby lowered her voice and leaned into him. "Travis, no one drinks beer at these parties."

"Oh, sorry." He should have figured that.

Ruby's smile brightened. "No problem. We'll take my car. I'll follow you to your house, and you can leave your truck there."

Travis considered teasing her about wanting to know where he lived but knew she was just being practical. "Sounds good. I'll load up the poles and wait for you in the truck."

She ran up the hill to the house. Travis hoisted the poles and tackle box. They hadn't caught a thing, not even had a nibble. But the past hour had been one of his all-time favorites.

"God, if You're up there, please note I'm in love with this woman. I don't want to hurt her. But I sure want to kiss her."

Chapter 5

Ruby followed Travis as he weaved through some of the back roads she'd never known existed in Verde Point. After fifteen minutes, she pulled in behind Travis into the driveway of his home.

"I'll be right out." He flashed her a smile and ran into the house. She noted he hadn't taken any keys out to open the place. And yet he'd insisted on a security door for her home. On the other hand, she lived relatively close to town, and her house sat on a bluff overlooking one of the fingers of Canyon Lake.

Ruby tapped her fingers on the steering wheel. Had it been a mistake to invite Travis to Bill's? He seemed pretty at ease about going. He slipped out the front door and headed toward her car. His teal-colored silk shirt hung loosely but looked light and casual.

"Is this better?" he asked, referring to her earlier comment about his T-shirt.

She honestly didn't mind the way he looked in a T-shirt. "It's nice." And truly it was. The green in the teal brought out the brown in his eyes. "You'll have to guide me out of here. I was lost after the third turn."

"Not a problem. Do you know where Bill lives?"

"Yes. Out by County Road."

"Okay, there's a back road that will cut off fifteen minutes of our driving time."

Ruby did as instructed, doubting she could ever find his house again. But the locale would make a great place for a chase scene in one of her novels, she mused.

"What?"

"Nothing. I was just thinking how these twisted roads could be wonderful as the backdrop for an intense chase scene in a novel."

"I suppose you're right. Speaking of chase scenes, have you finished your review on that latest R. J. Mack novel?"

"Yes."

"Can I borrow it? I'll still purchase my own copy, but I'd love to read it. It's been bugging me ever since I saw it at your place."

"Sure, just don't tell 'whodunit' before it's released."

"Of course not. Do you review all of R. J. Mack's novels?"

"I don't write reviews for them, I—edit them," she partially confessed.

A long silence fell between them as they drove down the country roads. He'd point in a direction; she'd turn. "Fishing was fun," she said at last.

He beamed. "I'm glad you like it. Can I take you out on the lake with my canoe tomorrow?"

She thought over the work she'd been planning on

doing with Bryce out of the house. "I'd like that, but I need the morning to work on some projects."

"We're here."

Ruby pulled into Bill's driveway.

Travis sat ramrod straight and rubbed his palms on his knees. Ruby reached over and placed a reassuring hand on his shoulder. "You'll have fun. You probably know everyone anyway."

He nodded and opened the car door.

"Will you help me carry in the food?"

"Sure." He opened the rear passenger door and lifted out the cake carrier. "Did I hear Bill request Black Forest chocolate cake?"

"Yup." She reached for the taco salad.

"Yum. Did you make a second cake?"

Ruby chuckled. "No." If she wanted to win Travis's heart, the old adage "The way to a man's heart is through his stomach" certainly applied.

"Maybe there'll be a couple of pieces left over for our fishing trip tomorrow."

"Not likely." Ruby led the way to the front door and raised her hand to knock, but Bill opened the door before she had a chance.

"Come on in." Bill peered behind her, holding the door open for her to pass. "Hey, Travis, good to see you. Welcome to my home."

"Thank you." Travis took hold of the door, and Bill released it. "Ruby, let me introduce you to my wife, Beth."

Ruby had longed to meet Beth. She'd been praying for Bill and Beth to reconcile for the past six months, along with all the others in their small group. Travis took the taco salad container from Ruby's hands. "You go ahead; I'll find the food table."

She glanced over her shoulder and prayed Travis would find someone he could talk to, someone he knew.

After Bill's introduction, the two women talked for a few minutes; then Ruby excused herself to find Travis. She found him with a plate full of food, talking with Mike Bentley. "Hey, Ruby, I didn't realize Travis was your contractor. He'll do a fine job."

"Yes, he did some renovations when I moved here last year."

"Super. Well, man, it's great to see ya again. I better go find the wife. I hear one of the young 'uns hollerin' over something."

"How are you?" she asked Travis after Mike left.

"Fine," Travis lied, looking more ill at ease than she'd ever seen him before.

"We don't have to stay too long."

"No, no, I'm fine. Wanna fix yourself a plate of food?"

"Sure." Ruby filled up her plate. She hadn't eaten much all day. "Let's find a spot to sit." She pointed toward the backyard patio, where they placed their plates on a glass-topped table and sat down. Ruby felt horrible. Travis was obviously quite uncomfortable. "So, how's the work on the addition going? We haven't spoken much this week."

"Excellent. Bryce's room is nearly ready for paint. Then I'll begin work on the knotty pine wallboards for the den. Are you planning on making the den your office?"

"I'm not sure. I like the view of the lake from the room

I'm in now. But the den allows a bit more room to spread out." Ruby reached for the fried chicken leg and gave a silent prayer of thanks before she ate it.

Travis cut up a slice of ham and dipped it in his baked beans, covering it with brown sugar and molasses.

"Ruby, Travis, long time no see. How are ya, you old dog? How's work treating you?" Neal Frank pumped Travis's hand.

Travis engaged in a lively conversation with Neal while Ruby cleared her plate, praising God for providing someone Travis could relate to. Perhaps it had been a bad idea to take him up on his challenge, but she really did like him and would really like to see him right with God, even if they were never meant to develop a personal relationship.

"Excuse me, can I get you more of anything?" she asked Travis, then turned to Neal. "Neal?"

"Nah, I'm fine. So, I hear you're helping Joe out with the tournament this year."

As she stepped back inside the house, she heard Travis say, "If it weren't for Ruby, I'd still be hunting and pecking those addresses into the computer. The woman is phenomenal."

Ruby smiled. It was nice to have someone appreciate her. *And I should really tell that someone who I am*, she chastised herself. It had been hard to sit there and listen to his praises about her writing without telling him. Now it felt too awkward and embarrassing to bring it up. *Lord, I need Your help, not the lawyer's on this one.*

Bill Turner walked up to her and whispered, "How'd you get him to come?"

"I simply invited him."

"You know he's not a Christian, right?"

"Yes, Bill, and we're just friends."

"Don't you fool yourself, Ruby. I've seen how he looks at you. And to be honest, I've seen how you're looking at him."

"He knows a relationship can't develop if he's not a Christian."

"Just be careful," Bill cautioned.

"I will. And how'd you get Beth to come?"

"She finally agreed to come back home. We're going to counseling, and it's looking pretty positive. I can't believe the Lord answered this prayer."

Ruby smiled and patted Bill on the forearm. "He's an awesome God."

"Amen."

"Well, I better get back to my guest. Although Neal's been chewing Travis's ear off, for which I'm grateful. He needs male friends who know the Lord."

Travis was amazed by how much fun he had last night. Just as Ruby had said, he'd known most of the folks who were there. Some were men he worked with, others he fished with—and even some of the women he'd known from school. No one pinned him down about religion or even pushed him to come to church. One or two invited him to Sunday service or, better yet, to the one on Saturday night. That sounded marvelous. He'd still be able to get his Sunday-morning fishing in.

Someone mentioned last night that Jesus' first disciples were fishermen. Travis hadn't thought about that. Then, as if to hit him with a double whammy, someone else mentioned that Jesus was a carpenter, just like Travis. That hit below the belt. Carpenter or not, he knew he lived a life far from that of what Jesus would have lived, being God and all. No one should put down God by comparing Jesus to Travis.

Admittedly it did seem odd that two of his favorite things to do had been a part of Jesus' life. He'd never considered that before.

The morning hours dragged. He wanted to call Ruby to see when she'd be free to go fishing this afternoon. He'd restrained himself last night. He hadn't attempted to kiss her good night, even though every part of him screamed to do so. He had to respect her and her wishes.

Travis sat back in his recliner. "You know, God, if You're really up there, I hear You're doing some mighty fine things. I can't believe Bill and Beth are getting back together. I've never heard of such a thing."

No man he'd ever known who had a wife leave him ever wanted his wife to return. "I'm hoping for Beth's sake Bill doesn't go back to drinking. It sounds like he got a little rough when he was drinking." If there's one thing Travis couldn't fathom, that was how a man could hit a woman. He prided himself on having high morals. Even if he didn't have a real belief in God, the Ten Commandments were a good way to live one's life. *Not that I obey all ten*, he silently admitted.

"Ya know, God, I can't admit to Ruby that I'm talking out loud with You. I don't want her to think I'm just doing this for her. Well, I know I am. But I know enough that if—and I do mean if, God—if I'm to commit myself to You it has to be on my own account, not because I want a woman. Although she's pretty strong motivation, if I do say so myself." Travis coughed to clear his throat, realizing what he was revealing to God. *You can't go telling God the truth*, he reprimanded himself.

Why not?

Travis looked around the room. "Who's here?"

No one answered. Travis shook himself and jumped out of the chair. That was just too weird. "I'm hearing voices. Wow, I must be crazy."

Travis left the house, hopped in his truck, and drove over to Ruby's. He didn't care if she was ready or not. He wasn't going to stay a moment longer in that house.

Fifteen minutes later, he knocked on Ruby's door.

"Hi," he said once she opened it.

"Hi." She knitted her eyebrows together. "Is something wrong?"

"Ah, no, not really. I should have called," he stammered. "I can come back if you're still busy."

"No, come in. I'm just about through."

"Can I help?" he offered as he stepped into the living room.

Ruby hesitated. "You know, I can just let it be. Why don't I run upstairs and change? I'll be right down. Oh, there's a surprise for you in the kitchen." She winked.

Travis grinned. The woman was pure medication for

the soul. A visit with her was like an hour fishing. He stepped into the kitchen and found an entire Black Forest cake in the cake dish on the counter.

He searched through the cupboards and found some small plates and cut himself a slice, as well as one for Ruby. Then he found a couple of glasses, filled one with milk for himself and another with water for her. He'd never seen her drink milk and wasn't sure if she liked it.

She came into the kitchen and smiled. "You found it, I see."

"I can't believe you made another cake."

"I couldn't sleep last night, so while I wrote, I baked it. I frosted it this morning."

"You make a mean Black Forest cake."

"Thank you. It's a favorite of Bill's, as well as several others', so when you hoped we'd have a couple of slices left to bring home, I didn't think it was probable."

"Would you believe I didn't even get a slice last night?" He smiled and ate another bite.

"Yes. I'm not sure it even makes it to the table sometimes." Ruby sat down at the table and pulled her plate closer.

"Mind if I have another?"

The lilt of Ruby's laughter was like the hum of the fishing line going out during the perfect cast—tantalizing, full of promise.

"Help yourself. The cake is for you."

"Me? I can't eat an entire cake!"

"Well I can, so you'd better take it home." She slipped a forkful of the rich chocolate into her mouth. He felt drawn to those lips.

Travis coughed and turned toward the counter. *God, help me! I can't do this! She's way too much temptation.*

The phone rang. Ruby immediately slid into deep conversation and silently excused herself to the other room. Travis had some time to collect his thoughts.

Ruby came back into the room. "Travis, I need a huge favor."

"What's up?"

"That was my publisher. Someone at the publishing house goofed and forgot to inform me I'm supposed to be on a network magazine show tomorrow morning in New York."

"New York?"

"Yes." Tears started to fall. "They weren't supposed to do this, at least not without my approval. I need to call my lawyer, my agent, and probably get on a plane to New York. My problem is Bryce. He's due back Sunday morning, and it's possible I won't be able to get a return flight. I don't even know if I can get an outgoing flight."

Travis ran up beside her. "Wait. Didn't you say you used a pen name? Couldn't someone else do the interview? Like the one who booked it?"

Ruby smiled. "That would be nice. I honestly don't know what to do. I need to call my agent. I can't possibly go fishing with you this afternoon."

"No problem. I understand. Hey, I have a friend who has a private jet. Would that help? I don't know if it's available, but I can call and ask. You'd have to cover the fuel cost, though, unless he has business in the area himself."

"At this point, I'd pay whatever it costs. Sure, call. I'm going to run into my office and call my agent."

Travis flipped open his cell phone and went through his directory. He had a fishing buddy who came every year for the tournament down from Louisville where he owned and operated a horse farm.

"Hello?"

"Jason, it's Travis Wells from Verde Point."

"How's it going, Travis? Is the tournament going to be good this year?"

"I hope so. The reason I'm calling is, I have a friend who might need a jet flight to New York City this afternoon, and you're the only one I know with his own plane. She's willing to cover the fuel costs."

Jason Clay laughed. "Be happy to help. I can send my pilot down there and pick her up in a couple of hours."

"Excellent. I'll call and confirm. She's trying to get out of the deal, something with her publisher messing up something or other."

"Who is she?"

"Ruby Townsend, one of my customers."

"Never heard of her." Travis didn't bother to explain that he wouldn't have, seeing how Ruby used a pen name.

"Well, I won't keep you. Thanks again."

"No problem. Always glad to help a friend. Although you might owe me and let me win this year."

Travis laughed. Jason joined him; then they said their good-byes.

Ruby came in, crestfallen. "I've got to go."

"Jason Clay said you could borrow his plane. His pilot

can be here in a couple of hours. I just have to call him back and confirm."

"Confirm. Can you watch Bryce?"

"Sure, but with Jason's plane, you should be back in plenty of time."

"You're probably right. I need to call Bryce. I need to pack. Oh, I hate this. I really, really do."

Travis took her in his arms and held her for a moment. "Ruby, you said prayer helps you when you're stressed. I think you might need to do that. Or you can try it my way and go fishing," he teased.

Ruby shook her head from side to side. "You're impossible but right. Thanks for reminding me."

"No problem. Hey, I've got a question for you. When you pray, do you hear voices?"

"Huh?"

"Nothing, never mind. You've got a lot to do to get ready. I'll be happy to take you to the airstrip if you'd like."

"That's okay. I'll need my car there when I return."

"Right, okay. I'll see you when you get back tomorrow. Call me if anything comes up."

"Thanks." Ruby paused with her hand on his chest. He wondered if she could feel his heart pounding.

Chapter 6

Ruby couldn't believe it. Not only had someone in the PR department set up the interview, but it was on Sunday, not Saturday. Jason Clay had no problem with his pilot being away for another night. He hadn't asked to be reimbursed, but Ruby told her editor the publishing house would need to come up with the cost of her private flight to New York. It was the least they could do. After an hour on the phone with her lawyer, they agreed she should do the interview, not because of any legal ramifications, however, since she was within her rights to refuse the interview. The problem came that the network had invested some major expense into the advertisements for the show. After all, R. J. Mack never did interviews. They did agree to keep her in the shadows, no cameras or lights directly on her.

In the end, Travis had agreed to take care of Bryce. The interview had gone well, and the journalists held their composure when they discovered R. J. Mack was a woman. Ruby had never been so pleased to go home.

Travis sat on the recliner flipping through the channels. He'd gone to church last night and actually enjoyed it. When the preacher asked if anyone wanted to come forward and give their life to God, he'd almost been compelled to go. But something held him back. He needed more time. He glanced at his watch. Ruby had called to say she was leaving New York City and to remind him that Bryce would be home in two hours.

The announcer's voice said, "Today we have an exclusive interview with R. J. Mack, the author of several best-selling mystery novels."

"R. J. Mack. Cool." Travis set the remote down on the coffee table.

"R. J., may I call you R. J.?"

"That would be fine."

Travis squeezed the arms of the chair. "R. J.'s a woman?"

He sat mesmerized by the shadowy form of a woman, with a hat on her head, talking about her next novel. Travis grabbed the advance copy, as Ruby had called it, and thumbed through to see if this woman really knew what she was talking about.

He never would have guessed it. R. J. Mack was a woman. *Weird*, he thought.

Travis found himself caught up in the story, and an hour had slipped by without his realizing it. He closed the book and hurried off to Ruby's house. When he arrived, no one was there. He looked toward heaven and prayed. "Lord, You know Ruby couldn't take it if her ex-in-laws were to deceive her and try to take away Bryce. Please bring him back home."

He let himself inside and sliced himself off a piece of the Black Forest cake and poured another tall glass of milk.

Ten minutes later, as he polished off his piece of cake, Bryce came running in the door. "Hey, Mom, I'm home!"

Travis left the kitchen. "She's not home yet, son."

"Oh, okay. You're here to watch me?"

"That's the idea. Wanna go fishin'?"

"Sure. Let me tell my grandparents?"

"Of course."

Two minutes later, a thin, bony-faced woman marched into the house. "Who are you?"

"Travis Wells." He extended his hand. "Just a friend."

"Lovers, more like it," she spat. "Harold, we're taking him back home with us."

"Over my dead body," Travis replied. "You don't have the right. Ruby will be here shortly."

"Humph."

"Gertrude, stop it. Ruby's entitled to a relationship."

"We're just friends."

The not-so-thin man scanned him from head to toe and evidently didn't believe a word Travis said.

Bryce stomped off to his room in tears.

"You two take a seat," Travis ordered. "It's not my place to mess with private family business; but Ruby's too sweet of a gal to tell you the way things are, and I don't want to see that boy hurt any more than he already has been. You two ought to be ashamed of yourselves. How can you be ignorant about who or what your son was? But that's neither here nor there. If I understand things correctly, you tried to sue for custody and take Bryce away from his mother. And yet she's willing to let you have visitation rights. She's never stopped you from visiting or even having him stay at your home for an entire weekend. And all you can do is think she's some kind of evil woman. That woman doesn't have an evil bone in her body. And if you truly loved Bryce, you would know that you're hurting him every time you lie to him about his mother—or his father, for that matter. A boy needs his mother."

"And a father," Mrs. Townsend added.

"Yes, and it wasn't Ruby who killed him, was it? The courts proved that the claims your son made in their divorce were false. Ruby proved it to the courts and to you. So why can't you let Bryce have as normal a life as he possibly can? He loves both of you, and he loves his mother."

"You see, Harold; I told you he was her lover. Just like Gil said, she had lots of lovers."

"I am not Ruby's lover," Travis fumed. "I wouldn't dishonor her and reduce her to being just my lover." And he knew it to be true. For the first time in his life, he wanted a wife, not a lover. Not a companion but a wife. He wanted Ruby, and he wanted her God.

"Harold, Gertrude," Ruby said and smiled as she walked into the room. "Did you have a good visit?"

Travis stomped off to Ruby's office to give her some privacy. There were papers strewn all over the room. He fingered the papers and glanced at the pages. "No way."

"Who is that man?" Gertrude huffed.

"My contractor and a friend. As I told you over the phone, I had to go to New York."

"And that's another thing. What do you have to do in New York?"

"Gert, calm down."

Ruby held her tone with her ex-in-laws while she evaded the meddling questions. Some she could have answered but chose not to because the Townsends needed to learn her life was just that: her life. With plans set for Bryce's next visit, they finally left.

"Bryce?" Ruby called. "You can come out now."

He ran to her arms. The red puffy rings around his eyes made it apparent he'd been crying. "I'm sorry I wasn't here to meet your grandparents," she whispered against his ear.

"It's okay. I love you, Mom."

"I love you, too."

"Mr. Wells let them have it."

"Oh?"

Bryce bobbed his head up and down.

"Perhaps I should go speak with him. He went into my office—oh no!" Ruby ran to her office. Her fears were realized when she saw him holding the one-sheet bio she'd been preparing for the release of who she was.

"You're R. J." It wasn't really a question, more like a pronouncement.

"Ruby Jean, yes. I'm sorry I couldn't tell you."

"Couldn't or wouldn't?" His anger was palpable.

"Travis, not now. I need to talk with Bryce."

"He's right behind you. Have you told him?" He dropped the sheet back onto the pile.

"I'll see ya around, R. J." Travis exited.

"Mom? What's going on?"

"Bryce, sit down. There's something I've been meaning to tell you." Bryce sat down in the soft chair she kept in the office for reading. Ruby pulled up a folding chair she used when working at the portable table. "Honey, you know I'm a writer."

Bryce nodded.

"Well, I've used what the writing business calls a pen name so most people don't know who I am."

Bryce knitted his eyebrows the same way she did when trying to reason something out. *Lord, help me explain this in a way he'll understand,* she pleaded.

"I started writing when you were a tiny baby. . . ." Ruby went on to explain who she was, how her job worked, and how popular her books were.

"I still don't get why Mr. Wells was upset."

"Mr. Wells wants to be more than a friend. I like him. I like him a lot. But he doesn't go to church, and I can't get involved with a man who doesn't believe in Jesus the way I do."

Bryce scrunched up his face. "I still don't get it."

"My friendship with Mr. Wells is, was. . ." She amended her words and hoped she would be able to talk with Travis about this in more detail later. "We were becoming good friends, and friends don't keep secrets from each other. So he's probably feeling betrayed and hurt that I didn't tell him who I was."

"Mom, I just don't get it. Grown-ups can be so weird. I think I'm not going to grow up."

Ruby's heart lightened. She pulled Bryce into a hug and kissed the top of his head. "I love you, Bugman, but you will grow up. Sorry about that."

Weary from her flight, and weary from the confrontations at home, Ruby felt like she could sleep for twenty-four hours straight. She and Bryce played a couple of games before bed; then Ruby filled the tub and poured herself a luxurious bubble bath. Bryce understood her reasons for keeping the information from his grandparents. She didn't tell him about the book that, to this day, she wondered if Dory had read before she killed Gil. The similarity was a bit too close for comfort. She hoped and prayed her ex-in-laws never read that book, for their own sanity if for nothing else.

The next morning, Monday, Travis arrived and worked on the addition. He didn't stop by the entire day to speak with her. Ruby had slept in. Bryce disappeared for a while. She suspected he was in the addition working with Travis. She probably should have gone in and dealt with Travis about last night, but she just didn't want to deal with another confrontation for at least one day.

When Travis still did not come and speak with her on Tuesday, Ruby decided to try to find his house and speak with him. She spent two hours running around the back roads but never did find Travis's home. Frustrated and exhausted, she went home and decided to deal with Travis in the morning when he came to work. Instead, she found a message from Travis saying he wouldn't be able to come in for the rest of the week but would be able to return to the job by Monday.

Sunday morning Ruby dressed for church, and she and Bryce mingled with some of their friends in the parking lot before the service began. A television crew from a local network pulled into the parking lot. Word quickly spread that they were looking for R. J. Mack and had heard she attended this church. Pastor Hayden came out and told the crew that this was not the place for an interview. Her care group came to her support and helped Ruby and Bryce escape into the sanctuary. She had confessed to her group on Thursday who she was, and someone must have blurted it out to a friend. Apparently it was big news. Hurt that one of her closest friends wouldn't keep her secret, Ruby suddenly felt like a fish out of water. They'd been told that what was shared in their small group was to stay in their small group—unless Travis had spread the word. *He wouldn't, would he?* she pondered.

Her agent told her it would only be a matter of time before the media found her. She wasn't prepared for this. Not that anyone could be. It was entirely possible the source could have come from the television station. A young reporter had followed her. But that couldn't be. She'd flown home in a private jet.

Ruby shook off the distraction and tried to concentrate on the morning service. *Father, help me understand what's going on.*

Somehow she made it through the morning service

and, with a little help from her friends, left without the news reporters following her car.

"Mom, how famous are you?" Bryce asked once they left the church parking lot.

"I'm not. I'm just a news story. Each of the media photographers wants to be the first one to get a picture of me." Ruby glanced in the rearview mirror. Thankfully no one was following her.

Ruby's cell phone rang. "Hello?"

"Ruby, it's Travis. Sorry to be so low profile. I've been helping Joe with the fishing tournament. But I heard what happened at church this morning. For your peace of mind, I want you to know it wasn't me who tipped off the media."

Thank You, Lord. "Thanks, Travis, I appreciate your calling." She hesitated for a moment. "We need to talk."

"Yes, about many things. Go home and pack a bag or two for you and Bryce. I'm working on a plan to keep the media out of your hair. And I've got several folks who are willing to help. Trust me, Ruby; we're going to help you."

"Where are we going?"

"My place. No one can find you there."

"I don't know how to get there."

"Not a problem. I'm almost to your house now. You can follow me."

"All right, thanks."

Ruby hung up with Travis and called her agent. "Hi, it's Ruby. It's time. The media was at my church this morning."

"I'll get right on it." Ruby had been working on a media package and had sent it to her agent to release to the public at the proper time. She'd been hoping to wait a couple more months, but the mess-up with the publicist brought the time line up to the present.

"Bryce, Travis said we could stay at his house for a few days so the reporters can't find me. What do you think?"

"Awesome. I like Mr. Wells. And, Mom, I like fishing. Can I get my own rod and reel? Oh, and a tackle box just like Mr. Wells's?"

"Sure. Maybe we can do that tomorrow."

When she drove up to the house, Travis was leaning against the right front fender of his truck, looking all too handsome and desirable. Ruby checked her feelings. As much as she wanted to be in this man's arms, she couldn't.

"Hi." He wrapped his arm around her shoulders and escorted her into the house.

She should disengage but couldn't. The comfort of a man's protective embrace washed over her. *Sometimes a girl just needs a hug.* And that was what she felt from Travis's gesture of kindness. "Bryce, run to your room and pack three pairs of shorts, a pair of jeans, three shirts, socks—three pairs," she amended. "And definitely three pairs of underwear. We can always come back for anything you miss."

"Would you like me to pack up your laptop?" he offered.

"Sure. The briefcase is in the closet. Everything is in it except the power adapter for the wall socket. That's attached to the laptop. Do you know how to use a USB memory stick?"

"Yup."

"Great. On my hard drive, the password is 'God's gift,' capital *G* on God. Copy the folder marked 'Slip Sliding'."

Travis chuckled. "As in the Paul Simon song?"

Ruby nodded, and Travis roared with laughter as he walked into her office. Ruby giggled and ran to her room to pack.

As she exited her room, Travis pulled her to himself. "Ruby, we need to talk, but know this: I love you." He bent down and captured her lips. His were soft and sweet as black cherries ripened to perfection. Ruby closed her eyes, lost in the oneness of their kiss. Then logic prevailed, and she pulled away. "Travis, no, we can't."

"Trust me—we can." He pulled her back and kissed her again, the impact so intense she had to remind herself to breathe. This time he pulled away and placed a finger on her swollen lips. "I'll explain later."

Please help me, Lord. I won't get involved with a man who doesn't love You. Even if he can kiss like that.

Chapter 7

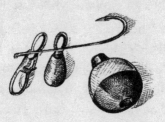

Travis savored Ruby's sweet kisses all the way home. He should have waited until he had told her about his profession of faith in God, but she needed reassuring after being overwhelmed by this media frenzy. Not that he could blame her for that, but he had hoped to shield her from some of it by letting her stay at his place. What he hadn't told her yet was that he planned on staying at her place. That way if a reporter should find out where she lived, all they would see was him working in the yard, fishing off the dock, and working on the addition. Hopefully they'd reason they had gotten the wrong information and this wasn't R. J. Mack's house. At least that was the plan.

Seeing the fear and confusion in her eyes when he kissed her the second time, he prayed she'd understand and trust him, but he could feel her resistance in the kiss.

Once they arrived, he immediately gave them a brief tour of the house. "There's an old tree house in the backyard, Bryce. You're welcome to check it out."

"Can I, Mom?"

"You bet." Ruby still held her suitcase in her hand. Travis reached over and relieved her.

"Ruby, have a seat. Can I get you something to drink?"

"No, but you can explain what just happened at my house."

Travis felt the heat rise on the back of his neck. "Sorry, I couldn't resist. At first, I just meant to comfort you. I guess how I really feel about you kind of took over."

Tears welled in her eyes. "I can't, Travis. I'm sorry."

"Shh, don't cry. It's okay, trust me."

"Travis, you don't understand."

"Yes, I do."

"No," she cut him off.

He lovingly placed his right index finger to her lips. "Shh, and let me explain. All right?"

She nodded her assent.

"Honey, I've been talking with God, praying actually. I even heard His voice; at least that's what I hoped it was. Otherwise, I'm going nuts or something. Bill challenged me to look at God's creation and reflect on my self-centeredness. I'm still wrestling with that one. But when you went to New York, I went to church on Saturday night, and again last night, and the preacher explained things in a way that made sense. All that talking with God and the preacher and Bill, well, I got to thinkin' God can't be all that bad. Then I called up Neal. We used to hang out, go drinkin' and lookin' for girls together when we were kids. And Neal helped straighten out a few things in my mind. Basically it comes down to this: I'm a sinner, compared to God, and I asked Him into my heart this past week. Now, don't get me wrong. I love you. But I needed to do this for me, not for you. Although a relationship with you would be a mighty fine gift, but—"

Ruby leaped into his arms and planted a kiss on him that twisted around his heart as tight as a fishing line with a thirty-pound bass pulling on it. "Whoa, woman, there's a young 'un in the house."

"Mom?" Bryce stood in the doorway with his mouth gaping.

Ruby pulled herself away from Travis and straightened her hair with her hands. "Hi." Her cheeks were bright red.

Bryce simply looked back and forth between them, then smiled. "You told her about God?" he asked Travis.

"Yup."

"Told ya." Bryce beamed and walked back outside.

"You told Bryce before me?"

"Afraid so. Sorry."

Ruby just shook her head.

"Look, I know we'll need to go slow, but I do love you, and I do want to be with you."

Ruby sat back and folded her hands in her lap. "I want to say I love you in return. But I need to pray, and I need to wait and see if your relationship with God is real. I'm sorry. I wish I could just simply accept it, but—well, I need to wait."

"I understand, and, Ruby," he said as he placed his hand over hers, "I wouldn't want it any other way. Also, I'm going to move into your place and give the impression that it's my home for a couple of days."

"This should all be over in a couple of days. Possibly

just one, after my agent sends out the PR material we've been working on. Every media source that wants it will have my photo so no one has to pay for a photo of me. My Web site will be launching a new look that reveals who I am and why I chose to reveal myself now. I'm not including the information about Bryce's custody battle.

"Oh no!" Ruby jumped back and scanned the room. "I've got to call my ex-in-laws. They have to hear it from me first, not the media."

"Phone is in the kitchen. Feel free to use it. I'm going to pack my bag. I'll remake my bed with fresh sheets while you make your calls."

Inside his room, he closed the door and knelt by his bed to pray. "Father, give Ruby the wisdom to handle this media frenzy, and help me understand all that she'll be going through over the next few days and months. I know I want her as my wife, but I figured it would be a bit much for me to ask her today. Help me know when the time is right. Please, please protect Ruby and Bryce. In Jesus' name. Amen."

He pulled apart his bed and dressed it with clean sheets and pillowcases, packed a few necessities, and left the room. He put the sheets in the washer and set it in motion. Ruby was leaning against the door frame, curling the phone cord around her index finger. "Harold, Gertrude, I just felt you should know before it was released to the media."

Travis could see the strain this phone call was causing Ruby. There was a short pause; then she spoke again. "Yes, I'm aware of that."

Tears fell down her cheeks. Travis came up beside her and held her. "I'm not responsible for Dory's actions, and I'm sorry you feel that way. Bye." She hung up the phone and sobbed into Travis's chest. It didn't take a rocket scientist to figure out that her ex-in-laws blamed her for her ex-husband being murdered by his second wife.

Travis held her and prayed. What else could he do?

The next day, Ruby found it hard to concentrate on work, so she opted for some fishing with Bryce. They borrowed Travis's canoe and paddled their way around Canyon Lake to the inlet near her home. She could see her house sitting on the bluff. Travis had spent the night there and was probably working on the addition now.

"Mom?"

Bryce's voice pulled her away from her wanderings. "What is it, Bryce?"

"I was just wondering."

"About what?"

"If you marry Mr. Wells, do I still keep my name?"

Marry—we haven't even gone out on a date yet. But to an eight-year-old, kissing meant marriage, she supposed. "Bryce, you'll always be a Townsend."

He nodded in acceptance of that fact. "Grandma and Grandpa don't want me to live with you."

"I know, son. Your daddy said some untrue things about me to them, and I'm praying that, in time, they will see that your daddy didn't tell the truth." She wondered if she should forewarn him about the latest accusation they'd made yesterday. Her eyes still watered just thinking about it.

"Mom, Mr. Wells said they said some unkind words to you on the phone last night and that's why you were crying. I don't want to visit them anymore."

Ruby rested her paddle across her lap and allowed the canoe to drift. "Honey, I won't force you to visit with them, but we need to be patient. They think your daddy was perfect."

Bryce let out a yell that echoed across the water. "No! They don't know him like we do."

Bryce had never said a negative word about his father. Ruby wanted to tread lightly, but she also needed to understand what kind of thoughts Bryce was having. "What are you thinking of in particular?"

"Like last night. Mr. Wells didn't leave till you felt better. He made dinner for us. He made sure you were okay before he left. Dad would've told you to stop it and walked out the door. I know Dad wasn't a good husband, Mom."

"He had some good points. After all, he gave me you." She ruffled his curls.

Bryce nodded. "Are you going to marry Mr. Wells?"

Ruby let out a nervous laugh. "Honey, I—"

"Ya kissed him."

Self-control. She definitely needed more self-control. "I don't know, son. We'll just have to wait and see what the Lord has in mind." Ruby glanced back at her house. Travis stood on the dock with his hands on his hips.

"Hey." She waved. The canoe wobbled.

"Mom!" Bryce screamed and held on to the edges for dear life.

"Bryce, we're fine." She paddled toward the dock. Bryce didn't remove his hands from the side rails. *The kid probably thinks I've never canoed before.* She'd done some in college and even a bit of white-water rafting. She'd done quite a few things before she met Gil. Would getting involved with Travis mean another relationship with a man who never cared to go anywhere? Didn't he say he'd never traveled?

The paddle seemed heavier with each stroke. The man had powerful kisses, but— She cut her thoughts short and brought them back to bringing the canoe up to her dock.

Travis's voice rumbled off the water. "We've got a problem."

Travis didn't know how to break the news to Ruby but felt the straightforward approach was best. "Your lawyer called. Your ex-in-laws are suing you." He cut off his words and glanced to Bryce.

"He knows enough. Go ahead," Ruby encouraged.

"According to the lawyer, and I'm leaving out the legal mumbo jumbo, they called their lawyer last night, who worked up the paperwork to petition the court for a lawsuit against any monies earned off of the death of Gil and—"

Ruby held up a hand. "Don't bother. I get the picture."

"Mom?"

"Bryce, one of my books that was written before your daddy was killed had a murder scene in it very similar to what Dory did to your dad. Dory claimed the book caused her to react that way and tried to say it wasn't her fault for killing your dad."

"Oh, I read that one."

"You did?" Travis's words echoed Ruby's.

"When?" Ruby pushed harder.

"Before I came to live with you."

"Bryce, I know you read well, but that's an adult book. Who let you read it?"

"Grandpa." Bryce giggled. "You're one of his favorite writers."

How ironic, Travis thought. "She's mine, too, but you're only eight. How can you read—" Travis paused "—something so complicated?"

Ruby turned to him. "Bryce has been reading since he was three. He's gifted."

Bryce smiled.

"Okay." If an eight-year-old could read murder mysteries now, what would he be reading in the future? "One good note, the media hasn't found you yet."

"I have an unlisted number."

Travis reached out and lifted Bryce from the canoe.

"Your agent called and said the media packet went out and should be on the evening news tonight at the latest."

"What are you going to do about your ex-in-laws?" Travis whispered in her ear as he helped her out of the canoe. She smelled heavenly. He wanted to kiss her neck but restrained himself.

"Go to court, I guess. My lawyer has a prepared statement to these charges. We anticipated this would happen once they knew who I was."

"I'd like to—never mind, it's not a kind thing to say or think."

Ruby squeezed his forearm gently and smiled. "I know," she said. "Travis, I've done a bit of thinking out on the lake today, and I've decided to return home, whatever comes my way. The media won't be on my trail for too long, and I'll have a news interview with a local radio station this afternoon."

"Oh, your picture has been circulating all over the place with some of the media trying to hunt you down. My buddies have been sending those reporters all over the countryside, up through the back roads, everywhere. I doubt they'll ever find you." Travis couldn't be more thankful to his fishing buddies. They knew how to deflect any snooping reporters. "However, I heard a few of the boys heard about your Black Forest cake somehow and are hoping you'll be making some soon."

Ruby smiled. She looked exhausted. Travis couldn't imagine the emotional toll all of this was having on her. He wrapped his arm around her shoulders and kissed the top of her head. "I know it's too soon—but, Ruby, I love you."

He thought he heard a quiet whisper say, "I love you, too."

Chapter 8

Ruby thought back on the month gone by since the media frenzy. It had been excrutiating. The battle with her ex-in-laws proved to be extremely painful but was taking the course her lawyer predicted it would. Bryce refused to speak to his grandparents on the phone. She couldn't force the child; and she tried to explain to Harold what the real problem was, but Gertrude just didn't get it. Frankly Ruby wasn't sure she ever would. She prayed they would come to terms with what really happened to their son and how much Gil had been responsible for.

Travis and Ruby had been together every day and a good portion of each evening. Their relationship was growing. She knew she loved him, and she even trusted his newfound faith.

The media never did find her house. Ruby'd made more Black Forest cakes in the past month than she had over the past five years. It seemed every fishing buddy of Travis's had a story to tell. She suspected many were like the old fish stories of the one that got away.

Ruby checked her hair and makeup in the mirror. Tonight, she and Travis were going out. Bryce was away at a Christian youth camp for the week.

Travis knocked on the front door looking like heaven on a stick. "Wow," she said.

He scooped her into his arms and captured her lips with his own.

Her mind spun from the intensity. She loved him. She knew it and planned on telling him tonight. She'd vowed never to tell a man she loved him until she was 100 percent certain and that he was God's chosen spouse for her.

Slowly he pulled away. "The kid's gone, right?"

"Right," Ruby giggled.

"Phew. I don't want him catching us like he did the first time."

"I appreciate that."

"Are you ready to go?" Travis asked, running his fingers through her short hair and down the back of her neck.

"In a minute. How's the tournament coming?"

"Everything's just about done. Oh, Joe wants to know if you want to have a booth for selling your Black Forest cake."

"Not in a million years. I don't think I'm going to make that cake again for at least six months."

"Six months?" Travis held his hand to his heart. "Darlin', you wouldn't make a man suffer so, would ya?"

She eyed him carefully. She knew she would make a cake just for him, but not for a little while. "Depends," she teased.

"On what?"

"Whether you want to make this relationship more permanent."

"I'm waiting on you, love. You still haven't confessed that you love me. Not that I don't know the answer by that kiss. But I need to hear those words."

Ruby traced his jaw with the tip of her finger. "Oh, Travis, you've caught me hook, line, and sinker. I love you so very, very much."

They held each other tightly. "Come away, my beloved," he whispered in her ear.

Ruby's heart warmed at the recognition of the familiar passage from the Song of Solomon and the fact that Travis knew it. "You mean after the fishing tournament, right?"

"Of course. I may be in tune with the Fisher of men, but I still have to fish. After all, it's where I was when God revealed Himself to me. Can't fault a guy for wanting to get closer to the Lord, can you?"

Travis led her back into her house.

"You're impossible."

"Yup, but you love me."

"Absolutely."

"When can we tell Bryce? I think he'll like the idea of us getting married."

"I told him before he left for camp. I didn't say that it was definite, but I did ask him what he thought about it. Not that I needed to. He asked me about marrying you the morning after our first kiss."

"That boy is sharp." Travis sat down on the sofa.

Ruby sat down beside him. "Yes, he is. We're talking a

lot about Gil and Dory. He's doing well."

"Yeah, he's been asking me a ton of questions, too. Mostly we've been talking about what being a real man is and isn't. How to be responsible and grow up well. He's a good kid, Ruby. You should be proud."

"I am. Speaking of children, are you wanting to have some?"

"A whole school of 'em."

"Ah?"

Travis's laughter flitted its way down to the tip of her toes. "How about a couple, and then we'll see about more after that?"

Ruby nodded. "That's doable. I do have one problem, though. Would you be willing to go on a book tour with me?"

"When, where, and how long?"

"When is somewhat flexible. Close to the release of the next book is best, which is this fall. They're talking about thirty days. I was thinking of buying an RV and going across country and taking three or four months. I have an idea for a story set in the Rockies. What do you think?"

"We could call it our honeymoon. I won't go if you don't marry me first." He winked.

"Demanding, aren't you?"

"You betcha. So?"

"So, I'll marry you—" she paused "—first."

Travis pulled her onto his lap and tenderly kissed her. "Is a month long enough to plan a wedding?" He kissed the tip of her nose.

Ruby closed her eyes and prayed.

"Father," Travis's voice called out, "bless our marriage and help us to be fishers of men through the example of our love for You and each other."

"Amen." A tear squeezed out of Ruby's closed lids. Who'd have thought another carpenter who loved to fish would come into her life and fill her with this much joy? "I love you."

"I love you, too."

LYNN A. COLEMAN

Lynn A. Coleman is a best-selling, multipublished author and speaker, writing historical and contemporary novels that entertain and hopefully encourage Christians to go deeper with their faith. She is the cofounder of American Christian Fiction Writers (ACFW). She lives in north-central Florida with her husband, the senior pastor of Friendship Bible Church. She loves hearing from her readers and invites you to check out her Web site at www.lynncoleman.com.

Reeling Her In

by Jennifer Johnson

Dedication

This book is dedicated to my grandma, Patsy Marsh.
This precious woman was my constant encourager,
always believing in me even when I didn't believe in myself.
On May 24, 2005, my birthday,
she left this world for heaven.
I praise God for allowing me to know her for
thirty-two years and for allowing me the honor
of celebrating my birthday knowing
she was running into the arms of our Abba.

*For it is by grace you have been saved,
through faith—and this not from yourselves,
it is the gift of God.*

EPHESIANS 2:8

Chapter 1

T hanks, Sally." Ken Marsh hung up the phone, sucked in a deep breath, stuck two fingers in his mouth, and let out a whistle loud enough to be heard in the next county. The customers and other barbers stopped, turned, and gawked at him. He grinned, unable to hide his mirth at their gaping mouths and widened eyes.

Ken cupped his hand over his mouth. "Pete! Beth!" he called out. "Barb's on her way."

In a flash, both barbers stopped clipping and cleaned their stations. Stunned customers watched the escapade in silence. Ken couldn't hold back a chuckle. "Don't worry, folks. We'll be with you in just a minute." He leaned toward his customer, Travis Wells, and whispered, "It's Doll Lady."

Travis smiled. "The inspector who looks like a fashion doll but has the heart of Darth Vader?"

Ken grinned and nodded. He grabbed the broom, then swept up the hair around his barber's chair. "The one and only." He cleaned off his mirror with a towel, then pulled his barber's certificate from a drawer and hung it on the wall. "She wasn't always that way, but that's another story."

Ken wiped his hands on his jeans, then picked up his comb and scissors to resume Travis's haircut.

The bells on the door jingled.

Through his peripheral vision, Ken could see Pete and Beth had both returned to their stations and were clipping hair. A laugh formed in his belly. He swallowed hard to keep it there.

"Come on in. We'll be with you in a minute."

Though his station faced the entrance to the shop, Ken didn't have to look up to know the most arrogant, hoity-toity woman in Kentucky stood inside the building. Forcing himself to keep a straight face, Ken lifted his gaze toward the inspector as she closed the door. He feigned surprise, fully aware she could see through his charade. "Why, Barb, what a pleasant surprise."

Barbara held a briefcase in one hand, her other rested on her hip. One high-heeled shoe, connected to a long, slender foot and leg, tapped against the floor. Shiny, straight blond hair raced past one shoulder. Hot pink lips puckered. Their color matched the two-piece business suit to exactness.

There was no denying it. Barbara Elliott was a sight to behold.

He looked into eyes the color of his favorite pond filled with phytoplankton—rich, natural green. She squinted back at him. Fury wrapped around her gaze.

"Kenneth Marsh, how did you know I was coming?"

Ken patted a wet comb against his arm, then used

it to straighten the back of Travis's hair. He clipped the scraggly hairs that had escaped his first cut. "Why would you accuse me like that?" He looked up at her, placed his hand over his heart, and puckered his lips. "It hurts that you trust me so little."

Barbara's shoes clicked against the gray-speckled linoleum floor as she walked toward him. She flailed one hand in front of her face. "Never mind. It doesn't matter."

Once she was in reach, Ken touched the comb to her arm. "While you're here. . ." He looked into her eyes. Their cool, green water begged him to dive in and relish their depths. They mesmerized him, held him frozen in time.

She looked away.

Ken blinked and shook his head to jar his memory as to where he was, who he was. What was it he had planned to say?

Distracted, Ken looked around the room. Travis stared back at him, a full, knowing smile on his lips. That single moment of weakness infuriated him, and he bit his lip to refrain from saying something foolish to his friend.

Barbara flipped through files in her briefcase, then pulled out his shop's folder. Manicured fingernails flipped pages until she reached the last. "This won't take long."

Ken didn't respond.

It irked him that his thoughts had responded to her with such power. He didn't even like Ms. I'm-a-Perfect-Do-Everything-by-the-Book-Fashion-Doll.

He lifted the top of Travis's hair and looked in the mirror to be sure he'd cut straight. The smirk on Travis's face reflecting back at him incensed Ken. The tips of his own hair would most likely be singed and in need of a trim after this visit by the state inspector.

Within moments, Barbara had completed her inspection and walked toward him. "Everything looks good."

That's a first. Ken grunted. In ten years of inspections, Barbara Elliott had never once left his shop without giving him some kind of chastisement. Of course, their relationship hadn't always been so hard. Barbara had changed all that right after high school.

She bit the top of her pen, and Ken noticed her straight, white teeth. He cringed. Sure, Barbara was beautiful. It was part of the joke. Today, however, like too many times before, her appearance distracted him.

"Just one more thing." Barbara's words tore him from his thoughts. Her heels clicked toward the wall that held his barber's license. "The last time I was here, I told you to get a picture on your lic—" Her words stopped when she reached her destination.

Ken relaxed. He crossed his arms in front of his chest. Once again, he was in control.

Barbara yanked the license from the wall and thrust it in Ken's face. "What's this?"

Ken grinned at the photograph of himself wearing only a pair of trunks with fish swimming on the front. In the picture, he held a fashion doll in one hand and gave a thumbs-up with the other. He'd wanted to get her all riled up. Obviously it worked.

He looked at Barbara and shrugged. "What? It's a photo of me on my license."

"This is not appropriate for the shop." She faced the picture toward her and gasped again. Her eyes squinted as she looked more closely at the photo. "Are you holding a doll, Mr. Marsh?"

His grin split his face from ear to ear. He could feel it. "Yes, ma'am."

"Why, Mr. Marsh?" She slammed the frame against the vanity. Her teeth gritted, and her nose wrinkled like a dog about to attack. "Why is there a doll in your hand?"

Undaunted by her fury, Ken placed his hand on his chest and batted his eyes. "It was for you—Doll."

"That's it." Barbara shrugged away from him and grabbed her briefcase in one motion. "Consider yourself officially cited." She stomped toward the door.

A laugh erupted from his stomach. "Don't be mad; I was just messin' with you. No one else saw it."

Barbara swung around and tromped toward him. One two-inch heel snapped. She squealed and fell to the floor on her hip and hand.

Ken gasped and walked toward her. "Are you okay?"

"Don't touch me." She stood as well as she could with one leg two inches shorter than the other and pointed her finger just centimeters from his face. "So, you admit you haven't had your license and picture on the wall? You admit someone told you I was coming?"

He stepped back and swallowed. "I—I don't admit anything." He reached for her hand. "Are you okay? Did you hurt anything?"

"Don't act like you care." Barbara leaned over, pulled

her shoes off her feet, and grabbed the broken heel. She turned and headed across the room. "Watch for a letter from the state." The bells jingled as she opened the door, then fell to the floor as she slammed it on the way out.

Heat warmed Ken's cheeks when he realized the entire shop looked at the door, then back at him in unison. Quite a show he'd given them today. He feigned a laugh and walked back to Travis.

Travis shook his head. "You went too far this time."

Ken sighed. "I think you're right. I hope she's not hurt."

"You want to go check?"

"Nah. I don't think she'd want to see the likes of me right now." Ken turned Travis away from the vanity and handed him a mirror to see the back of his haircut. "Are we still on for the fishing trip in two weeks?"

"Yep."

Ken rubbed the back of his neck, then put the comb in the sanitizer solution. "Good. I think I'm going to need a vacation."

Barbara jumped into her new sports car and raced home. She grabbed her purse, briefcase, shoes, and broken heel; then she stomped barefoot from the car and up the steps to her apartment. Hot tears welled in her eyes as she twisted the key to the door. The lock clicked, and Barbara slipped inside. She leaned with her back against the entrance, dropped the articles, and slid down until her bottom hit the floor.

"Why does he do that to me?" She swiped her eyes and gritted her teeth to keep the flood of tears from breaking the dam.

Over and over, she replayed the scene at Shear Design. Every bone in her body had jarred when the heel snapped. The plunge to the floor had been painful in more ways than the physical. She remembered heat scalding her cheeks and knew they had burned crimson. Humiliating.

She looked at her wrist. Though not swollen, it throbbed. Her hip ached with each step she took. It even hurt as she sat, not moving, on the carpet. She dreaded the bruise that had probably already formed.

Embarrassment warmed her cheeks anew as the fall played again in her mind. So many people had been in his shop. Some she didn't know and hoped never to see again. She couldn't face them. She couldn't face him.

Barbara scanned her living room. Snow-white carpet cushioned her hands and feet. Dolphin gray baseboards and crown molding framed pure white walls. An indigo leather sectional sat against the wall on her left. Splashes of silver, contemporary decor added richness to the deep mahogany wood furnishings. The room portrayed the person Barbara longed to be—clean, soothing, perfect.

Except when she was around Kenneth Marsh.

"For it is by grace you have been saved, through faith— and this not from yourselves, it is the gift of God."

The verse Barbara had committed to memory surfaced. She sighed; then she grabbed her purse, briefcase, shoes, and broken heel, and stood. After walking into the kitchen, she dropped the shoes and broken heel in the trash.

"It's by grace I'm saved." She placed her briefcase and purse on the table, and then slunk into a chair.

Grace.

For years, Barbara had battled her self-imposed rules and guidelines. Many times God had shown her mercy and love in the midst of imperfection. Still, her obsessive notions were like a cobra rearing its ugly head, sticking out its tongue, and waiting for a chance to sink venomous teeth into her skin.

She assumed the inner battle came from her militant father's no-nonsense treatment of his family. It had been right after high school when Dad left that Barbara's perfectionism seemed to come to a head. And yet she didn't blame her dad. She was a grown woman, a new creation in Christ. This matter was between her and God. Somehow she had to release this yearning for perfection.

Barbara walked to the refrigerator and grabbed a yogurt and an apple. *I'm sure that's why Ken likes to tease me so mercilessly.*

Trudging into the living area, she flopped onto the sectional and plopped her feet on the coffee table—an old habit that hadn't died when perfectionism wound its way into her life. If she were honest, she couldn't deny that part of her wished she could be as laid-back as Kenneth Marsh. He teased everyone, and they all seemed to love it. Nearly the whole town received haircuts from Ken. In their last ten years of acquaintance, since she'd graduated college, Barbara had only addressed him as Mr. Marsh or Kenneth—always formal, always direct. No fun. No games. A twinge of jealously tweaked her heart.

Course, it wasn't always this way. "Help me, Lord. Only You are perfect."

She leaned back on the couch and took a bite of apple. Juice rolled down her chin; she wiped it away with her hand. Closing her eyes, she remembered when Uncle Joe, the bait-and-tackle-shop owner, had introduced her to Kenneth. Of course, Joe wasn't really her uncle; nearly everyone just called him that since he didn't have any children of his own but loved to fish with the area's youth.

Barbara had been an insecure, late bloomer of a freshman, fishing with her favorite partner, Uncle Joe, when the most popular, good-looking junior in high school strode up to them and cast his line beside Joe. Barbara had thought she might die of embarrassment, but Joe introduced them, and Kenneth treated her like an old friend within no time.

How many times did we fish together at Canyon Lake? Too many times to count. But that was history, and she couldn't change it.

If I had laughed at Ken's joke instead of getting mad, I wouldn't have humiliated myself.

Barbara opened the yogurt and dipped in a spoon. If she had pretended to be amused at the ridiculous picture of him in swim trunks holding a doll, maybe he would have backed off. For that matter, if she had loosened up about his "fashion doll" jokes years ago, maybe she'd have made some kind of repose with him. After all, was his teasing really all that much of an insult? He ribbed everyone about everything. Fashion dolls were actually very pretty, even if they did have an unrealistically tiny waist and legs that didn't end.

On the other hand, Kenneth Marsh needed to grow up. He could see how much discomfort his words caused her but refused to stop. That really annoyed her.

Still, she couldn't control his actions, only her own. Barbara was unable to make him quit, but she could choose how she reacted to his childishness.

She sat up, placed a cloth napkin on the coffee table, then set the fruit and container on top. She closed her eyes. "I haven't been a very good witness to him, Lord. Forgive me."

A proverb slipped into her mind. "Do not answer a fool according to his folly, or you will be like him yourself." Barbara sighed, picked up her yogurt, and licked the tip of her spoon. She didn't have to join Kenneth Marsh in his game of foolishness.

Tomorrow morning she'd drive to his shop, apologize for her outburst, and give him another chance to put an appropriate picture on his barber's license.

Her plunge to the floor swept through her memory again. Her pulse quickened. She'd be embarrassed to see that man again so soon. A hint of renewed anger seeped into her skin.

No, I must pray for him, be good to him. God promises vengeance to be His. He would take care of Kenneth's treatment of her.

The memory of the fall ran through her mind again. She clasped her hands and rubbed them together. The remembrance of seeing him kiss cheerleader Kim Mavis at "their" spot on the lake also swept through her mind. She shook her head, dismissing the thought. "I'm heaping hot coals on your head, Ken."

Chapter 2

Ken released the handle of the push mower, and the engine died. Pulling up the edge of his muscle shirt, he wiped the sweat from his face. Just past midmorning and already the day was a scorcher. He pushed the lawn mower into his grandparents' shed. More perspiration trickled down his back and chest, soaking the rim of his jogging shorts.

He sighed as he surveyed the acre of land he'd just mowed. For years, he'd encouraged his grandparents to purchase a riding mower. They insisted the yard wouldn't look as nice, and there was no arguing with the eighty-year-old couple. Ken had quit trying.

Besides, grass cutting gave him some weekly exercise. A man didn't use too many muscles snipping scissors and reeling fishing poles, and those two things pretty much summed up the activity of his life.

He squinted against the sunlight toward his favorite spot on earth—his family's pond. He didn't live with his grandparents, though he could probably pitch a tent down by the water because he spent so much time there.

His grandparents were the only parents he'd known. Ken's mom and dad had died in a car accident when he was a baby. Grams and Pa never fully got over the tragedy. They fretted over the years Ken would never experience with his real mom and dad. As it turned out, Ken had grown up spoiled but still responsible. He hadn't wanted for anything, but he wasn't allowed to avoid real work either. The upkeep of the house and land belonged to him, and he took his job seriously.

Ken sneezed. He had spent his entire life in the country, but at thirty-four, fresh-cut grass still triggered his allergies. He trudged toward the old farmhouse.

"We still goin' fishin'?"

His white-haired, blue-eyed grandmother—wearing blue jeans rolled up to her knees, a button-down plaid shirt, and a fishing hat—met him at the door. Ruth held a tackle box in one hand and her fishing pole in the other.

Ken laughed. "Hang on, Grams. Let me wipe my face and get a drink." He hoped he could be like her four decades from now. She ran circles around most of the twenty-year-olds he knew. "Pa going?"

Grams huffed. "That ol' fuddy-dud. I reckon he won't be leaving that couch and book for the rest of the day."

A vision of Barbara Elliott swept through his mind. He could picture her curled up in a chair reading a novel of some sort.

Grams continued, "I'm surprised you'd ask. You know your pa doesn't take a likin' to fishin'. Never has."

He'd surprised himself with the question. He knew his granddad didn't fish. Since the last time Barbara had been in his shop, his perspective of people had been rocked. For quite some time, he'd considered Barbara an unfeeling, all-righteous beauty queen, but when she had fallen, he realized how wrong he'd been. There was fury in those pasture green eyes when she had looked up at him, but also hurt. A deep, down-to-the-core pain.

Ken wondered if there was a reason his pa didn't like to fish. He pondered whether his granddad might have been willing to try the sport, but Ken and Grams had never asked.

Nah. He inwardly pushed the thought away. In all the years he'd known his grandfather, Fred Marsh would not go anywhere near a pond, much less a tackle box. Truth was, Barbara wouldn't go within ten feet of a fishing pole, either—not anymore anyway.

"Your pa won't go within ten feet of a fishing pole."

Ken shook his head at his grandmother's words. She must have read his mind.

His grandma snapped her fingers in front of his face. "Snap out of it, boy. I'm ready to go."

He chuckled. "Okay, Grams."

Grams opened the back door and tottered out to his pickup truck. He loved his feisty grandmother. She'd chatter him into the ground at the house, but once at the pond, he wouldn't be able to coerce a peep from her. She wouldn't dare chance scaring the fish.

Glad he had put his fishing gear in the back of the truck before he came, he grabbed two bottles of water from the refrigerator. Ken walked into the living room. "I locked the shed."

"Hmm." Absorbed in his Bible, his granddad sat in a wingback chair with his feet propped on an ottoman. His bifocals had fallen to the edge of his nose.

"See ya."

"See ya, son." His granddad waved but didn't look up.

Ken shook his head and walked out of the house. How his grandparents ended up together, Ken would never know. His grandfather had his doctorate in English and had retired from a nearby university as a great, respected professor. His passions were literature and classical music.

His grandmother, on the other hand, graduated from college with an agricultural degree. She spent her life as what Ken lovingly called an "outdoors domestic engineer." She stayed at home but not in it. Grams spent more hours hunting, fishing, and gardening than she did anything else.

Even as a child, Ken could see their relationship made no sense. They were stark opposites, but Ken knew one thing: They loved each other and had for more than sixty years. In some important areas of life, the two agreed enough to be in love.

They said their love came from God, but Ken never could quite get a grasp on all that gospel and preaching stuff his grandparents made him endure as a child. It wasn't that God wasn't a good idea and all; it was just that Ken couldn't see any point in all that religious nonsense. His life was good enough as it was, plus he'd lost his parents. They'd believed in God, but that hadn't done them much good.

No, all that church stuff was not for him. Ken hopped

into the cab of the truck and started the engine. "Ready, Grams?"

She patted his arm. "Well, I imagine. I've been sitting out here waiting on you. What were you doin' in there anyway?"

"Just telling Pa bye."

"Oh. Guess that's all right. I'm anxious to get down there, you know. Don't want them little critters hidin' on us. The sun'll get too hot, and we won't catch us a single bite. Not a one."

Ken listened to his grandmother's chatter as he drove through the truck-made path to the pond. He jumped out to help her from the cab.

"Get my chair, son." She headed toward the edge of the pond. "No more gabbin'. Don't want to scare the fish."

Ken grinned. He'd spend the next two hours with his grandmother in complete silence, then get her back in the truck and never get a word in.

He pulled two chairs, his fishing pole, and a tackle box from the bed of the truck. He helped his grandma into her seat, then settled into his own. Pulling a night crawler from an old coleslaw container, he baited the hook, then cast it into the water.

For some reason, he wasn't in the mood to fish. He kept thinking about his grandparents and the odd relationship they shared. As a boy, he remembered his grandfather once telling him, "Son, if you can reach a level of mutual respect, there's nothing more enticing than loving your direct opposite."

His grandfather would wink and nudge his arm. "Add

just the right dose of Jesus to the recipe, and a man can love just about anyone, even Grams." Every time Grandpa said it, Grams would hear and give him a good fussing from the other room.

Ken smiled at the memory until his mind wandered to a long-legged, blond bombshell. If anyone fit the definition of Ken's counter, it was Barbara Elliott. He had no idea how to reach a level of compatibility with someone you completely disagreed with. Yet he couldn't stop thinking about her. It was the same every time he saw her, starting years ago when Joe, or rather *Uncle* Joe, first introduced them as teenagers.

Grams leaned over and whispered in his ear, "You ain't trying."

"Sorry, Grams." Ken reeled in his bait, then cast it into the water again.

"You wanna go back?"

"No, I'm fine."

"There's somethin' on your mind, isn't there?"

"Nothing important." He sat straighter in his chair.

She cupped his chin and turned him to face her. She stared into his eyes. He knew she was surveying his expression for any sign of worry. The woman had some kind of supernatural power to always know when something was wrong. He lifted his eyebrows and smiled in an attempt to fool her just this once. He knew how much she loved their weekly fishing trips, and he didn't want to rob her peace because he couldn't get his mind off Barbara.

His grandmother grabbed his arm, then shook her fist at him. Her eyes were lit with merriment. "You gonna tell me about it, or am I gonna have to beat it out of ya?" She clicked her tongue and winked at him.

He shook his head and chuckled at her silliness. "Grams, let's just fish."

Ken reeled in his line and checked to make sure he hadn't lost his night crawler. Finding the critter nicely stuck on the hook, he recast. His grandmother sat still beside him, too still. She wasn't even tending her line. A knot formed in his stomach. He knew what her brooding silence meant. He'd upset her. In only a matter of moments, Mount Saint Ruth would erupt.

"I never thought I'd live to see the day my own grandson wouldn't share his troubles with me."

Here we go.

"I've tried to be a good grams to you. Understandin', too. I even stopped fussing at you for not coming to church with us on Sundays."

Ken grabbed his grandmother's hand. He loved her, but at times she tended to be a bit of a spitfire. He didn't reply in hopes she would simmer down and return to her fishing.

Silence wrapped around them. Ken released a contented sigh. She must have decided to let it go.

"We're going back." She stood and reeled in her fishing line.

"No, Grams. You look forward to this all week. I'm telling you nothing's wrong."

Ruth picked up her tackle box and headed toward the truck. "Get my chair. We're goin' home."

Ken groaned. There was no use arguing with her. He

110

collected their things. He had ruined his grandmother's favorite day of the week. All because he couldn't get his mind off Barbara Elliott.

Barbara had been upset when Kenneth wasn't at work on Saturday. Most barbers made a great deal of money on the weekends and wouldn't or couldn't give up those appointments. Her curiosity was piqued, and she wondered if he'd had special plans and what they were.

I don't care what he does with his Saturdays. She applied mascara, then blinked several times to make sure her eyelashes were dry. She pulled her frozen-yogurt lipstick from her makeup case and smoothed the light beige color on her lips.

"There." She smoothed the front of the taupe short-sleeved silk shirt and looked in her full-length mirror. Crisp, cream-colored capris and light brown heeled sandals completed her favorite summer outfit.

Barbara had spent a good part of Saturday morning mustering the nerve to apologize to Kenneth. When he wasn't there, she'd been aggravated for the unnecessary headache and tense muscles that had accompanied her anxiety. Pete had assured her Kenneth had appointments Monday afternoon. With the day having arrived, Barbara had taken off several hours to prepare for this meeting.

Barbara took a deep breath and blew the air from her lips. *Help me, Lord, not to get mad at this man. Keep me focused on being a good witness for You.*

She grabbed her purse and keys and headed out the door. The drive seemed shorter than usual, and within moments, Barbara sat in front of Shear Design. She gripped the padded steering wheel as anxiety and embarrassment welled within her.

Barbara pondered how he would respond to her. Maybe he would laugh at her for falling, even try to mimic her fall to the whole shop. He might point at the photograph and tell everyone that she was the famous fashion-doll inspector.

Stop it. She opened the car door. *Just get this over with.* She walked into the shop.

"Be with you in a minute." Kenneth didn't look up. He squatted behind a small girl in his barber's chair, trimming the edges of her long, brown hair.

His tone sounded normal, almost professional. *Hmm. Pete must have forgotten to tell him I was coming. Good, maybe I'll catch him off guard.*

Barbara sat in a chair and picked up a hairstyling magazine. She flipped the pages and tried to think of anything except the reason for her visit.

"Barbara?" Kenneth's surprised voice shook her to attention, and she looked up at him.

He'd called her by her name. For the first time, he hadn't poked fun at her from the moment she walked through the door. Stunned, she sat glued to the chair.

Kenneth leaned toward the small girl in his chair. "Just a minute, Tabby." He crossed the floor toward Barbara. "Are you all right? That was a nasty fall. You didn't hurt yourself, did you?"

Barbara looked up at him. She couldn't move or speak. Kenneth Marsh was being kind and considerate. She wondered who this man was and what he had done with the real Kenneth.

He sat in the chair beside her and raked his fingers through his short, dark hair. His hazel eyes penetrated her soul with sincerity. "I went too far the other day. I'm sorry."

Barbara's eyes widened, and her mouth fell open. He had just apologized to her. She couldn't believe it.

"I came to apologize, as well." She looked away from his intense gaze. "I shouldn't have gotten so angry. I know you like to tease."

She glanced back at him. A smile spread across his lips. Not only did his mouth smile, but his eyes did, as well. His square jaw with a hint of stubble added masculinity to his expression. She couldn't remember a time she didn't love his face.

Her heart raced. She stood on shaky feet and wobbly knees and extended her hand to his. She had to get out of here. "We'll call it a truce. I won't cite you for the picture as long as you promise to get a legitimate one up on the wall."

Kenneth stood and grabbed her hand. "Agreed."

After years of jokes and jests, a compromise seemed awkward. Warmth covered Barbara's cheeks. She was at a loss for words.

Kenneth cleared his throat. "Just so you know, it's a compliment when I call you a fashion doll."

"I thought you said she was Darth Vader."

Barbara glanced down at the small girl who'd been

sitting in the barber's chair. Her hands were on her hips. She'd apparently gotten tired of waiting.

"Pete, come get your daughter!" Kenneth hollered. Barbara looked up at the man. His face had turned bright crimson. He shoved his hands into his front jean pockets and shuffled from side to side. "I—"

"What?" Barbara furrowed her brows. She had no idea what the girl could have possibly meant.

"Daddy, it's Vader!" the girl yelled and pointed toward Barbara.

Pete appeared from behind his station. "What are you talking about, Tabby?" His eyes widened when he saw Barbara. He snatched the girl and fled toward the back of the shop.

Barbara could hear the muffled reprimands. "That's what Ken said," the girl's voice echoed from the back.

Realization dawned. A deep hurt pinched Barbara's heart until rage welled inside her. She could feel the stirring in the pit of her gut, gripping and punching until the fury exploded. "Darth Vader!"

The words erupted from her mouth. Four customers whipped their heads toward them, mouths gaping. Silence dropped in the room. Déjà vu. He'd done it again. Humiliated her.

The apology, the concern, it was all just an act. He didn't want to be cited, so he tried to kiss up to the mean ol' state inspector.

She glared at him. He looked like a mouse caught in a cat's trap. He thought her a villain; she shouldn't disappoint him.

Barbara stomped toward his station. She pointed to the barren wall. "No license. One citing." She yanked open the drawer below his vanity. "No sanitizing tablets. Do you have any?"

Kenneth didn't speak. He just stood there with his mouth open.

"Well?"

"I ordered them. They're coming today."

"Citing number two!"

Barbara stomped to the sinks. She pointed at one of them, then spun around and looked at Kenneth. "There's hair in here."

Kenneth walked toward her. Anger lit his face. Good. She couldn't stand that he talked about her behind her back, then kissed up to her in person.

He grabbed a towel and wiped the hair out. "I just used this, *Doll Lady*. I haven't had time to clean it out."

Barbara held three fingers in front of his face. "Citing number three." She turned away from him and walked toward the front desk. "Maybe I should go home, get your folder, and redo my evaluation." She faced him again and batted her eyes. "I may have missed a few things."

Kenneth balled the towel, then threw it on the floor. "Go ahead."

Barbara straightened her shoulders and headed out the door. "I'll be back."

"I can't wait," he called out before the door could slam behind her.

She stomped to her car and slid inside. *I'm going to heap my own coals on your head, Mr. Kenneth Marsh!*

Chapter 3

I can't believe you talked me into this," Barbara quipped into her cell phone as she slammed her car door shut and headed into the retail store.

Ruby Townsend's laugh boomed into Barbara's ear. "It'll be good for you. Loosen you up a bit."

"What if I don't want to be loosened?" Barbara whined.

"You know that you need it. You jumped at the idea, remember?"

Barbara remembered. God had been working on her to soften up, allow some spontaneity, some disorganization into her life. Now, as she walked toward the fishing equipment in the store, Barbara wasn't convinced her initial feelings had been right.

"Barbara, I gotta go," said Ruby. "Just get what's on the list. We'll have a blast."

"A blast." Snapping the phone shut, Barbara grimaced as she took in the dozens of fishing poles hanging above her head.

"May I help you, miss?"

Barbara turned to see a teenage store employee standing

beside her. His shaggy, brown hair fell in front of his eyes. A few pimples scattered across his face made him appear entirely too young to have a job. He looked about as happy to help her as a barber getting ready to cut a squirming toddler's hair. She sighed. "Yes, you can help me. I need poles to fish with. . . ." She looked down at her list. "Bluegill and bass. I need different poles for different fish?"

The boy smiled, exposing more silver than she owned in her jewelry box. "Yeah, it helps." His eyes seemed to dance over a joke—her.

Barbara felt heat rush up her neck. The boy obviously thought she knew nothing about fishing. "I used to fish quite regularly. I just didn't pay much attention to what I was catching."

He nodded as if he didn't believe a word she said. "Yeah. Yeah." He motioned her to follow him. "Come on. I'll help ya."

"Surely not." Ken gawked at the slender, blond bombshell placing a fishing pole in her cart. He remembered the younger version of Barbara standing beside him and casting her bait into Canyon Lake. Her light yellow hair had been pulled back with a scrunchie. She'd been all arms and legs back then, so gangly, so kidlike, so fun. Time had changed her in many ways.

Ken shook away his thoughts and headed for the next aisle. He would just grab the things he had to have for the trip and get out of there before she saw him. He was in no mood to deal with Barbara.

Still, he couldn't help wondering why she was buying fishing equipment. In his wildest dreams, he couldn't envision Little Miss Perfect baiting a hook with a worm, let alone touching a night crawler. Why, the woman might go into cardiac arrest if she got her nails dirty.

"Imagine seeing you here."

Ken turned when Barbara spoke. For a moment, he saw a long, gangly teen with a smile splitting her face and her hair pulled up in a ponytail. The facade quickly faded when one eyebrow raised and her expression took a hardened, more mature look.

Ken blinked, then folded his arms in front of his chest. "I'd reckon I could say the same to you. I'm a frequent customer to this section of the store. How long's it been since you were here?"

Barbara took a deep breath. She seemed to struggle with her thoughts. "I seem to have forgotten a lot of things about fishing."

Ken softened. "Been a while, huh?"

"Yeah." She looked into his eyes. Her intense gaze nearly sucked his breath from his lungs.

"How long has it been?"

Barbara shrugged. "High school, I guess."

Her vulnerable stance did funny things to Ken's insides. He wanted to hold her hand, caress her cheek, something, anything. *What am I thinking? This woman drives me batty.*

"I hope I can remember how to do this." She bit her bottom lip.

Ken shoved his hands in his pockets and tried not to

think about the soft color on her lips and how she smelled sweeter than Grams's flowers. "Well, you can't be any worse than you used to be." She gawked at him, and Ken gasped. "That didn't come out right. I meant you never fished for real anyway." He cringed. *That hadn't come out right either.* "I mean—"

Barbara put her hand up to stop him. "Look, Kenneth. You were too busy spending your time kissing cheerleaders to know how good I was." She placed both hands on her hips and stomped her foot. "As I recall, there was many a time I caught more fish than you."

Ken huffed. "Hmm. A little jealous, are we?" He grimaced. That came out a bit meaner than he'd intended. Why he had a tendency to go for the jugular with Barbara was beyond him. "Barbara, I'm—"

"No." She gripped her cart so tight her knuckles turned white. "No, Kenneth Marsh. I will not listen to another word from a heartless, immature, blabbering idiot. You have never grown up. You probably never will." She flailed her arms. "I'm sorry, so sorry that we ever spent time on that lake together. I thought you had been my friend. You make me so, so—ugh!"

Ken watched as she pushed her cart away. A heavy weight seemed to push down on his chest. *I am an idiot. I am always an idiot when it comes to Barbara Elliott.* He exhaled a long breath. "The 'why' is what I don't understand."

The sweet aroma of French vanilla wafted through the

stairwell as Barbara made her way down into the church's basement. The congregation's annual spring craft fair had long been one of Chelsea's favorite days of the year. Barbara had to admit her friend's obsession did seem to spill over into her own heart each year. Though crafty items were not her favorite things around the house, Barbara loved to find floral wreaths and whatnots for her door and patio.

Barbara scanned the room filled with women of all ages, as well as a few unhappy-looking fellows who held several craft arrangements. Their frowns held steady as their wives placed more items in their hands. A slight giggle escaped, and Barbara covered her mouth so as not to gain any attention.

"Barbara, look at this."

Barbara made her way to Chelsea and the four or five men surrounding a table. Chelsea held up a bright orange stringy-looking thing. "They're fishing lures. Have you ever seen the likes?"

"No, I haven't." Barbara grabbed one and wrinkled her nose. The thought of a slimy, floppy animal hanging from it made Barbara's stomach churn. She didn't know if she was ready for her trip.

"You're going to have a blast."

"What?"

Chelsea smiled. "On your trip."

"Am I going fly-fishing? Do I need another pole?"

Chelsea shrugged and scooped several into her hands. "We'll take these."

After paying for the lures, they moved to the next

table. Barbara looked at her friend. "I don't know how you do that."

"Do what?"

"Know what I'm thinking."

"We've been friends for years."

"Okay, what am I thinking right now?"

"You've had another run-in with the most eligible bachelor-slash-barber in town, and you need to talk about it."

Barbara's jaw dropped. A knot twisted in her belly, and her hands went numb. "How could you possibly—"

Chelsea laughed and shoved her arm. "I'm just kidding you. Willy's mom works at the insurance agency with me. He came by and told her about the fight he'd witnessed at work between Ken and some blond lady."

"Who's Willy?"

"The clerk at the discount store."

Barbara groaned. "It was that bad?"

"Enough to run home and tell Mom about." Chelsea laughed out loud, then leaned over and whispered, "Makes you feel any better, he said Ken was a royal jerk and you told him off good."

Barbara closed her eyes. The scripture, *"A fool shows his annoyance at once, but a prudent man overlooks an insult"* popped into her mind. She hadn't been very prudent with Ken. She could have and should have ignored his insults. "I hope no one else saw us."

"I think it's the talk of the store. Small town. You know how it is."

Barbara's legs felt weak. She rubbed her temples, begging

the oncoming headache to stay at bay.

"Come on, girlie." Chelsea linked her arm with Barbara's. "Let's ditch this joint and hit the nearest coffeehouse for some java."

"You mean Betty's Diner."

"The one and only."

Barbara grinned and nodded. "Sounds good to me."

"You really called him a heartless, immature, blabbering idiot?" Chelsea's eyes were as big as the complimentary cookies Betty had given them when she apologized for the jerky men running around this town. Evidently Ken and Barbara's argument had made it to the diner, as well.

"Yes." Barbara straightened the salt and pepper shakers next to the sugar packet holder. A woman couldn't even have a simple argument in this town; everyone knew everything about everyone.

"You, Miss Sweet-Prim-and-Proper, actually said those words."

"Yes, I did." Barbara grabbed the cloth napkin off the table and scrunched it. "I feel terrible about it now. I'm a Christian, Chelsea, a new creation in Christ."

"Well, he must have said something to get you all riled up."

"That's what I've been thinking about all afternoon. You know how Kenneth is. He probably didn't actually mean what he said. I could tell by his body language that his words were coming out wrong, but he made me so mad just the same." Barbara exhaled, then refolded the napkin and set it on the table. "In my heart, I know I have to apologize, but Kenneth Marsh always pushes just the right buttons. I don't know how he does it."

Chelsea leaned back in her seat with a Cheshire cat smile splitting her lips. "Hmm, makes a gal wonder."

"What do you mean?"

"I'm just thinking about *why* Kenneth Marsh would get you all riled up."

"Because he's mean and immature and his jokes aren't funny." Barbara took a drink of the warm cappuccino.

Chelsea leaned forward and stroked her chin with her finger and thumb. "Or maybe," she said and winked, "you have a thing for him."

"What?" Barbara nearly spit java in Chelsea's face. "Are you nuts?"

"Just a thought."

"Just a wrong thought."

"Didn't Elizabeth drive Mr. Darcy near to insanity? Didn't Rhett nearly go mad over Scarlett?"

Barbara frowned. "Those were all men feeling crazy over women."

"Maybe Ken feels that way about you."

Barbara swatted the air. "Not likely. I was always like his kid sister in high school."

Chelsea clicked her tongue. "Yeah, but you've grown up. You're a beautiful woman now, inside and out."

"Chelsea."

"Well, it's the truth. Maybe your ol' pal Ken has a fire lit for you."

Barbara shook her head and grabbed her purse. "I think you're the one who's gone crazy." She pulled a couple of dollars from her wallet. "I've got to go. Lots of paperwork to get done before tomorrow."

Chelsea smiled an annoying all-knowing kind of smile. "Okay, I'll see you later."

Barbara walked out the door and into the quickly cooling night. A slight breeze blew her hair away from her face. Preposterous. The very possibility, the very idea of Ken having feelings for her was completely ludicrous. Still, she felt a down-to-her-core knowing that once again she would have to apologize to Ken. *I don't know if I can do it again, God.*

She thought of the apostle Paul and the many adversities he faced in obedience to God—shipwrecks, hunger, and persecutions of all kinds. And yet Paul said he was content in Christ. "The least I can do is apologize to an immature thirty-four-year-old."

Scrounging through her purse for her car keys, Barbara envisioned herself walking into Ken's shop for a third time in less than one week. The very thought made her throat and chest tighten. *What am I going to say?*

"I love your new do," said one woman to another as they walked past Barbara.

"Thanks." The lighter-haired woman fanned one side of her hair. "Ken, of course." They giggled and disappeared into the diner.

Pushing the automatic unlock on her key fob, Barbara grinned. She had an idea.

Chapter 4

"Finally done for the day." Ken dropped his comb into the cleaning solution and then stretched his arms out in front of him. He grabbed the broom from the closet and swept up the hair from his last client.

"Don't pack up too quick," Pete quipped.

Ken looked at his watch. Four o'clock. He'd get to his grandparents' house in plenty of time to mow, eat, and fish with Grams for a while.

"You had a call-in earlier," said Beth. "You have an appointment at four thirty."

Ken sighed. "Cut?"

"Cut and color, I think," said Pete.

"Guess I'll call Grams. I'll be over an hour longer than I thought."

"At least." Pete nodded his agreement.

"And, of course, you'll have to do your best, just like every other appointment," said Beth.

Ken frowned and walked toward his appointment book on the desk. "What is going on here?"

"An appointment." Beth covered her smile with her hand.

"That I'm staying late to see!" Pete laughed.

Ken grabbed his book and read the name penciled in for his 4:30 slot. "No." He shook his head. "No."

"Yep. The famous inspector is coming in for a haircut."

"I'll be back in a sec." Ken escaped to the back of the shop. After shutting the door of the bathroom, he flopped onto the toilet cover. Barbara had to be up to something. *She could go to any shop anywhere. Why would she come to mine?*

Her reason smacked him straight in the face. She wanted to keep track of every single thing he did wrong so she could cite him even more. No matter how good he cut hair, that woman wouldn't rest until she cited him right out of a business. Barbara Elliott had ice running through her veins.

He stood and turned on the tap. After splashing some cold water on his face, he grabbed a towel and wiped dry. He hated what had happened in the store. His intention hadn't been to hurt Barbara, but he had. Her response had been painful, more painful than he thought it would have been. He cared what she thought of him. He didn't understand it, but he cared just the same.

The bell jingled at the front of the store. Knowing it was Barbara, Ken looked at his watch. She was early. Of course, she was early. Barbara Elliott couldn't be anything less than punctual, anything less than perfect. And he was drawn to her like a bass to a spinner bait.

Ken's knees grew weak. He tried to stretch the stiffness

of hours of clipping from his hands and wrists. Barbara had the upper hand, and he hated it. He looked at his reflection in the mirror. "She's just one person in a sea of people. Don't get so frazzled, Marsh."

I don't believe this was one of my better ideas. Barbara fought off the urge to hurl her lunch as she settled into Ken's chair.

"So, what are we doing today?" he asked as he snapped the heavy plastic cape around her neck. He pulled the clip from her hair and let her tresses fall past her shoulders. "Your hair is really thick."

"Yeah, it's a pain. I have to straighten out the waves every morning."

He tousled her hair and then raked his fingers through it. "I'd have never guessed. You must spend a lot of time on it."

" 'Bout an hour a day."

His touch shouldn't have felt so nice, shouldn't have felt so soothing. He shouldn't have smelled so good, either. Her favorite men's cologne seemed to wrap around her. She needed to get on with her apology, but somehow the words didn't come. She felt like a puppy getting her belly rubbed, unable and unwilling to move a muscle.

"I know a cut that would look beautiful on you." He smiled fully.

Barbara closed her eyes. "Nothing drastic, okay?"

"You're the boss." He lifted the front of the plastic cape. "Now let's get that hair of yours washed."

Ken hadn't prepared himself for the softness of Barbara's hair as it fell from his fingers like Grams's freshly tilled topsoil just before she planted in the spring. And the thickness—he'd never have imagined it. He turned the water on, allowing it to run over his hand until warm. All day, he swept his fingers through hair—coarse hair, fine hair, different colors and lengths—yet something about Barbara's hair beckoned him to drink in its feel.

"Go ahead and lean back." The fragrance of her light perfume mixed with the shampoo and surrounded him in a sweet aroma. As he washed her thick tresses, he couldn't help savoring her smooth skin. Sprinkles of freckles kissed her nose and cheeks from slight exposure to the sun.

He looked at the dimple in her chin and remembered teasing her about someone having stuck her with a pencil, leaving the dent. The dimple actually complimented her face perfectly.

Get a grip, Marsh. He finished rinsing the conditioner from her hair and wrapped her tresses in a towel. "Come on back to the chair."

Ken knew his voice sounded a little gruffer than it should to a client, but his attraction to her really grated on his nerves. He knew she wanted to slam him with one citing or another: one unwashed sink or misplaced comb. He had to keep his guard up. So far, she hadn't said anything. Not one word. He couldn't decide what to make of it.

"So, Barbara." He pulled off the towel and patted her head with it. "Do you want to try a new cut?"

She took a deep breath. Her eyebrows met in a concerned line. Barbara looked at his counter and bit the bottom of her lip. He could tell she had something to say to him.

Probably she had a problem with all his cartoon character memorabilia. He couldn't help it that Pete's daughter had some weird fascination with cartoons and that he was a glutton for entertaining kids. There was nothing in any barber school manual that said a fellow couldn't enjoy a few animated figures every once in a while.

"Well," she began, then stopped.

Ken sighed. It was late. He was tired. Grams would still want to go fishing. He didn't need to get into a fuss with Barbara today, and he was particularly miffed that her lips looked so kissable.

Barbara shifted in the chair. "This probably wasn't a good idea. Really, I just wanted to talk to you about the other—"

"How 'bout a good trim?" He sliced his comb through the back of her wet hair.

She sighed and leaned back. "Yeah, that sounds good."

"Pete had you down for a color, as well."

"He did?"

"Yeah."

Barbara shook her head. "No, that's not necessary. Anyway, remember when we ran into each other at the discount store? I just wanted to—"

He picked up his comb and quipped, "By the way, this is sterile."

"Yes, I believe you. About the other day—"

Before she could finish, he grabbed his scissors and a section of her hair. After pulling the lock straight, he ran the scissors along the length, contemplating where to snip. Ken decided an inch would be sufficient for a nice, blunt cut.

He positioned the scissors just above his fingers, as was his habit for the first snip of a haircut when an inch or more was involved. Ken would then show the cut piece to the customer, ensuring he or she wanted that amount and not more cut. He began the quick final motion closing the blades of the scissors when Barbara flung her head back and squealed at such a high pitch Ken feared she'd break his mirror. Her hands flailed wildly through the air. "Get it! Get it away!" she screeched.

Ken quickly pulled the scissors away from her head. In the same motion, he stepped back and moved the scissors behind his back. A bee circled and buzzed away from his station. Sucking in his breath, Ken looked at the snip that was a full three inches shorter than the rest of Barbara's hair.

"Did you see it?" Barbara squealed and pointed to the flying insect as it droned toward the back of the shop. "It nearly attacked me."

All Ken could see was the lock of hair, a full three inches of it, which he held between his fingers. He looked at the spot of missing hair. Beads of sweat popped out on his forehead as heat washed over him.

"Barbara, I am so sorry." He let his voice trail off. "I don't know how to tell you this. . . ."

Barbara looked into the mirror. Ken watched as her

eyes grew as big as bobbers when she saw the snip of hair he held between his fingers. She fought to swallow the obvious knot in her throat. He felt her entire body tense in the chair.

Barbara bit the inside of her lip when she saw the lock of hair between Ken's fingertips. Her lock of hair. She raised her hand and touched the back of her head. Sickness welled in her stomach when her fingertips ran across the cut that rested well above her shoulders. That was not the snip of any trim she'd ever had. *He didn't mean to. I screamed. I leaned back.*

There was no escaping now; all of her hair would have to be cut above her shoulders. It hadn't been that short since—middle school.

God, I've never liked my hair short. I'm going to throw up. She swallowed hard and tried to focus on breathing. She couldn't reattach that piece. *Breathe in.* It would have to be cut. *Breathe out. Focus, Barbara. Your intentions were to apologize. Deep breath in.* She needed to be a light to Ken, to show him how a Christian should act. *Cleansing breath out.*

Barbara looked at the mirror. Ken seemed to hold his breath waiting for her response. He looked apologetic, but he also seemed to expect her to blow her top, cause a scene, and run to the nearest barber she could find to fix her hair.

Swallowing hard, she knew what she had to do. Knew

it to the depths of her core. How she would make it through this appointment, she didn't know. It went against her nature, everything she knew, every way she behaved, but she couldn't argue with her spirit. She had to let Ken cut her hair. Pinching her lips together, she closed her eyes. She would trust God—and Kenneth Marsh.

"She didn't say a word." Ken glanced at Grams, who had been suspiciously quiet throughout his entire confession about what had happened at the shop. Normally Ken wouldn't have shared everything with Grams, but he was more than a little perplexed at Barbara's actions—or rather, lack of actions—during her haircut.

"How did it turn out? The haircut?" asked Grams.

Ken thought about the haircut and how the shorter length seemed to enhance her light complexion and made her eyes seem a deeper shade of green. The choppy style just above her shoulders gave her a less-kept look that made her very attractive. Ken couldn't keep his eyes off her. "She looked beautiful."

"Hmm."

Ken hit a bump in the truck-cut path to the pond, causing Grams to fall into him. "Sorry."

"So, this gal who you say has to have everything perfect didn't say anything about a three-inch accidental slip of the scissors?" asked Grams.

"Well, she did scream and lean back into the scissors, Grams." Ken shook his head. "But she didn't say a word."

"Sat there and took it, did she?"

"Grams, it was an accident. It really wasn't my fault, but I did figure she'd run off to another barber to fix it."

"So she stayed and put her faith in ya."

Ken frowned. As usual, Grams was trying to slip faith and Jesus into the conversation. But the truth was, Barbara *had* stayed right in his barber's chair and let him finish the cut, even though it didn't end up being what she'd intended.

One of their many high school fishing trips came to mind. Barbara had just come back from youth camp somewhere in upstate New York. She had told him how some of the kids had laughed at the "hillbillies" and their Southern accent. It had burned him up just hearing her talk about it, but Barbara didn't seem overly upset. All she could talk about was the Bible study and worship songs and how she wanted to stay longer and share her "hillbilly" faith with them.

Once he and Grams reached the pond, Ken hopped out, grabbed the chairs, poles, and bait from the back of the truck, and followed Grams to their favorite spot. After Grams had settled into her chair and cast her pole, Ken did the same. Grams leaned over and touched his forearm. "Thanks for sharing with me. I'll be praying for ya."

"Yeah." Ken never knew how to respond when she said that. He didn't really want her praying for him, but he didn't want to be disrespectful, either.

She patted his arm. "You can just think on it all a little while." Her mouth split into a full smile, and she winked.

"Besides, we don't want to scare the fish."

Ken shook his head. Grams would never change. They could chatter anywhere—at the house, in the truck—but not at the pond.

Chapter 5

Ken breathed in the fresh, country air as he and Travis headed for town before making their way to Canyon Lake for the fishing trip. The sky held clear and bright, allowing the sun to bathe them in natural warmth. Ken needed this break. His week couldn't have been any longer.

On Monday a lady brought in her four children, all under the age of seven, for haircuts. He had two hours blocked off for the wrecking crew. He should have set aside more like six. Between their crying every time he picked up his scissors to their squirming every time he stepped near them, Ken had his hands full. A part of him felt great pity for the frazzled mother. He even contemplated not charging her at all. Then he looked at his watch and the time he'd spent attempting to make each cut match the other and decided he'd earned his pay.

Tuesday wasn't any better. His favorite hair dryer blew up. Ten years. Ten long, faithful years, he'd had that dryer. The very thought of using another made him feel somehow dishonest or unfaithful.

Wednesday, Thursday, and Friday all rolled up into a disliked haircut and color, a too-tight perm, lost sanitizer tablets, a broken comb, a much-too-high phone bill, and a sick fellow barber who needed his appointments covered for him. Ken was plumb exhausted.

Thankful that Travis didn't seem to have much to say, Ken watched a rabbit hop away from the gravel road and toward a thicket of trees. The little guy was probably trying to escape a world of chaos, as well. Ken almost chuckled aloud at the mental picture of a papa rabbit trying to run from a continuously multiplying group of baby bunnies.

They passed the abandoned red barn that had been there as long as Ken could remember. He'd attended many a high school party there. Nothing good came of the get-togethers. Inevitably one or all of them ended up in some sort of trouble. Barbara had never been a part of all that.

I can't get that woman out of my head.

He had been thinking about her all week. Since the haircut, he couldn't get her out of his mind. He'd always enjoyed teasing her for being so stiff and uptight, which she was, but this week he'd come to realize that she was the real thing. He knew she thrived on perfection, but she sat there and willingly let him cut her hair in a way he knew she never would have chosen.

Even though the cut had been an accident, when Ken thought about it, he was willing to bet Barbara had made the choice to make the most of it and trust him. Made a willful decision, just like Grams's preacher always talked about when it came to being a Christian. He could hear him sounding from the pulpit, "It's a choice, your choice." The whole thing perplexed him.

"Since you paid for the gas, I'm buying the bait." Travis interrupted his thoughts.

"Sounds good to me."

Travis pulled into the parking lot in front of Joe's Bait and Tackle shop. They hopped out and headed into the store. As usual, Joe stood behind the counter helping a young fellow weigh his fish.

"Hey, Joe," Ken said and walked over to his longtime friend.

"Well, Ken. Good to see ya. How ya been?"

"Good. Whatcha got there?"

Joe patted the boy, who couldn't have been more than thirteen, on the shoulder. "This young man has caught himself some good fish. He's thinking on entering the tournament, and I reckon he'll be hard to beat."

The boy grinned, revealing a mouth full of silver. He bent down and pulled another fish from his cooler. "What do you think about this one, Joe?"

Ken had to admit the boy had caught himself a good-sized bass. The kid just might do well at the tournament. Joe grabbed the fish and set it in the container on the scale. "Yep, it's a good 'un."

"Are you ready?" Travis walked up to the counter with several containers of night crawlers and mill worms.

"Yep."

"Joe, how ya been?" Travis asked as he set the bait on the counter away from the boy's fish.

"Good. I think y'all have some competition this year."

He winked at the boy, and Ken had a fresh remembrance of how Joe was always ready and willing to encourage him in his fishing. He could almost feel Joe pulling the bill of his cap down after Ken had teased Barbara for not baiting her hook right the first time.

"We just might. See ya, Joe." Travis paid, scooped up the bait, and headed for the door. "Ken, you coming?"

Ken shook his head and followed him to the truck. "Yeah. Don't know what's gotten into me."

"You've been a bit preoccupied. Something bothering you?"

"Just tired. I need some R & R."

Travis grinned. "You do know the girls are coming tomorrow, right?"

"Not my girls." Ken smiled and stretched his arms. "It's your wife and her friend. I believe you, my friend, will be the one worrying about the girls."

Travis groaned. "Guess you're right."

"I'll be sitting by the lake, drink in one hand, fishing pole in the other, letting the sun just soak right through to my bones." Ken inhaled and exhaled aloud. "Oh yeah, I'll have it made."

Barbara looked at her filled suitcase. Everything inside would be filthy and stinky by the time she got home. Her nice white T-shirt—it wouldn't be white. But it was her favorite comfortable shirt, so she knew it had to go with her. Those finally-stretched-to-fit-exactly-right jeans that lay at the bottom of her suitcase would come back trashed, as well, but she had to take them. If she had to be stuck outside for a full week, she had to at least feel good.

"Chelsea, what was I thinking?" she whined into the phone. "I haven't camped in years." She gasped. "Make that over a decade."

Chelsea laughed so loud Barbara had to hold the receiver away from her ear. "You're going to have a blast. Let that cool new do be your guide."

Barbara groaned and turned to see her reflection in her bedroom mirror. Ken had really done a number on her hair. It stuck out in choppy pieces all over her head.

However, Barbara had to admit she liked it. She felt freer, more alive, with her hair like this. She couldn't decide if it was the cut or if it was the fact that she sat there and allowed Ken to do whatever he wanted that made her feel good. Maybe it was the listening to God and trusting Him to keep the crazy barber from ruining her hair completely. Whatever it was, she felt free, and she loved it.

"You're right, Chelsea. This is going to be fun. It's okay to get a little ruffled."

"I have waited so long to hear you say that."

"It's amazing what a haircut can do."

"I think it was more of a letting go of control that did it."

Barbara twirled a piece of hair. "Yes. God's better with the control things anyway."

"Amen to that. I've gotta go. Have fun tomorrow, okay?"

"I will. Bye."

Barbara clicked the phone off and zipped her suitcase. She grabbed her car keys and her purse. Before her week in the woods, she was going to splurge on the biggest sundae she could get her hands on.

Ken watched as Travis grabbed his Bible and a notebook from his duffel bag. His friend grabbed a soft drink from the cooler. "I'll be back in a bit," said Travis; then he strode toward the lake.

Bible study. Since he "found Jesus," the man was always studying his Bible. Ken didn't quite understand it. Sure, he'd been raised in church. Ken had seen many lost souls give their lives over to Jesus, but Ken didn't feel lost. He had a good house, owned a great business, had super friends. His grandparents had always been wonderful to him. True, he'd lost his parents when he was a child, but Ken had been small enough that he'd never really known them anyway.

Ken had always been a pretty good guy. He didn't steal from people—had never killed anyone. Sure, he'd played some pranks on people and had been known to party a bit when he was in high school, but who didn't do that? Ken just didn't see why he would have a need for God.

Why was he worried about it anyway?

Suddenly Ken felt curious about what Travis did when he read his Bible. Ken had seen Pa sit at his desk reading scriptures and writing down notes about stuff. Then Pa would lay his head on his desk, just as Ken, as a small boy, had at school when he was tired.

Grams loved to sit in her flower garden. She had a bench in the very middle of it. She'd go out there with her Bible, read just a very few moments, and then kneel in front of her bench. For some reason, Grams always looked so pretty at that bench. Ken figured it had to do with all the flowers around her.

Ken tried to walk quietly toward Travis. What did Barbara do when she read the Bible? Ken could imagine her sitting at an immaculate wooden desk with a perfect leather Bible, a silver pen, and a new notebook. Manicured fingernails would slice through pages as she searched for the "right" verse for the day.

After passing several trees, Ken saw Travis. He sat on a large rock next to the lake. He had his face lifted toward the sky. His eyes were closed. Ken was struck by how peaceful he seemed. Within mere seconds, Travis looked down at his Bible. He flipped the page and appeared to intently read.

Embarrassment welled inside Ken. Spying on a friend's quiet moments was not something he did every day. He shook his head and then swiped up a long, thin stick from the ground. He turned back toward camp, smacking at bushes and leaves as he went.

Seeing Travis bugged him. Bugged him right down to the tips of his toes. Ken didn't understand this need for time with God. Travis was a great guy and always had been, but now he had this deep-down happiness to him. A contentment of sorts.

Maybe his faith has something to do with that.

Ken frowned. His thoughts went back to a summer some twenty years before. *I must have been no older than fifteen.* He and a group of friends had gone to camp. About six of them decided to skip out in the middle of the night. No particular reason. Just see what they could find to do.

Zane Matthews would not go. He said something about not wanting to sneak out when they knew they shouldn't. Ken had been as ruthless as his buddies in teasing him.

"It's wrong, and you all know it," Zane had said, and then he crawled back into his bunk.

Ken left with his buddies, and they did a little of nothing. Mainly they just hung out and talked about girls. They never got caught, but Ken couldn't help watching Zane the rest of the week. The guys had been merciless in taunting him about the great time they'd had that night. Zane didn't seem to mind.

He never wavered, and for the rest of their high school years, Ken noticed that Zane always seemed to do what was "right" no matter what the other guys did.

The same peace that encompassed Zane also filled Travis. The two had Bible study in common. Ken had never before cared about what people thought of God, and he didn't know why he cared now.

Well, that wasn't exactly true. It was the sin thing that tripped him up. Ken just didn't feel like he was all that much of a sinner that he had to beg God for forgiveness. He never did anything that was all that bad.

A vision popped into his head of Barbara falling and then jumping to her feet in his shop. The hurt in her eyes betrayed the overwhelming embarrassment she felt. That was pretty bad. He smacked a cluster of leaves hanging from a low branch. But it wasn't really his fault.

"Barbara!"

Barbara smiled at Ruby's squeal and the astonished look on her face. She fluffed the bottom of her hair. "What do you think?"

"I'm stunned." Ruby grabbed Barbara's arm and twirled her around. "I love it, but it's so different from anything I could imagine you doing."

"Well, I didn't exactly ask for it."

"You didn't?"

Barbara giggled as Ruby touched one side of Barbara's hair. "It's a long story. Let's just say it involves Kenneth Marsh."

Ruby recoiled her hand as if she'd been burned. "You still don't get along?"

"Did we ever get along?" Barbara quipped. "Seriously. The man drives me bonkers, but lately God's been doing a work in me. Wanting me to chill out a bit." She laughed and shrugged. "Seems God's been using Ken to help me."

Ruby shifted her weight from one foot to the other. "Um." She scooped one of Barbara's suitcases off the floor and turned toward the door. "That's good."

"Put that down." Barbara tried to grab the luggage from Ruby's grasp. "Travis would kill me if he saw his pregnant wife toting my bag."

Ruby fidgeted and didn't look at Barbara. "I'm all right. Not helpless, you know."

Barbara frowned. "What's going on?"

"Nothing." She bustled out the door and down the walk.

A sinking feeling weighed in Barbara's stomach. She grabbed her other bag and followed her friend. "Tell me what's up, Ruby. I know you too well."

Ruby opened the back of the car and shoved the suitcase inside. She seemed to hide in the trunk. "What could be wrong?"

Barbara frowned. What could be wrong? Something with Ken. Ruby had gotten frazzled when Barbara mentioned Ken. A thought popped into her mind, causing Barbara's head to feel light. Her heart thumped in her chest. "Who was the friend you said Travis was bringing?"

The trunk seemed to swallow Ruby, she leaned so far into it. "I never said."

Barbara's palms grew clammy. Ken and Travis were friends, quite good friends. She looked up at her apartment, contemplating some reason she had to stay. Clean out the freezer maybe, or wash down walls. She had been meaning to go through her closet and give some clothes to Goodwill. "Who did Travis take?"

A muffled sound came from behind the trunk. Barbara walked over to her friend. Ruby had just shoved a handful of potato chips into her mouth.

"Ruby." Barbara crossed her arms in front of her chest. "Who's going?"

"I just told you." Ruby laughed when potato chips spit from her mouth. "I need a drink." She opened a cooler, grabbed a bottle of water, unscrewed the top, and took a big swig.

Barbara took the bag of chips from Ruby's hand. "Who was that again?"

Ruby sighed. "It's Ken."

Ken thought his heart would beat out of his chest. He sat in the folding chair he'd brought to fish with. Looking at the woods around him, everything seemed so alive and distinct. He watched a bird with a worm hanging from her mouth fly above him and into her nest. It reminded him of Grams bringing his Bible to his bed at night for a bedtime story. The bird's babies chirped so loud they seemed to drown out the other creatures dwelling around them. As a boy, he'd yearned for her stories, as well.

He looked at the campfire and remembered a missionary visiting their church during their annual campout. Their whole congregation had gathered around a campfire and listened to the man share his experiences in another country.

Biting into a piece of beef jerky, Ken leaned back in his chair. Constant memories seemed to taunt him. The time he'd taken Grams's car without permission. The time extra supplies had been delivered to the shop, but he just let it go. He shook his head; doing wrong had been a part of his life.

Nature, fresh and clean, beckoned serenity. Serenity that he just couldn't seem to feel. Grams had always said that if you doubted God, all you had to do was look at nature to see how wrong you were. Ken couldn't even look around him. Everything screamed of a God Ken didn't know.

Travis strode toward camp. Sweat beaded on Ken's forehead, and bile rose in his throat. The time had come. Ken motioned for Travis to sit beside him. "We need to talk."

" 'Bout what?"

"God."

A light breeze swept through Barbara's hair as she walked around the back of the car to get her things. Nature smelled more wonderful than she remembered. The trees, lush and green, swayed with the wind. They seemed to beckon her to the camp.

Hefting her bags on her shoulders, Barbara followed Ruby up the path toward their campsite. She had an overwhelming urge to take off her tennis shoes and feel the beaten grass beneath her feet. Barbara had spent many a barefoot year in these very parts.

"Hi, Barbara."

Barbara jumped at Ken's voice. She hadn't heard the guys approach. The crush she'd had on him arrowed its way back to her heart. He belonged at this lake, in these woods, when she was here. Most of her fishing memories included him. She smiled. "Hey."

"Let me get those for you." He took the bags from her. "I'm glad you came."

Shocked by Ken's actions, Barbara nodded. "Yeah, me, too."

They walked toward the campsite in silence. Barbara tried to focus on the beauty around her as her mind continued to wander to Ken. Being in nature was his element. He looked rugged with his day's growth of a beard, yet his features had softened. He smelled clean and natural, the way she remembered him from years before. It nearly astounded her.

By the time they reached camp, Travis and Ruby had already started unpacking her gear. "You and Ruby are sharing your tent, right?" asked Ken.

"Yeah."

"I'll help you get it set up."

"Okay."

Barbara watched as Ken took the tent and pegs from her bag. She grabbed one side of the floor, and he grabbed the other. They stretched it out. Within no time, they had the frame up and Ken had all four pegs secured into the ground. Together they secured the tent over the frame.

Pulling her folding chair from its bag, she set it up and then grabbed two drinks from her cooler. She handed one to Ken. "You still like Ale-8-One?"

He pulled his chair beside hers and opened the bottle. "Yeah, but I thought you hated it."

Barbara wrinkled her nose as Ken took a long swig of the sugary, caffeine-filled drink that was native to Kentucky and a staple to many of its residents. "I don't hate it; I'd just be so jazzed on caffeine and sugar I'd never fall asleep again in my life."

Ken laughed. "And yet you brought some with you camping."

Heat rushed up Barbara's neck. She'd bought them for him. Once Ruby told her that Ken would be there, it just seemed right to see him fishing with an Ale-8-One in his hand as he had all those years before.

Ken must have noticed the red creeping up her cheeks, because he smiled. "Thanks, Barbara."

For once, he didn't say anything to taunt her. Barbara shifted in her chair when she found herself wanting to count the many dark flecks in his hazel eyes. She looked away from him. "Where do you suppose Travis and Ruby went?"

"Maybe they went down to the lake for some time alone."

Barbara nodded and gazed toward the path that led to the lake. "It is beautiful there."

"Yes, it is."

Ken's voice held such a winsome tone that Barbara couldn't help looking up at him. Her heart raced at the sincerity in his gaze that fell fully upon her. She wondered what had happened to him.

Chapter 6

Ken yawned and stretched his arms above his head. The fresh scent of coffee filled his tent. After unzipping his sleeping bag, he pulled off his long johns and put on a pair of sweatpants. He grabbed his favorite Jeff Foxworthy, You-Might-Be-A-Redneck T-shirt off the ground, shook it free of any nighttime eight-legged inhabitants, and then put it on.

Stepping out of the tent, he almost fell over his own two feet at the sight before him. He rubbed his eyes with his knuckles. Surely he was dreaming. He blinked and then opened his eyes as big as he could. With her back to him, Barbara leaned over a skillet holding a spatula in her hand. A second later, she scooped up a flapjack and flipped it in the air.

Her dark jeans fit snug against her long, slender legs. One of the back pockets was ripped and fell over the rest of the pocket. The crisp, pale pink T-shirt she wore added just the right touch of Barbara to her worn, out-of-character jeans. She had her hair pulled up in a ponytail. Wisps of hair fell down her neck and behind her ears, giving her the most tantalizing, bedraggled look he'd ever seen.

"Sleep well?" Her soft voice nearly scared him out of his britches.

"I, uh. . ."

She giggled and turned to face him. Without makeup, her freckles seemed to take over her complexion. Deep green eyes smiled at him. "You sounded like a grizzly, yawning like that. Want a pancake?"

Ken cleared his throat. "Sure."

Barbara pointed the spatula to her left. "Coffee's over there. Ruby made it a bit strong."

"Fine with me." Ken grabbed the sole unused mug and filled it to the top. Lifting the cup to his nose, he inhaled deeply. The brew was strong enough to wake up the weariest of campers.

Barbara handed him a plate stacked high with pancakes. She pointed to the syrup and butter on the table. "Everything you need is there. Hope you don't mind that I made them like my grandpa's."

Ken put several on a clean plate, poured a glob of syrup on top, cut off a piece with his fork, and shoved it into his mouth. "Mmm, tastes like—"

"Peanut butter. My grandpa always made pancakes with biscuit mix and peanut butter." She grinned and piled a couple of flapjacks on a second clean plate. Pulling off a large piece, she popped the whole thing into her mouth. She grabbed her coffee and swallowed a large gulp. "One of my favorite memories of him." She wiped her face with a paper towel. "I think it's just you and me today."

Ken lifted his mug to his lips and took a slow drink.

He hadn't seen Barbara act this freely in years. She perplexed him but intrigued him, too—not to mention attracting him in the most primitive of ways. He had an almost uncontrollable urge to scoop her into his arms and plant a big kiss on her lips.

"Unless you'd rather fish on your own."

He looked up to see her frown. She'd mistaken his silence for disinterest. But what could he say to her? If he spoke, he'd end up telling her things that should be left unsaid.

She stood, brushed her hands on her jeans, and then turned away from him.

"I made a commitment to God yesterday." The words flew from his lips before he'd had time to think. She was the first he'd told besides Travis.

She turned around. "What?"

"Yeah, I'm a changed man."

"Wow." She shoved her hands in her jean pockets and looked up at the sky. "That's wonderful."

Ken looked at his plate. "I've wasted a lot of time feeling like I didn't need God."

"But you've got lots of time yet to depend on Him. I've kind of learned some lessons about that myself over the last few weeks."

"Really?"

She pulled out her ponytail and shook her hair loose. "This was my breaking point."

Ken's heart filled with remorse. "I'm sorry about that."

"No, it's okay. Don't you see? I feel better, too. Everything doesn't have to be perfect."

Ken gazed at his fishing pole leaning against his tent. "If memory serves me right, it's been awhile since you've been fishing."

Barbara smiled. She walked to her tent and disappeared inside. Within moments, she came out holding a fishing pole in one hand and a tackle box in the other. "It's been awhile, but I'm ready. Bass, right?"

Barbara followed Ken down the narrow dirt path toward the lake. Though still morning, the sun had already risen high, promising that a warm day lay ahead. Twigs and small branches snapped and popped around them as they pushed their way down the trail.

Barbara inhaled deeply when the lake came into view. Deep blue water extended as far as she could see. The bank was worn and dusty from obvious frequent visits from passersby. She'd been a teenage girl the last time she'd seen this water. Gangly, awkward, and completely unsure of herself.

Ken pulled his chair out of the bag and unfolded it. Barbara put the tackle box down and followed his lead. "So, where are Travis and Ruby?" Ken picked up his pole and fixed his line and bobber.

"They're out on a boat Travis rented for the day. They'll be back after lunch. We'll join them then."

"Needed some time alone, did they?"

Barbara grabbed her pole and tried to remember how to get the line fixed properly. "Well, with Bryce at home and a new baby coming, they probably don't get a lot of alone time." The reel popped. She wasn't doing this right.

"Here. Let me help." Ken took her pole and fixed her line and bobber. He handed it back to her.

"Thanks. I hope this is like riding a bike."

Ken laughed. "Don't worry. It'll come back." He opened a container of mill worms and squished one onto the hook.

Barbara scrunched up her nose. She'd hated this part of fishing. Not wanting to wimp out, Barbara fished through the sawdust-filled container and pulled out a mill worm. She looked at it and frowned.

"Want some help?"

Ken looked entirely too pleased with her moment of weakness, but she didn't care. Barbara handed him the worm and let him put it on her hook.

After he handed her pole back to her, Barbara watched as Ken cast his line with ease. She took a breath. *Okay, let's see. I hold the button and then flick the pole like I'm throwing a softball. At the highest point of the flick, I let go of the button.*

Barbara mimicked the action. The line was supposed to fly through the air, and the bobber would land in the water. Hers fell flat at her feet. *That's okay. Just try again.*

She pushed the button and flicked the pole a second time. Again it fell at her feet. She peeked at Ken from the corner of her eye. A full grin split his lips. He didn't look back at her—just bit the bottom of his lip.

Squishing her pride as far down in her belly as she could, she determined that by the third time she'd have it. She tried again. This time, her line made it a few feet away from her. She straightened. Now, she could do it. She reeled the line in again, then flicked it once more. This time, the bobber flew through the air and landed a good ways from her.

"Good job. I knew you could do it."

Barbara's heart swelled. "Thanks."

Ken sat in his chair beside her. Barbara didn't quite feel ready to sit. A slow breeze caressed her cheeks. She shouldn't have spent so many years away from the lake. The air smelled clean and crisp. Trees, reaching for the sky, surrounded them and the entire lake. Their full green leaves swayed with the wind.

Her parents' divorce had been devastating to her as a teen, but now she regretted that she had stopped coming here. God seemed to wrap His majestic arms around her. She thought of Ken sharing his newfound faith. *God, You are awesome.*

Bending down to scratch her leg, she sneaked a quick peek at Ken. His gaze was transfixed on the water. He had changed, but not completely. He was still Ken. She could still see mischief flitting through his eyes, but he'd been kind to her and didn't make fun. The attraction she'd spent fifteen years trying to squelch welled inside her. This time, she wondered if she should let it grow.

"Are you ready to do some tubing?" Travis scraped the remains of his lunch into the trash bag.

Barbara nearly swallowed her fork. She pulled it away from her mouth before she gagged. "Are you serious?"

"Yeah."

"I didn't know we were tubing." Fear sped up her heart.

"Have you ever been?" asked Ken as he stood and started cleaning up the food. She handed him her plate, and he tied the top of the trash bag into a tight knot to ward off any hungry critters.

"No."

Ruby grabbed Barbara's arm and helped her up. "Wipe that deer-caught-in-headlights expression off your face." Ruby chuckled and led her to the tent. "Get your swimsuit on. You are going to enjoy it."

Barbara stepped inside her tent and zipped it shut. Fishing through her suitcase, she found her red one-piece bathing suit. Hesitantly she took off her clothes and slipped into it. *What am I getting myself into?*

She grabbed a pair of white running shorts from her bag. A large black thing scurried across her hand, and she screamed.

"What? What is it?" Ken called from outside.

She unzipped the tent and pointed toward her suitcase. "Over there." The spider that had to have been half the size of her hand moved toward the edge of the tent. "Get it." She swatted Ken on the shoulder. "Get it—quick!"

Ken shivered and stepped back. "Have I told you how much I hate spiders?"

"Ken," she squealed, "please!"

"Okay, okay. Give me a shoe."

Barbara slowly reached down and picked up one of

her tennis shoes. She handed it to him. Ken crouched toward the arachnid. The thing seemed to know its doom was near, because it scurried back toward her clothes. Ken jumped and took a step back. Barbara covered her mouth as giggles welled inside her. The muffled sound escaped a bit.

"Do you want to do this?" Ken, his face as white as shaving cream, turned and tried to hand her the shoe.

"No." She shook her head and pushed the shoe back at him.

"Then don't laugh."

Barbara bit her lip, determined not to utter a peep. Ken crouched down again. He smacked the shoe on the ground. The spider scurried to his right. Ken smacked it again. This time, he got it. Barbara clapped her hands. "My hero."

Ken walked out of the tent and fell into a chair. Beads of sweat covered his forehead, and he looked as if he would be sick. Barbara grabbed a bottle of water from the cooler and handed it to him. "Are you okay?"

He half smiled, unscrewed the cap, and took a quick drink. "I really don't like spiders."

Barbara sobered. "Well, then I really appreciate it."

He grabbed a towel off the table and wiped his face. He looked at her. "You know, you do look like a fashion doll."

Barbara gazed down at her bathing suit. She hadn't had a chance to put on any shorts or even a T-shirt. Heat rose up her neck and cheeks. "I'll be back."

She ran into her tent as Ken started to laugh. "Shake

your clothes before you put them on," he called. "I always do."

Ken watched as Barbara applied sunscreen to her shoulders and arms. He couldn't deny his attraction to her. The woman was beautiful. She wiped the top of the lid when she popped it shut, then opened her bag and stuck the sunscreen in its own place inside. Many of her things were labeled; all of them were organized in perfect order. He wouldn't doubt if they were alphabetized.

He huffed. He was lucky if he could find his toothpaste in the morning. A relationship with Barbara would be ludicrous. They'd drive each other crazy.

"Okay, Travis and I are going to ride together first," said Ruby. "Then y'all can have a turn."

"What if we want to go first?" Ken teased her.

"I just figured since Barbara hasn't—"

"No, no." Barbara touched Ken's arm. "By all means, I need to see you do this."

Ken liked the feel of her hand on his arm. It was soft, and her nails barely scratched his skin, giving him goose bumps. She moved away. Ken rubbed the spot and then grabbed the wheel of the boat. "Go ahead."

Travis and Ruby stepped into the tube. Barbara pushed it away, letting the rope loosen. When Travis gave a thumbs-up, Ken started the boat and drove them around. Ruby laughed as the water bumped them up and down. Ken watched as Barbara's eyes lit up. *She wants to take a turn.*

He loved seeing a different side to Barbara. A side that made him contemplate more than a bachelor pad and a great business. She moved closer to him. "Is it our turn yet?"

Ken smiled. "Sure." He stopped the boat and then pulled the tube up to it. "Our turn."

Travis helped Ruby onto the boat. "That was great."

Ken hopped down into the tube. He reached for Barbara's hand and helped her down beside him. "Hold on to the handgrips."

A bit of fear lit her eyes. "What if I fall off?"

"Travis will turn the boat around and pick you up. I'll even jump out with you."

"Promise?" The hesitant look in her eyes made him want to melt into a thousand pieces.

He touched her hand. "You'll be fine. Just hold on."

"Ready?" Travis called from the boat.

Ken looked at Barbara. She grabbed the grip and then nodded. He gave a thumbs-up sign to Travis. The boat started.

They hit a few bumps, and Barbara laughed. "This is fun."

Ken smiled. The water splashed her face, and she blinked several times. The wind whipped her hair straight back. They hit a bump. Barbara let go of the grip. She squealed, and he grabbed her arm and pulled her to him.

After she collapsed on top of him, her eyes widened in surprise. He held her by the waist as the boat slowed. Her lips, wet and red from the ride, seemed to beckon his. Without thinking, he kissed her.

Barbara didn't know what to think about Ken's kiss. When they got back into the boat, he didn't speak to her. Even when they pulled up to the dock, Ken said nothing. She chatted with Ruby as they walked back to camp, but nothing from Ken.

Exhausted and confused from the day, she declined dinner, grabbed a snack, and headed into her tent to change into her pajamas and go on to bed. Nestled in her sleeping bag, she listened to the crickets chirping. Night had fallen sometime before, but she still couldn't sleep. *God, what am I to think about Ken's kiss?* She sighed and gazed at the top of her tent.

She knew God wanted her to allow Him control of her life. He wanted her to trust Him. Opening up was hard, but she'd enjoyed the last few days. Freedom was so much easier than all the rules she had for herself. *God, I'll just wait and trust You.*

Her stomach growled for the third time. *That snack wasn't enough. I don't think I can make it until morning.*

As quietly as she could, Barbara stood, unzipped the tent, and tiptoed toward the truck. She opened the door, then popped open the cooler and grabbed a banana and some peanut butter crackers. Whispers sounded behind Ken's tent. Not wanting to disturb whoever was talking, Barbara tried to move silently to her tent. Then she heard her name. Curiosity took over as she felt sure the voice was Ken's.

She sneaked toward them. Ken and Travis sat in their

chairs. Travis shut his Bible. "I'm sure Barbara would love to do a Bible study with us. We could do it as couples."

"Barbara and I aren't a couple."

"Oh." Travis frowned. "I just assumed. Ruby saw you kiss her."

"I don't know why I did that." Ken rubbed his jaw. "It just happened. I shouldn't have—"

"Does Barbara know it just happened? You can't play with a woman's feelings, Ken."

Ken smacked the arm of the chair. "Can you see us together? I don't know if there are two people on the planet who are more incompatible. I've always teased that she's got Darth Vader somewhere in her family's lineage. How could we possibly. . ."

Barbara gasped and backed away. Unwanted tears welled in her eyes. She swiped at them and headed toward her tent. *At least I know exactly how he feels.* Lying down in her sleeping bag, she zipped it up to her neck. She didn't need or want Kenneth Marsh in her life anyway.

Chapter 7

The phone rang. Barbara popped another piece of popcorn in her mouth and looked over at Chelsea. She swallowed her drink of pop. "You gonna get that?"

Barbara shook her head. "I'd rather watch the movie." She and Chelsea watched the same movies once a month throughout the year. This month was *Seven Brides for Seven Brothers*. She looked at the television. Gideon had just gone up to the cabin to tell Adam that Milly was having his baby and he was a fool not to come back and take care of his wife.

The answering machine picked up just as Gideon punched Adam in the jaw. "Hi, Barbara. It's me again. I really wish you'd give me a call." There was a pause. "I guess I'll. . .talk to you later."

Barbara shoved another piece of popcorn into her mouth and willed her hurt away. It had been two weeks since the camping trip, and she couldn't get her mind off Ken and the brief kiss. She wanted to talk to him, but his words to Travis had sliced through her.

"How many times has he called?"

"I don't know. Maybe a dozen."

"Why don't you call him back?"

Barbara pushed the popcorn away from her. Several kernels fell to the floor. "I told you what he said to Travis."

"But you walked away. You said you left before they'd finished talking." Chelsea touched her arm. "Eavesdroppers always miss a key piece of the truth."

Barbara scowled at her best friend. "I am not an eavesdropper. I didn't mean to listen to their conversation. Not really anyway." She smacked her leg with her palm. "He said I was related to Darth Vader."

Chelsea giggled, and Barbara snarled at her. "Come on, Barb. It's funny. You've got to admit it's funny."

Barbara grabbed a couch pillow and hit Chelsea on the arm. "You better hush, or I'm gonna use 'the Force' against you."

"Seriously, did you ever talk to Ruby about it? She could ask Travis exactly what Ken said."

Barbara sighed. "I haven't told anyone but you. The man kisses me, then mocks me. It's too humiliating to talk about."

"But, Barbara, you missed part of their conversation. I've heard Ken is really serious about his newfound faith. He joined Travis's church and has been going to Bible study with their pastor twice a week."

"I'm glad."

Chelsea flicked the television off. "Talk to Ruby—better yet, talk to Ken."

"I can't." Barbara swallowed her wayward emotions.

She grabbed the remote and turned the TV back on and pointed to the screen. "Don't be turning off my favorite part."

Chelsea smiled and leaned back on the couch. "Wanna play a game of Old Maid when the show is over?"

"Chelsea!" Barbara forced a laugh and then took a drink of her pop. Her heart yearned to race to the phone and give Ken a call, but her head knew better.

With only minutes left in Canyon Lake's annual fishing tournament, Ken carried his day's catches up to the weighing station. He'd caught several good-sized bass and a few bluegill, but he felt fairly sure he hadn't done well enough to win.

"How'd ya do?" asked Joe when Ken put his bucket on the table.

"Don't know. We'll see, I guess."

Joe pulled Ken's fish from the bucket of water, weighing them one at a time. He tallied the weights on his calculator and clicked his tongue. "Sorry, 'bout that, Ken. You're in second place so far, and not everyone's weighed in yet."

Ken swatted the air. "Wasn't figurin' to win anyway. I enjoyed myself though."

"Yep. Always have a good time fishin'."

Ken pointed to the scoreboard. He didn't recognize the name of the fisherman in first place. "Who is that?"

"Remember my teenage friend who I told ya would give ya a good run?"

"Him? It costs fifty bucks to enter."

Joe grinned. "He mighta had a sponsor."

Ken smiled and nudged Joe's shoulder. "You ol' softie. I hope he wins."

Joe frowned. "Don't be sayin' stuff like that." He huffed and turned away.

Ken scooped up his bucket and carried it out to the dock. He dumped his fish back into the lake, and they quickly swam away. A lot of people kept them to cook up for dinner, but Ken didn't feel like skinning and cleaning them.

He walked back down the dock to see how Travis had done when he saw Barbara standing beside Ruby. She was wearing a pair of cutoff jean shorts and a white T-shirt. Partially pulled back in a clip, some of her hair stuck out around her cheeks and down her neck. She looked so natural and carefree and different, like she had while they were camping.

Ken picked up his pace. She hadn't called him back, though he'd tried for nearly a month to reach her. Deciding he'd offended her by kissing her when they were out on the tube, Ken was determined to apologize and take her to dinner, to start over.

The last few weeks as he had grown closer to God, he'd come to realize he was ready to settle down, to have more than fishing trips with Grams and a haircutting business. He wanted a wife, and every time he thought about it, Barbara Elliott popped into his head.

"Hey, Barbara." She jumped when he said her name. He was glad she hadn't seen him; she couldn't run away.

"Hello, Kenneth."

A growl formed in his gut. They were back to "Kenneth." He'd been "Ken" the whole week of camping. He needed to apologize and get back in her good graces. "Can I talk to you a minute?"

Barbara stood still for a moment. She looked at him and then at Ruby. Ruby nudged Barbara toward him. At least she was on Ken's side. Barbara sighed. "Okay."

They walked toward the dock. It was empty, as most of the people had gone to hear Joe announce the winner. Ken grabbed Barbara's hand. She gently pulled it away. He turned to face her. "I'm sorry I kissed you like that."

She shrugged. "It's okay. It didn't mean anything to me."

Ken felt as if he'd been punched in the stomach. He looked at her face. Her eyes were moister than usual. "It meant something to me."

She turned away from him and raised her hand to cough. Ken noticed she swiped at her eyes, as well. He tried to grab her hand again. "I'd really like to take you to dinner. I want to get to know you—"

"Why, Ken?" She looked back at him, her eyes flashing with anger. "I'm a relative of Darth Vader, remember?"

"Barbara, I'm a new man. I said those things before I knew Jesus. I've always been attracted—"

"No, Ken. You said that while we were camping. To Travis. The very day you kissed me. I heard you and Travis talking. I didn't mean to eavesdrop. I was hungry, and I went to get a snack and. . ." She pulled away from him. "Just forget it."

"Barbara." He grabbed her hand again. "You must not have heard all of it. I told Travis how my view of you had changed. I teased you so hard because you stirred things in me that no other woman ever had, and it scared me."

She turned to him again. A tear had fallen down one cheek, leaving a glistening path. He wiped it away. "Barbara Elliott, you are so beautiful." He touched a strand of hair that lay on her neck, remembering her willingness to trust him with the cut. "In every way."

"You mean that?"

Ken nodded. "I think it was this haircut that made me realize it was more than your physical beauty that drew me to you; it was your inner beauty, as well." He let go of the wisp and gazed into her lush green eyes. "I wanted to know more about that inner beauty."

"Oh, Ken."

"May I kiss you, Barbara?"

Her lips parted slightly as she nodded and closed her eyes. He leaned close to her and held her cheeks with both hands. Lowering his lips to hers, he basked in her soft touch and fragrance.

"So, what anniversary is it today?" asked Chelsea.

Barbara laughed into the receiver. She stuck the last plate and fork into the dishwasher and shut the door. "You better quit making fun of me, or I'm gonna hang up on you."

Chelsea laughed. "Okay, okay. So, are you and Ken going out tonight?"

"Yeah." Barbara wiped off her hands on a dish towel. "And it is our two-month anniversary."

"I knew it!"

Barbara chuckled. "Seems like a lot longer."

"Well, you've known each other since you were what, two?"

Barbara gazed out her apartment window. The older couple who lived across the street sat on their porch. He read the paper while she talked. Barbara sighed. "Fifteen years. We've known each other fifteen years."

The doorbell rang. Walking to the door, she looked at her watch. "Ken must be early. I better go. See ya, Chelsea."

"Have fun."

Barbara clicked off the phone and laid it on the back of the couch. She opened the front door. No one was there, just a shoe box wrapped in cartoon-character paper. She smiled as she bent down and picked it up. Glancing left to right, Barbara knew Ken had to be nearby.

She cleared her throat and announced in a loud voice, "Hmm. Someone has left me a present." She shut the front door and sat on one of the chairs on her front patio. "Wonder who it's from."

After untying the yellow ribbon, she gently tore the edges of the paper. She opened the shoe box. A blond fashion doll lay inside. Her hair had been cut to her shoulders, and she wore a white wedding dress.

Barbara's heart sped up. Only one person would buy her this. She was afraid to think what the wedding dress could mean.

"She's awful pretty, don't you think?"

Barbara jumped. "Kenneth Marsh, I knew you had to be somewhere around here, and you still managed to scare me."

He laughed. With one hand behind his back, he grabbed her hand for her to stand beside him. "I have something for you." He brought his hand around and handed her a box of red roses.

"Oh, Ken, they're beautiful." She kissed him and then set the box on the patio table. Opening it, she pulled out one rose and smelled it. "Thank you."

He reached into his pants pocket and pulled out a black velvet box. Barbara thought she would faint. All her blood seemed to rush from her head to her toes. He took the rose and set it back in the box. Taking her hand in his, he caressed it for several moments. Barbara watched as Ken's chest rose and fell in nervous anticipation.

"I love you, Barbara," he said finally. "I don't know how long I've loved you." He gazed into her eyes, and Barbara feared she would melt. "Maybe it was when I first saw you at fifteen, and you were catching more fish than me." He smiled and touched the tip of her nose. "It doesn't matter, I suppose."

Barbara swallowed the lump in her throat. She couldn't take her eyes from him. She wanted to savor every word and every expression. The crush she'd always had on him had swollen inside her to something more than youthful dreams and wants. Ken was the man she wanted and needed.

"I didn't buy this for you." He half chuckled. His voice

wavered. "It's kind of an odd story actually. You know how much Grams and Pa mean to me, and you know how different they are, as well." He cleared his throat and shifted his weight. "I had told Grams I wanted to ask you to—well, she gave this to me. To give to you."

He shook his head. "Here." He opened the box. Inside sat an antique-looking engagement ring. The round diamond in the middle sat in a square, white gold setting. Two smaller diamonds sat on either side. A second pair of even smaller diamonds sat on each side of them. "It's Grams's ring."

Barbara looked up at him. "What?"

"I told Grams I wanted to ask you to marry me. She wanted me to give you her ring." He smiled. "She says we remind her of her and Pa."

Barbara touched the top of the ring. Ken scooped the ring from the box and grabbed her hand. "Barbara, I love you. Will you be my wife?"

Barbara closed her eyes and envisioned Ken's grandparents, who truly were as opposite as north and south and yet loved each other with a complete, godly love. "Absolutely."

He put the ring on her finger. She wrapped her arms around his neck and kissed him fully on the lips. She squealed in delight as he lifted her in the air and twirled her around.

"Life will never be boring," he whispered.

"Never."

"What do you say we go fishing tonight? Back to the place we first met."

Barbara grinned. She'd never realized how sentimental Ken could be until they'd started dating. She loved that about him. "I can't think of anything I'd rather do." She touched his cheek and then moved her fingers down his jawline. "Don't get mad when I catch more than you."

He growled and pulled her close to himself. "I'm not worried. I've already reeled in the best catch."

JENNIFER JOHNSON

Jennifer Johnson and the world's most supportive red-head are happily married and raising the three cutest girls on the planet. Jennifer is a new eighth-grade math teacher in Lawrenceburg, Kentucky. (Pray for her!) She is also a member of American Christian Fiction Writers (ACFW). Jennifer loves to read, write, and figure her checkbook—when the numbers match. She also likes to talk to Robin, scrapbook, and chauffeur and cheer for her daughters' soccer, basketball, singing, and youth events.

Blessed beyond measure by her heavenly Father, Jennifer hopes to always think like a child—bigger than she can imagine and with complete faith. She would love to hear from you at jenwrites4god@bellsouth.net.

Lured by
Love

by Gail Sattler

Trust in the LORD with all your heart
and lean not on your own understanding;
in all your ways acknowledge him,
and he will make your paths straight.

PROVERBS 3:5–6

Chapter 1

T"he eyeballs are over there." Nicole Quinn pointed to the left. "About the middle of the aisle."

"Perfect," came the barber's response.

She turned to Ken. "I don't understand what it is you're doing. But if this is another one of your bad jokes, you can get your body parts elsewhere."

Ken grinned and shook his head. "No, this is quite legit. Barbie told me that sometimes our lives' biggest treasures are right under our noses, and in this case, she's right. Or if not under our noses, then they're next door." His grin widened. "We've been operating side by side for years, and I can count the number of times I've been inside your store on one hand."

Nicole raised her hand and ran her fingers through her latest haircut. "On the other hand, I can't count the times you've given me a great cut on short notice. Anything you want, name it, and you've got the same discount."

"I was counting on it."

Without another word, Ken sauntered through her store to the aisle she'd shown him.

Whistling.

Nicole shrugged her shoulders and returned her concentration to what she'd been doing before Ken walked in, which was sorting her selection of new embroidery cotton skeins by color, according to the sequence of a rainbow. Then she began tacking them to the display board.

Within minutes, Ken returned. He spread a large assortment of mismatched paraphernalia all over her previously tidy counter.

"This is it. The only thing you didn't have was hooks."

Nicole pointed to the center aisle. "All my hooks are over there."

"I don't need knitting hooks."

"It's not *knitting hooks*, it's *crochet* hooks and knitting *needles*." She shook her head. "Men," she muttered under her breath.

"Whatever." Ken looked up at the clock on the wall behind her, another of her handmade creations. She'd designed it from a piece of driftwood, decorating it with dried seaweed; then she'd used tiny plastic fishes instead of numbers. With fishing being the prime attraction for tourists, as well as the main hobby of the inhabitants in their lakeside town, she'd had many requests for similar clocks over the years. Instead, she gave everyone who asked a list of materials and a map of her craft store and told them how to make one themselves. Hers was the prototype and one of a kind, and it wasn't for sale.

Nicole picked through Ken's pile, punching in the discount she'd promised as she rang each item into the cash register. "This thread you picked really isn't suitable for crocheting. It's rather stiff, and you'd need a very small hook. I didn't know Barbara did crafts. The only things she's ever bought from me were kits for assembly—nothing intricate—and I had the impression she was buying them as gifts, not to make herself."

"You guessed right about Barbie but wrong on this. This isn't for her; it's for me. My next stop is Joe's Bait and Tackle shop where I'm going to get myself some *fishing* hooks. And then I'm going to win Joe's next tournament."

"Well, good luck," Nicole said as she dropped everything into a bag and handed it to him.

"Now to go back out to visit Joe," Ken said, and, true to his word, instead of going left to his own store, he turned right.

Nicole returned her attention to her project.

She'd almost finished her new Rainbow of Threads display when the bell tinkled, indicating another potential customer entering Nicole's Kraft 'N' Knack Shack.

Nicole couldn't help staring.

Another man had come into the store, this time someone she didn't recognize.

In any given week, she could count the number of men who entered the store on one hand. But today it was very odd that she hadn't been open fifteen minutes and out of the two people who'd come in, both were men.

The man approached the counter. When she didn't say anything, he looked down at her, frowning. "Is something wrong? Are you okay?"

"I'm sorry. What can I help you with?"

His face softened, and he smiled.

Every coherent thought in Nicole's mind fled.

Not only was this new customer a man, he was a handsome man. As he smiled, crow's-feet appeared at the corners of the bluest eyes she'd ever seen, which contrasted vividly with hair so dark it was almost black. His strong jawline emphasized a large nose, but strangely they only added to his appeal.

"I need an Egg-Sucking Leech," he said.

Nicole's stomach did a flip-flop. "I'm—I'm sorry," she stammered. "I think you've come to the wrong place."

The man ran his fingers through his hair. "But I just saw Ken headed out to Joe's place. He said he was here and bought a Sofa Pillow and Bug Eyes."

A mental picture of Ken's purchases flashed through her mind. Ken most certainly had not purchased a cross-stitch pillow kit. He'd purchased two kinds of flashing metallic thread, one small spool of plastic thread, yarn, some marabou, three different kinds of feathers, a packet of plastic beads, a small bag of wiggle eyes, and some glue.

"I'm sorry, but Ken didn't buy a pillow, although he did buy the eyes."

"Maybe I misunderstood then." His brows furrowed. "What colors did he have?"

"Everything he bought was in shades of rust orange and bright pink."

"Hmm." The man crossed his arms and tapped one foot. "It sounds like a Sofa Pillow, but I'd certainly never use one of those this time of year. I do better with a Crystal Butt-Hopper."

Nicole stood. "That's enough. I think it's time for you

to go. In fact, I think you should go straight back to Joe's Bait and Tackle. He sells all kinds of disgusting bugs and critters." Just the thought of the abominable things in Joe's display case turned her stomach. The frozen dead bugs were almost acceptable because they were already dead. But the thought of a small dairy container full of live, squirming worms was too much for her stomach first thing in the morning.

"But. . ."

Before the man finished his sentence, the bell tinkled and two more men sauntered in.

"Hey, Vic," they both said at the same time.

Vic waved and smiled back. "Hi, Trev, Stan. I guess you talked to Joe."

"You bet." Trev grinned, glanced around the store, then turned to Nicole. "Can you tell me where a man can find some wings around here?"

"Wings?" Nicole stammered. She turned and pointed to the doll-making supplies, where she actually did have a couple of pairs of angel wings left over. For a while it had been trendy to sew angel wings onto stuffed teddy bears, and she still had a few pairs left in the store that she hadn't been able to return to her supplier because someone had opened the bags. "That way."

Stunned, she watched two men disappear down the doll-making aisle.

Today was Saturday, which explained how it was possible that she had men, who other days would be at their jobs, in the store first thing in the morning, but it didn't explain why. Men usually didn't come into her craft store unless their wives dragged them, always very obviously against their will. Most men insisted on waiting in the car while their wives browsed unescorted through the aisles of craft items.

Not only did she have men inside her store, but they were actually shopping. For themselves.

She couldn't hear what they were saying, but she could understand the general flow of the conversation that the angel wings were not satisfactory.

One of them returned holding one wing. "Uh, we were kind of looking for something smaller. And fluffier."

She turned to the side, but Vic had disappeared.

The bell rang, and two more men walked in.

Nicole didn't have to be a rocket scientist to know what they wanted.

She just didn't understand why. So she simply pointed in the direction she'd sent Ken, who apparently was very pleased with the miscellaneous mismatched supplies he'd purchased.

Vic returned with a pile similar to the one that Ken had gathered, only in different colors. He laid his collection on the counter, beaming from ear to ear as he spread everything out. "Now I just have to go to—"

"Joe's Bait and Tackle for some *fishing* hooks," she muttered.

Vic's grin widened. He was so happy he nearly glowed. "Yeah."

The other men returned, all with similar items—which made Nicole wonder how many feathers she would have left in the store by the end of the day.

While she entered Vic's items, two more men walked in. Without a word exchanged, she pointed to the same aisle she'd shown to all the other men and continued on with the transaction.

"So what do we do now?" Trev asked.

Nicole looked down at the mismatched array. "I have no idea," she replied.

Vic laid his hand on the counter, forcing her to look up into his face. His smile dropped, and his eyes—eyes framed by the longest eyelashes she'd ever seen—turned intently serious.

"I thought you and Joe had this all worked out, but I just realized that you have no idea what we're doing," he said. "We're making fishing flies."

"Fishing flies?" Nicole stared down at the conglomeration of feathers, thread, yarn, and marabou in front of her. As she analyzed the pile, a lightbulb went on inside her head. She'd never actually seen a fishing fly, but she'd heard about them. Now she knew that they were made from feathers and marabou and tied together with shiny thread. "Of course," she said. "This all makes sense now." She looked up at the men. "I'm sorry, but—"

Vic held up one hand, cutting off Nicole's words. "Excuse us, Trev. I need to ask the lady about something."

Chapter 2

Vic Thompson quickly glanced at the business card holder; the cards told him he was talking to Nicole Quinn, the owner of the store.

When he was sure they were out of hearing range of the other men, he turned to her so their conversation would remain private.

"You made all this stuff you've got displayed all over the store, didn't you?" he asked as he raised his hand in the air and motioned in general to all the handmade creations that were hung on every wall and displayed on top of the shelves.

"Uh. . .yes."

"So you're obviously really good at making stuff?"

Her cheeks turned a charming shade of pink. "Uh. . . yes."

"One of the guys I work with said his wife had their daughter here for some kind of preschool arts and crafts thing you did a couple of months ago. He was saying he couldn't believe the stuff his kid brought home, how good it was."

Her eyebrows scrunched, like she was trying to remember and couldn't. "Thanks. . . ." Her voice trailed off. "I guess."

He glanced from side to side, just to confirm the other guys weren't listening in on their conversation. "What I'm trying to say is, if you can help little kids make something recognizable, then you must be a good teacher. I'm not the only one who's heard that, because Joe sent me here, and the same with all these other guys. I already tie my own flies, but these guys are expecting some help."

"But I've never made fishing flies before."

"I can show you. It's not hard, really, but there is a knack to it."

Her eyebrows crinkled even more. "But I don't understand why you want *me*," she said, pressing one hand over her heart, "to show them."

Vic stared into her face. She really was perplexed. He didn't understand how it all began. Joe knew that Vic knew how to tie good ties, but Vic didn't know why Joe would send a bunch of inexperienced men to make their own. The end result, though, was that there were a bunch of men ready to do some serious shopping at Nicole's store if they received the proper instruction.

As a businessman himself, Vic couldn't ignore the potential dollar signs. Every business needed new customers, some more than others. He didn't know why Joe was so insistent that all the men come here; he only knew that Joe was adamant about it. Vic had to trust that there was a reason he'd been caught in the middle, when all he wanted to do was buy his supplies and go home. He could only pray that whatever happened, he was doing the right thing.

"You should show them because Joe said you'd be good at it," he finally said. "Otherwise, they'll be asking me."

Her eyebrows arched, and a silence hung between them.

Vic raised both palms in the air. "I didn't mean it like that. It's just that I know these guys. They aren't going to pay attention to me the same way they'd pay attention to you. I also know that if they don't get it the first time, they'll expect that I'll do it, just to shut them up. I don't have the time or the inclination to make everyone else's flies. I just want to make my own."

"I suppose I could help them. As long as you gave me detailed instructions."

"I can do that. Also, if you have trouble, there are lots of Web sites that have step-by-step instructions, even pictures, on how to do them."

"Then why can't your friends do the same thing?"

Vic stiffened and pressed his hand over his heart. "Because we're men. Real men don't need to read instructions."

"Then why do real men need someone to show it to them?"

"That's different."

Her expression told him that she didn't understand, but he didn't have time to try to explain it a different way. As they spoke, more men were walking into the store, no doubt all expecting to buy what they needed, which included help with making a recognizable fly pattern.

"You said you don't get a lot of men in here." He

looked down at her hand, which was still pressed against her heart. No rings, which meant she wasn't married and didn't have a man around the house, either, which probably explained why she didn't understand the way men did things. "There's even more coming. I'm just trying to help."

She turned and stared at the door as the bell tinkled and another man entered, just as he'd predicted. "I have a bad feeling that I don't have a choice. I guess it can't be too hard. I give out written instructions for a lot of the things I sell to the ladies because kits aren't always available. I guess men just need to be shown rather than reading a sheet. It must be a men-are-from-Mars-women-are-from-Venus thing. I have to get back. There's a line at the counter."

Vic didn't quite understand the reference. All that mattered was that she agreed to do it.

They hurried back to the counter. When Nicole had his total tallied, Vic reached into his back pocket and pulled out his wallet.

Instead of taking his money, she stared at his wallet.

"Your wallet is made from duct tape."

"Yeah," he said, prouder of himself than he'd been for a long time. "I made it myself. Isn't it great?"

"Couldn't you find a nice leather one?"

He ran his fingers through his hair. Being a craft-making person, she should have understood his hand-made wallet and what it meant to him. "It's duct tape," he repeated, trying to get her to understand the significance. "A handyman's secret weapon." He leaned closer. "Real men only need two tools. If it moves and it shouldn't, use duct tape. If it doesn't move and it should, use WD-40."

Her blank expression told him that she couldn't tell if he was being serious.

"Come on, move it, Vic," a male voice called from behind him. "Pay the lady and step aside. I've got places to go."

Vic glanced over his shoulder. "Sorry, Trev, but I was just talking to Nicole about all this, and she agreed to teach a class on fly tying."

"A class?" she sputtered. "I didn't—"

Trev turned around to Stan and the line of men behind him, which now numbered almost a dozen. "Did you hear that, guys? They're doing fly-tying classes here. That's why Joe wanted us all to come here."

Vic flinched when Nicole's fingers wrapped around his forearm. "They? There's no 'they' here. It's only me. And I didn't say I would teach a class. I just said I'd give out instructions—that *you* said you'd give to *me.*"

A man Vic didn't recognize stepped up to the counter. "Is class size limited? I want to sign up right away."

As soon as the men heard the words suggesting a limited enrollment, the line fell apart and a circle formed around the counter.

"Where's the sign-up sheet?" another man asked.

Nicole sighed, pulled out a piece of paper, wrote out the numbers from one to twenty-five, and set it on the counter, along with a couple of pens.

Vic couldn't help being impressed. Giving the illusion of a large number of openings, and that it wasn't first come, first served, brought everything back to a quiet order while each man took a turn at the paper to write his name down. Nicole obviously knew how to handle people in a group situation.

When the last man was done, Nicole picked up the paper without looking at it. "I didn't really expect to do a class," she muttered, only for Vic to hear, then cleared her throat. Her voice came out loud and clear as she continued. "If anyone wants to know how much it's going to cost, I first have to. . ." She blinked repeatedly and stared at the paper.

Something settled like a rock in Vic's stomach. "What's wrong?"

She looked up and counted the men in the room, not including him.

"There are eleven men here. How did we get twenty-one signed up?"

The first man in line replied, "I signed up my neighbor to go with me. We were talking about doing flies this year for the tournament, and he was just like me: He would rather have his own colors, but he doesn't know how to put one together either."

Similar comments resounded throughout the crowd.

"The tournament is coming soon," one of the men called out from the back of the crowd. "Can we start this week?"

Nicole scanned the crowd. "But I have to order supplies. The soonest I could do this would be Wednesday or Thursday."

"That's fine by me," the same man called out.

All heads in the room nodded. Not one person said they couldn't be there.

"I can't be with twenty people at once."

"Uh, that's twenty-one," Vic corrected, double-checking the page.

Her gaze tightened. "Since this was your idea, consider yourself drafted."

"Me?"

"Yes, you." She crossed her arms and glared daggers at him.

Vic should have felt resentful, but he didn't.

He suddenly didn't mind the thought of teaching the guys how to tie flies.

In fact, he didn't know why, but he was downright looking forward to it.

Chapter 3

Nicole signed for receipt of her latest order and returned the signature board to the driver.

"You've got twice as many boxes as usual. Business must be good," the man said as he tapped in the delivery time, making the transaction complete.

She wasn't sure how to answer him. Initially she'd replaced the stock the men had bought, but she'd also had to order quantities of everything needed to construct more various kinds of flies for the ten men who were signed up but hadn't been in the store yet. She'd even ordered three sizes of fishhooks from a different supplier who thought she was crazy by the time she figured out what Nicole wanted.

For now, all that she knew would sell would be enough for each of the remaining ten men who hadn't been in the store that day to make one fly each. After that, she didn't know if she'd ever sell the materials for another fly. First, she had to successfully run the course, then take her chances that either the men would want to make more than one, or that there were more men in town who wanted to catch fish with something other than Joe's disgusting collection of worms and frozen dead things.

Nicole honestly didn't understand why a fish would want to eat a bug made of synthetic materials when, to a fish, the real thing had to be far tastier.

But hers was not to reason why. Her job was only to provide for her customers, male or female, even if she'd never had a male customer before. But in order to do so, not knowing exactly the right colors to choose, she'd bought a large variety of colors and types of thread—too much for twenty-three flies. She'd also had to buy some special eyes and other supplies she'd never seen before.

She wondered if it was possible to begin a trend of constructing something else made of bright feathers and marabou, shiny metallic thread, and wiggle eyes.

Nicole shuddered at the mental picture of the monstrosity she'd created in her overactive imagination.

"Yes, I guess business is good," she replied lamely to the poor deliveryman, who had been staring at her the whole time she'd been standing there lost in thought.

At least she hoped business would be good. If she did manage to sell all the supplies she'd purchased, business would be *very* good. If not, that would be very bad, because she couldn't return incomplete cases.

When the driver walked away, Nicole picked up the first box and began to carry the unassembled fly parts into the storage room.

"Need some help?" A male voice resounded behind her.

"Vic. Hi. Sure. You're early."

"Yeah. That's me. Mr. Punctual." He picked up a box

and followed her to the back of the store. "I had some time coming to me, so I left work a bit early to beat the traffic."

Nicole could think of a few names other than *punctual* for a man who was proud of a wallet he'd made out of home-repair supplies.

"I'm glad you're here. Things have been slow all day, but that won't last now that people are getting home from work. Hopefully we'll have enough time for you to show me how you put these things together."

"That's what I'm here for. Have you decided what night you'll be running the class?"

"Yes. I thought Thursday evening would be a good time."

He stopped moving, then pushed the box onto the shelf very slowly. "That's the only evening I'm busy."

"Wednesday then?"

"That works better for me."

It didn't work better for Nicole, because that only left her one day—today—to learn what she was supposed to do. Of course, since she wasn't paying Vic for his time, she couldn't make any demands of him. She'd actually been surprised at his acquiescence. She didn't think it had been her imagination that he didn't want to show the other men how to assemble the flies. "We should get started."

"I brought my needle-nose pliers, just in case you don't have an extra set."

"Pliers?" Her stomach did a nosedive into her shoes. "I don't own pliers. Please don't tell me that I also have to buy twenty-one pairs of pliers for the class."

Vic shook his head. "No, all the guys should have a pair at home. When you phone everyone to tell them what day you're going to run the class, tell them to bring pliers. Just make sure you tell them to bring needle-nose pliers, not the regular ones."

Immediately she was thankful that the men were able to bring their own tools. For most of the classes she led, she had to supply everything required, even glue guns, which she thought was something any crafter should already own. The usual supplies were bad enough, but she definitely couldn't afford a case of pliers.

Before Nicole tucked away the last box, she pulled out a few feathers and all the other things she thought she would need. "Let's get to it," she said softly, then walked back to the counter inside the store.

"Wait! What kind of colors do you have?"

"Why? Does it matter?"

Vic smiled, and the same thing happened as the first time she saw him—namely, that she wondered if some of those flies they were supposed to be making were fluttering around in her stomach. The man had a killer smile and long, thick eyelashes to die for.

"The colors are very important. The idea is to imitate reality, or if you can't do that, then you're supposed to attract the fish. You're not going to attract anything with those colors."

Nicole had actually thought about making a display from her finished project. "I don't want to attract anything," she said. *Unless it's you. . .* Nicole's breath caught, and her heart pounded at the possibility that she'd actually said out loud what had just flashed through her head. Had she really just thought she wanted to attract Vic? She wasn't into foolish dating games.

All she wanted to do was run her shop. She couldn't allow failure to beat her. She couldn't live through the same thing again.

"What's wrong with the colors I've chosen?"

"You really should either have tones of browns, greens, and grays, or reds and oranges. Some of the attractors can be pink, but there really isn't anything blue like that."

"This color is called skytone." *The color of your eyes.*

He stared at the delicate feathers as she held out her palm.

"Skytone? Right. Those are *blue*," he mumbled. "Let me think for a minute. If you want to use that color, I think we can build you a Silver Thorn Dressed."

Nicole stared blankly at her feathers. She struggled to recall some of the ways she'd already heard the men refer to the feather creations. "You mean all these things have names?"

His eyebrows quirked. "Of course. Every fly has a name, some based on what they are imitating, and some include the name of the person who designed that particular fly. There are also names for their categories."

"Categories?"

He nodded. "Yes. There's attractors, salmon patterns, steelhead patterns, emergers—"

Nicole raised her empty hand. "I think I get the message. Am I going to need to do a lot of research for this? It sounds like I'm at least going to need a directory or guidebook. Plus a set of pliers."

"I already told you. Most of the common patterns are online. We can go look them up."

"My computer is in the back."

"Then I have an idea. You can print off some of the noncopyrighted instructions, and we can study the rest. It shouldn't take long to find a few prime sites."

"But I can't leave the store unattended while I fool around on the Internet."

"No problem." Vic grinned again, his baby blue/skytone eyes sparkling with delight. However, this time, Nicole wasn't going to be caught off guard or distracted. She was learning the hard way that Vic's grin meant there was a catch coming.

She gritted her teeth. "But?" she asked.

"Nothing. I just think I'll go back home and get my extra pair of pliers. I'll come back just before you close, and when you lock up, we can pick up where we left off, when there's no one here to distract us. See you in a couple of hours."

Chapter 4

Slowly, trying to balance everything and not drop any of the bags, Vic pushed the door to the craft shop open with his hip.

Above his head, a bell tinkled.

Nicole looked up at him from her spot behind the counter. She nodded, but she didn't smile.

Vic didn't think that was a good sign, but he chose not to dwell on it. The only sign he needed was the one he got from Joe, even if he didn't understand exactly what Joe meant.

Joe had said Nicole needed him—insisted actually—and then didn't say anything else. Because Vic, Ken, and Joe had been talking about using flies versus live bait for the next tournament, Vic had assumed that Nicole knew Joe was sending a bunch of men into town to buy the pieces.

But she didn't know. So, therefore, Vic had assumed that Joe had taken it upon himself to send everyone to the store to help her financially. He had figured that she needed the business and the revenue that went along with it. But the store didn't look bad or shabby. It was quite nice, and she had all sorts of extra handcrafted items everywhere that she had clearly marked as not for sale. So that assumption got blown out of the water.

Then he had assumed that she would jump at the suggestion to teach a class, because some people just liked to do that. But she didn't seem very enthusiastic. And then Vic had found out that she didn't know how to tie a fly. He didn't know if it was good or bad that she'd drafted him quickly when she realized she was in over her head.

And now, he'd assumed that she would think it was a great idea to sit together after the shop was closed and go over everything she needed to know.

She sat behind the counter staring at him like he was something green that had just floated in from outer space.

Vic lowered his tackle case to the floor and held up the fast-food bag. "I brought supper."

"Oh. . ." Her voice trailed off, and she stared at him like a deer caught in the headlights—just before it got run over by a big truck.

He stiffened, once more kicking himself for assuming that she was willing to eat dinner with him. He hadn't considered until this moment that teaching her how to tie flies in the back room after the front doors were closed for business maybe wasn't the best idea, especially when they didn't really know each other. "Uh. . . There isn't someone else you're supposed to be having dinner with, is there? I thought"—*assumed*, he kicked himself for thinking—"that this would be the best thing to do."

Her voice came out husky, immediately making Vic feel guilty for asking. "No, there isn't anyone else. I just wasn't expecting you to bring me anything. How much do I owe you?"

Not that he'd considered this anything close to a date, but Vic still felt stung. He hadn't intended for her to pay, and he especially hadn't intended for her to feel obligated.

"You don't owe me anything. We should get busy. I have an idea, though. Since you're not officially closed yet, why don't we start by looking at the flies I brought with me right here, while we eat right here? I know people might still come in, but these burgers are bad enough when they're warm. When they're cold. . ." He pretended to shiver. That, at last, produced a hint of a smile, a positive response.

"That's a good idea."

He handed her a burger and an envelope of fries. "I didn't know what kind of drink to bring you, so I brought us both coffee. I figured that was safe."

She gave him another hint of a smile. "That's very considerate. Thank you."

Considerate?

Vic forced himself to smile back. "You're welcome," he said, for lack of something better to say.

He proceeded to open the wrapper for his burger while Nicole did the same, except when he dumped his fries onto the wrapper, Nicole started eating without waiting for him.

He always paused to say a prayer of thanks before he

ate, even if it was a bad burger. If he couldn't pray for the goodness of the food, the least he could do was thank God that he had a good job that provided the money so he could afford bad burgers.

It would have been nice to pray together. Failing that, it would have been nice to know if she didn't pray just because she didn't know if he would or if she didn't pray because she didn't have a relationship with God.

It was also something he wanted to know. Something about Nicole touched him, even though he didn't know what or why. He'd never had that happen when he first met a woman, which scared him, because this was only the third time he'd been with her, and he had the feeling that she wasn't a believer. Tonight, when he had time alone and in private, he would ask God what he was doing there.

But for now, that wasn't an option.

Vic closed his eyes for a brief two seconds to give the quickest prayer of thanks in his life, then reached for his burger with one hand and for his flies with the other.

Before he actually touched one, he turned to Nicole. "It's okay to eat while I'm doing this. These flies are all new. I haven't used them yet. No fish has touched them. They haven't even been wet."

"That's good to hear," she mumbled between mouthfuls.

Vic couldn't help watching her eat. He couldn't remember ever seeing a woman eat so fast. He wondered if she was accustomed to eating fast because she had to run the store while she ate and didn't have time to stop, or if perhaps she was just that hungry, the quality of the burger aside.

He turned all his concentration back to his tackle box, where he had all his flies sorted by category.

He picked up a Mayfly. "This one is called a Lightning Bug. See how the colors and shape are chosen to imitate the real thing?"

"I'm sorry, but I really don't know that much about bugs. I usually do my best to avoid them."

Vic thought of his sister, whom he'd once loved to tease endlessly with bugs and spiders. Eventually he realized that he did better to "save" her from such creatures to earn her favor, especially after he turned sixteen when he could reap the rewards of also saving her friends from nature's little horrors.

But those days were gone. They were all adults now, and even though it was flattering when his sister's friends tried to flirt with him, he was more interested in hooking up with a woman from his church, who shared his faith.

Vic blinked and again returned his concentration to his tackle box, unable to believe that he'd let his mind wander. Usually he was quite focused when he set his mind on something, especially his fishing.

He picked through the pile until he found what he was looking for, then grinned from ear to ear as he held up his pride and joy. "This one's a Cutthroat; it's called a Rolled Muddler. It's my favorite."

"You're sounding very specific again. Do these things all have special names?"

"Yes, they do. Usually they have buggy names. They're named first after the different categories, like chirono-mids, midges, caddis flies, and leeches, and then they're individually named, sometimes by a special feature." He carefully placed the Rolled Muddler back in its compartment and selected another example.

"This one is a shrimp pattern, and it's called a Pregnant Scud."

"Ew. That sounds disgusting."

"They're just bugs, Nicole. Little creatures made by God so bigger creatures can eat them and get bigger, so bigger creatures can in turn eat them. Such is the cycle of life."

"Except the fish don't get to actually eat something good before they die. It's not fair. Those are fake."

"Yes, but most of the time, I don't kill and eat the fish. Most of the time, I catch and release them."

She stared into his tackle box, studying his collection of flies and other assorted fishing gear, at least that which he'd brought with him. "You mean you spend all this time and money to catch fish, just to let them go?"

"I don't do it for the food. I do it for the fun."

"Fun? I can't imagine it's much fun for the fish."

"Maybe not, but even when they lose, it's still a win-win situation. They get to carry on to wherever it is they were going. I just make them late. But I'd imagine they have quite a story to tell when they get there."

She stared at him like she couldn't tell he was kidding. He wanted to tell her to lighten up, but he had a feeling it wasn't that she didn't have a sense of humor—he had a feeling there was something else, something deeper involved.

Something that he wanted to know, even though he didn't know why.

He continued to show her samples, and then instead

of moving to the back room to give her the instructions from the Internet, as soon as Vic was finished eating, he picked up the fire orange thread, some pink marabou, and yarn.

"We can make a Bug Eyes right now, because it's an easy one."

Her brows knotted. "Believe it or not, I've heard of that before. But I can't figure out where."

"I think this is the last one Ken made." But the real reason he'd picked a Bug Eyes was that it was mostly pink and just seemed like a girl kind of fishing fly.

"First, we secure barbell eyes on the hook near the eye; then we wrap it like this." He steadied the hook firmly with the needle-nose pliers and carefully wrapped it in a figure eight motion. As he wound and pulled, Nicole's head tilted in the most endearing manner. Just like one of those moments in the movies when the hero turned and kissed the girl.

Vic nearly choked at his thoughts.

He cleared his throat and fixed his attention more closely on his work in progress. "Next, we tie in the marabou tail. Like this. You have to do the next part real tight; then we put in clumps of yarn and pull it like this."

"Can I check your tension?" Without waiting for his response, she reached toward the fly. Her hands brushed his as she gave the thread a gentle tug while he was still holding it, and then she curiously poked at the wound section.

This time, Vic's chest tightened. He felt the almost-overwhelming urge to embrace her and save her from all the evils of the world. Which didn't make any sense. Yet he couldn't turn off the feeling that she needed protection. His protection, to be exact. And that really didn't make sense, either; she was an independent business owner, and he just worked a nine-to-five.

He reached into the open package for more yarn. "Now we add another clump here, against the first clump. We keep adding more until we reach the eye of the hook. See how I'm wrapping around the barbell eyes?" He picked up the scissors and trimmed it into the shape of an egg. "Now I just do a whip finish, cement the head, and we're done."

She stared at the Bug Eyes, mesmerized. "Wow. That's quite a process."

He lowered the fly to the counter. "That's why these guys need a class to do this properly. You can't have your flies coming apart when they hit the water."

Nicole picked it up. "You know, except for the rather deadly hook, it's kind of cute."

"Don't ever say *cute* in front of the guys."

She tipped it and did that tilt thing with her head again. "I could make these in a variety of colors, and it would make a wonderful display. If I could find something else to use instead of hooks, these would make a very entertaining mobile."

"Uh. . ."

She reached into the bin and picked up another fly. "I really like this one. What's it called?"

"That's a Skunk."

All Nicole's motions froze. "Ew."

"You've been saying that a lot."

"Sorry." She returned the Skunk to the steelhead bin and left the Bug Eyes on the counter. "On one hand, this seems doable, but at the same time, I feel like I'm in way over my head."

Vic stared into her eyes. Honest eyes. Eyes that hid nothing, including her hesitation and nervousness. Of what, he didn't know. He was harmless. He'd even do his best to protect her if a gun-toting robber barged into the store, although he certainly hoped that wouldn't ever happen.

"Have you locked the front door yet?"

She glanced up at the clock. "Oh! I was so interested in watching you that I forgot. I'll be right back."

He watched as she flicked the lock shut and flipped the sign in the window so it read CLOSED from the outside. "I was thinking," she said as she returned to the counter. "A couple of the men asked how much I was going to charge for the course. I usually run free workshops, but this is a unique situation. Usually the cost of the materials for a craft, when multiplied by the number of participants, covers my time, but this time it doesn't. For the amount of materials used, this really takes a long time. Also, often you can make copyrighted items for personal use, but I'm going to be making money running the course. I think for the purpose of the class, I'm going to pick my own colors and design, and that way we'll all be doing the same thing at the same time. That's really the most efficient."

"That's actually a good idea."

Her voice lowered to a point that he could barely hear. "I hope so," she muttered, then turned her back to him, not giving him a chance to ask what she meant.

"Can I help?" Vic blurted out. "If I'm going to be showing the guys during the class, I should have made at least one before the class begins. I think that makes sense."

She turned around slowly. "It does make sense, but the class is tomorrow. That means I have to put something practical together tonight."

He shrugged his shoulders. "I've got nothing better to do."

Without waiting for her approval, he walked into her storage room. "So pick some colors, and we'll get started," he called out. "Just don't pick pink."

Chapter 5

Nicole sucked in a deep breath as the last chair was filled.

She'd set up three tables with ten chairs each for the class, thinking that with twenty-one participants, both she and Vic would have ample opportunity to move around and sit in different groups as the men needed more help.

All thirty chairs were filled, and neither she nor Vic was in a single one of them. Word had apparently traveled.

The murmur of low voices unnerved her. It was a graphic reminder that she was the only one present of the female persuasion.

"We're ready to start now!" she called out, and the drone died off.

She held up her blue and green creation. "We're all going to make a Nick of Victory today. Did everyone get a bag of supplies at the door?"

All the men nodded. Vic, who was still standing at the door, flashed her a thumbs-up.

Now she was doubly thankful that he'd offered to

help. When more people came than expected, Vic ran into the storage room and put together the additional bags of supplies, which allowed her to stay at the counter and not leave the store unattended.

She locked the cash drawer and took her place in front of the three tables.

"This is a special design, made exclusively for this class. If anyone wants to make another Nick of Victory later, just ask for another bag of supplies. The cost will be minimal."

One of the men started to laugh. "I get it. Nicole. Nick and Vic! The Nick of Vic. Tory! Ha-ha."

A few of the men also laughed. Vic didn't, but he smiled from ear to ear, and if he'd been a peacock, his chest would have been puffed out and his tail would have been in full bloom.

Memories of the previous evening they'd spent together cascaded through her head while the men enjoyed their little joke.

She couldn't help it. She liked him, but that really was no surprise. Vic had been so kind and helpful; he was everything most women would want in a man. Tall. Dark. Handsome. Funny. Kind. Intelligent. He had a good job and was trustworthy and honest to a fault, which was what she needed most in someone, friend or otherwise.

She cleared her throat and raised the borrowed pair of pliers in the air. "Please! Let's get started!"

The room again became silent. Thirty men, thirty-one if she counted Vic, all with needle-nose pliers in their hands, watched her.

"For those of you in the back who can't see me that well, please turn and face the other way and watch Vic."

Vic held up his pliers and bag of supplies.

"This is just like the preflight thing on how to fasten your seat belt and work the oxygen masks!" one of the men called out. "But instead of a 'flight' attendant, Vic's a 'fly' attendant!" This time, every man in the room burst into gales of laughter.

Nicole froze, not sure what to do.

Women never would have acted this way. They just would have mentally calculated the dividing line, and those in that half of the room would have repositioned their chairs, and the class would have continued.

Vic took a bow, then made a big production out of removing the hook from the bag. He held his pliers at chest level but raised the fishing hook above his head in a theatrical display, turning it for everyone to get a view of every part of it from every angle, as if they'd never seen a fishhook before. Which was cute, and would have been okay if any one of the men in her half of the room would have been watching her and ready to begin the class.

"We really should get started," she called out.

The correct number of men turned around.

Nicole proceeded through her instructional display just as they'd rehearsed, with Vic doing everything at the same time she did. When it came time to check the men's thread tension, Nicole and Vic did as they had agreed, each starting kitty-corner from each other at the far ends of the tables and meeting in the center of the middle table.

They finished only ten minutes later than they esti-mated, and every man present had a fly Vic guaranteed wouldn't fall apart when it hit the water.

That was the good news.

The bad news was that all the men were so excited about their flies that they came to a unanimous agree-ment that they wanted to make more. One session wasn't enough.

Before Nicole could say anything, the group agreed to meet every weekday, with the exception of Thursdays because Vic was busy that night, at fifteen minutes before she closed the store, as a drop-in session. They even agreed on a flat-rate fee per session, which included the materi-als. Even considering materials, the amount was generous. They insisted because they wanted to be fair, but mostly because no one wanted to bother with change.

She really wasn't sure what to do, but she couldn't look a gift horse in the mouth. It was income, and she needed it.

Soon, all who remained was Vic—and the mess on the tables.

"That went well," he said as he swept the clippings into a pile with his hand.

"Yes, it did. Thanks for your help. I couldn't have done it without you. I know we've already talked about this, but are you sure I can't give you half of the class fee? You certainly deserve it."

"No, but there is something you can do for me."

She smiled. He didn't know how much she needed the money, and though it had been hard to offer it to him, she wanted to do the right thing.

"Sure," she said. "Name it."

"We're having a barbecue instead of a Bible study meeting tomorrow night, and I'd like you to come with me."

Chapter 6

I think it's time to stop for a word of thanks, and then we can all dig in!" one of the church elders called out.

Everyone in Kathy and Hank's backyard quieted.

As usually happened with Vic's church crowd, everyone reached out to hold the hand of the closest person.

While a few of the women shuffled their purses to free up their hands, Vic sucked in a deep breath for courage, then reached out for Nicole's hand.

Someone on the other side of her automatically did the same. Vic felt her flinch at the contact with a stranger, but since she didn't pull her hand away, he praised God for small miracles.

The whole time Hank prayed aloud, Vic's heart pounded.

He could tell Nicole felt out of place, but she was being very gracious and going with the flow.

She was also holding on to his hand very tightly.

A couple of people who were there knew her, and they'd been both surprised and happy to see her, which confirmed what Vic really didn't want to know.

Not only did she not go to his church; she didn't go to any church.

It wasn't what he wanted to find out. He wanted her to tell him that she went to another church, somewhere, anywhere.

But she didn't.

He'd been through this before. There had been just once, the only time he thought he could be seriously in love with a woman, except she didn't share his faith. For a while, they had simply agreed to disagree, but it hadn't taken long for the gap to widen. After a while, Elsa refused to go to church, and she'd made it clear that she thought his friends were weak, that they were using God as a crutch.

It didn't take Vic long before he wondered if she felt the same way about him, even though she gladly went out with him and accepted everything he gave her. No matter what he said or did, nothing could show Elsa that God was real, except for His being the grand Creator of the universe, which was true, but not enough. Vic wanted Elsa to have the same love for God that he did, but Elsa would have no part of God that wasn't to her convenience. She was completely self-sufficient and independent, and she refused to allow God to interfere with her life.

Vic looked down at Nicole.

She was short, like Elsa, and being a business owner, Nicole was also independent and confident, which was probably why he liked her.

It was also why he should keep away from her. He'd fallen for the same type not long ago, except Nicole was far more quick-witted than Elsa. Still, the results had been devastating. He didn't want to lay his heart and soul open to be stomped on and kicked around the block again.

But he couldn't help it. In the last few days, he had felt a connection between himself and Nicole. He didn't really know why he'd invited her to the barbecue, but now that they were here, it forced him to make a decision. If she was a believer, then he could open the door and take a risk. And if she wasn't, then starting tomorrow, the connection between them would be limited to business only. Just because he wasn't making any money didn't mean all the time he spent at her store helping with the fly tying wasn't business—not that he would call it charity. But he found he was enjoying teaching the other guys about fly tying, something he hadn't foreseen. Doing something he enjoyed and getting free supplies were payment enough.

He hadn't even wanted to accept free supplies. He hadn't meant to look, but when he rushed to the back storage room to make up the extra bags of fly supplies for the class, he'd seen some past-due invoices she'd left on one of the shelves. They weren't huge invoices, but they were over thirty days overdue. He'd already refused to accept payment or a wage for his work, but seeing that she had unpaid bills confirmed in a second that he'd done the right thing.

When the amen came, Nicole didn't let go of his hand.

He probably shouldn't have felt that way, but Vic liked it, so he didn't let go, either. He laid his free hand on top of their joined hands and patted. "Let me show you where to go. I know you hardly know anyone here, so let's not get separated in the crowd."

At the reminder that they were in a crowd, his church crowd to be exact, her eyes widened and she glanced around.

Vic didn't think that was a good sign.

"Are you okay? You don't have to be nervous. I know everyone here. I know it's hard to memorize so many names, but I can help you."

"It's okay. I'm fine. I've just never been to a thing like this before."

"Certainly you've been to a backyard barbecue before."

Her cheeks darkened. "Of course. But I've never been to one where everyone was so. . .uh. . .religious." All the color drained from her face, and her whole body went completely stiff, causing him to release her hand. She raised both hands and pressed her palms to her cheeks. "I'm sorry! I didn't mean it like that."

Vic suddenly lost his appetite. At least Elsa had put up with his church friends. It was his own fault that he didn't realize sooner that Elsa had no intention of letting his church friends or God interfere with her life. "We're all just normal people, Nicole. No one here is full of warts or smells bad. We just all believe and trust in the same God, and we know that because of His love, we're all going to heaven."

"Do you really know that? I mean, really?"

"Yes, I do. But it's not quite that simple. While we should do good deeds, that doesn't get a person into heaven. All we have to do is believe. I know that sounds simple, and it can be simple, but it's not always easy. Most people will say they believe in God, but they don't really. It's like when you're halfway to work and it runs through your head that you've left the element on when you were making your breakfast. If you did, that means there's the chance that your house will burn down. If you really believed that, you'd turn around, knowing it would make you late for work, and you'd go home and turn it off. But if you didn't really believe it, you'd continue on to work and forget about it. The belief you need to get to heaven is the kind that makes you late for work."

A familiar male voice sounded behind him. "Well, I've never heard it said quite that way, but you make a good point."

Vic spun around. "Hi, Larry."

"I see you brought a guest." Larry smiled and turned to Nicole.

"Larry, this is Nicole. Nicole, Larry."

"Nicole. . ." His voice trailed off. He turned briefly to Vic, raised his eyebrows, and turned back to Nicole. "Are you the owner of that craft store on the main drag where they're teaching fly tying? Do you have any openings?"

"It's a drop-in. There are always openings."

"Great. You'll probably see me and my son there tomorrow night. I'm taking him fishing on Saturday to practice up for Joe's next tournament. Billy doesn't like putting worms on the hook, and he thinks making his own fly is the perfect solution."

"Then I look forward to seeing you both."

Larry glanced over his shoulder. "Excuse me, it looks like my wife needs me. It was nice meeting you. I'll see you tomorrow."

He walked away with a pleasant wave and joined his wife at the barbecue.

"Apparently word continues to travel. He seems very nice."

"Yes. He is. He's the pastor."

"The pastor!" She gulped. "He didn't look like a pastor."

"What's a pastor supposed to look like?"

"I, uh, don't know. I've never met one before."

"Now you have. He's just the same as everyone else here, except his day job is church administration. We're all equal in God's eyes."

She didn't reply, so he wondered whether she agreed, disagreed, or didn't know.

"Let's go get some food. The line is shorter now."

They both chatted amicably with people on either side of them in the line, and soon they were sitting under a tree, just the two of them.

As they talked, another one of the group's regular attendees introduced himself to Nicole, expressing interest in the fly-tying drop-in before he went on his way.

"Wow," Nicole muttered as Mike walked away. "I don't know what to say. This little venture is going to change my business entirely. A few of the men who were there have asked me to supply guy-type craft things, and a few have asked for materials they can use to build scenery for model-train sets. I've got so many new ideas. If it weren't for you, this wouldn't have happened. I don't know what to say."

Vic smiled. "Actually it was Joe who sent me, but I don't believe in coincidences. I think it's been in God's hands all along. He cares about you."

Her face clouded over, and Vic didn't know what he'd just said to cause such a reaction. He'd meant to be encouraging, to show her that God cared what happened in her life.

As well, Vic cared, and not just in a ministry kind of way.

It was getting personal.

Very personal.

Too personal.

"Nicole, what's wrong?"

She stopped eating and started pushing clumps of potato salad around her plate with her fork. "I just don't believe that God does care."

Vic's thoughts raced. If she didn't believe that God cared, at least she believed that God was there. But Elsa had believed that God existed, too. That wasn't enough for Vic.

It was time to find out exactly what Nicole thought, because this time if he was going to fall in love, he was going to be smart about it. He would find out what she thought, and why, and where her heart was *before* he was past the point of no return.

He sucked in a deep breath and forced himself to smile when, deep inside, his heart was pounding and his supper was sitting like a rock in the pit of his stomach.

"Why do you say that?" he asked.

"You know, I don't belong here. I'm really sorry, but if you don't mind, I think I should go home now."

Chapter 7

While Vic drove her home, Nicole stared out the car window.

She really didn't belong there. Everyone there was happy, talking in small groups and generally having a good time, as if nothing bad had ever happened to them.

They all believed God cared when really He didn't. Either that or God cared for everyone else and not for her.

It would be many years before she would be able to get back to where she'd been in her life—if she ever could.

She wasn't a bad person. She'd never hurt anyone, she'd never been mean, and she gave money to the poor. At least she used to.

A caring God wouldn't have let such a thing happen.

"Nicole? What's wrong? Do you want to talk about it?"

She turned to Vic as he drove.

Vic was the first good thing to happen in her life in a long time, but that apparently came with strings attached.

"I just don't believe that God really cares."

"I get the feeling that you have a very personal reason for saying that. Can I ask what happened? Does this have anything to do with your business?"

She stared out the car window again, unable to look at him as she spoke. "In a way. There was a time when I was doing okay with my business. I wasn't making millions, but I was comfortable and able to put money aside, hoping to be able to pay off my mortgage early. I was also putting some money away every month as a nest egg. I was even going to get married. But then, my fiancé took all my money and disappeared. All I had left was the mortgage, my current stock, a lot of unpaid bills, and a broken heart. It's been over two years, and I'm still not into the black. I don't think a God who cared about me would let things like that happen."

The car slowed, and Vic pulled off to the side of the road.

"Did you report this to the police?"

"Of course. But we'd already signed everything into joint ownership because we were getting married. Everything except the mortgage and the business license. Since Shawn had legal access to all my assets, there was really nothing the police could do. I tried to find him, but with limited resources, I didn't get very far."

"I don't know what to say. God gives everyone free choice, and your fiancé made some bad choices that unfortunately you took the brunt of."

"I know what you're trying to say. Even though you think God is helping me now, I can tell you that although it helps, a small class for the limited duration of the fishing season isn't going to make the difference I need to get myself out of my financial troubles."

"What will it take?"

She stared out the window, even though they weren't moving and there was nothing to see.

"It would take a miracle, and I'm afraid I don't believe in miracles anymore."

"But I do. Small ones and big ones. Maybe instead of one big miracle, this is going to take a bunch of small ones."

She turned back to him. "You almost make me believe it could happen, but I can't get my hopes up when I don't see any reason to."

"I see lots of reasons."

All Nicole could do was stare at Vic. Ever since they'd met, she knew there was something different about him. She didn't think it was just that, like her, he enjoyed making things with his hands. Most of the men in the class had enjoyed making the flies, even if a few of them found parts of the process a little frustrating.

She now wondered if it was his relationship with God that made the difference in how he dealt with people and problems.

She also couldn't help it, but she liked him. He had an inner strength and a quiet confidence she hadn't experienced before, which was something she needed very desperately in her life right now. But then, she couldn't allow herself to do something stupid like start to like him too much, just because she was still feeling weak and vulnerable. That was especially why she couldn't allow herself to lean on him. She'd learned the hard way that the only one she could trust was herself.

Nicole crossed her arms over her chest and leaned back into the door, as much as her seat belt would allow. "What reasons do you see that things could be turning around for me?"

"Short of winning the lottery or some rich relative dying and leaving you a million dollars, it's not realistic to think that everything is going to go back to the way it was overnight. I believe that every large journey starts by taking a few baby steps, and I think this fly-tying thing is the first baby step. You said that since a bunch of men have discovered your shop, you're going to be opening a section devoted to guy stuff. I think there's great potential there, and that's the second baby step."

"If I'm ever going to get out from under this debt load, it's going to take an awful lot of those baby steps."

"That could be so, but you can't say that it won't ever happen."

Nicole stopped to think. "It could, but by then, the interest will kill me."

"We'll see. I think this is just the start. I'm just asking you to give God a chance and not to shut Him out."

At her agreement, Vic started the car again and drove her the rest of the way home.

"It feels funny dropping you off at the front of your store."

"You picked me up from the store."

"That was different. It was like picking you up from work."

"That may be so, but I do live here, too, in the suite upstairs. It's small, but it's home, and that's where I live. The back has a separate entrance, but the lightbulb is burned out. For now, dropping me off in front is just easier," she said. *And probably safer*, she thought.

As if he could read her thoughts, when she exited his car, Vic also got out and followed her to the door, waiting behind her as she unlocked the door, then shut off the alarm.

When she was done, she turned to him.

"Good night, Vic."

Nicole stood, waiting, her heart pounding. Without thinking about it, she'd automatically hoped that he would kiss her good night. Not that it had been a date, because if it had, it hadn't been a good one. But they had spent the evening together in a social situation. She'd seen enough of him at the store where she had come to know him to some degree, so a parting kiss felt like a natural thing to do.

"Yeah. Good night. I guess I'll see you tomorrow night for the drop-in."

He turned and walked to his car, slid in behind the wheel, and drove off quickly.

Instead of a warm kiss, the cool night wind chilled her cheeks as she stood in the doorway until his taillights disappeared around the corner.

Chapter 8

Vic poked at the thread with his finger.

"No, Trev. Tighter here—and looser here."

"Maybe I should get Nicole to show me." Trev turned his head. "Hey, Nicole! Can you show me how to do this?" he called over his shoulder.

Vic gritted his teeth. He was quite capable of showing Trev how to position the chenille on the Lazy Nymph. In fact, he was probably more capable than Nicole because he was the one who'd shown Nicole how to do it in the first place.

But most of the guys didn't want his help—just as he'd told her the day they met. They wanted Nicole.

The trouble was, Vic wanted her, too. And not just to tie his flies.

He didn't know exactly what it was he wanted, but mostly he wanted to get to know her better.

Except he knew he shouldn't go any further toward a relationship with her if she didn't love God the way he did.

"Hey, Nicole! Can you help me?" one of the men from

another table called out.

She very graciously excused herself from the man she was helping and began to assist the next man who needed her.

"I'm next!" Trev called out, while Vic was still leaning over, trying to correct Trev's tension without having to take the whole thing apart.

Vic pressed his palm over his ear in an attempt to clear the ringing. "Thanks, Trev," he mumbled.

Trev only laughed.

Trev's laughter faded when Nicole approached him.

"Having trouble with something, Trev?"

He nodded and even frowned. "Yeah. I can't seem to get this even. My fly is all lopsided. I need your help."

"You're pathetic," Vic grumbled as he stood and walked away.

As he stared at Nicole helping Trev, something inside him burned—proving that he was even more pathetic than Trev.

But instead of obsessing about it, Vic carried on to help one of the other men, someone whom he'd never met before. They exchanged a few jokes about Vic helping his competition for Joe's next tournament by doing the flies and then had a great conversation about the new pier being built at Canyon Lake, where the tournament would be held.

Except that he couldn't help himself—he kept watching Nicole float around the tables, helping all the men.

All the single men were openly flirting with her, each one hoping to snag her attention.

And she didn't seem to notice. Every smile, every compliment, every time they called out to her and ignored him, vying for a turn with Nicole when Vic had nothing else to do—she simply took it all in stride, as if she couldn't tell what they were doing or why, or as if it didn't matter.

But Vic knew that a passionate heart lay beneath that facade of indifference. Last night it had been getting dark by the time he took her home. She'd squished herself up in the corner against the door, but she couldn't hide the anguish in her face when she tried to be casual about being left with a broken heart after her fiancé took off with all her money. He'd heard the little break in her voice, trying to hold back how much it still hurt. It was probably none of his business, but he hurt for her. He knew the pain of being abandoned. Even if it was for a very different reason, it still hurt.

But that was also the reason he didn't want to get involved, either. He was still feeling the effects of being abandoned himself. When the time came to start again, he was going to be better prepared, taught well by his past poor choices. He now would date only a woman he knew was already a believer. For his own protection, he wasn't going to allow himself to be caught on the rebound before he was ready, and to be fair, he wasn't going to catch someone else on the rebound before she was ready.

If he could be practical and look at the situation from a distance, neither of them were ready. He knew that.

When he was fishing, he did catch and release, but in the game of love, when he cast out his heart, the person who caught it had to be a keeper.

As the men finished their newest flies, they began to filter out. The married men all must have been more skilled at tying flies, because they were the first to leave.

Mentally Vic kicked himself for noticing.

"Can I help you clean up?" he asked after the last man left.

She didn't reply immediately, so Vic stood still and studied Nicole. Her brows knotted, and she glanced at the door, the clock, and then back to him as if she didn't know how to answer.

So instead of waiting, he grabbed the broom and started sweeping. "I think today went pretty well, don't you?"

Nicole picked up a cloth and began wiping down the tables. "Yes. But again, everyone wanted to make the Parachute Hopper so they could learn how to get the crown right. That's great for me, if this trend continues, to do one featured fly a night, because that would use up pretty much a case of the same materials in one lesson rather than different items from a dozen cases."

Vic nodded. "Maybe we should suggest a series so they can learn a new basic technique every time."

She stopped wiping and turned to him. "That's a great idea. I never would have thought there was so much involved in something that you just toss out for a fish to catch. In a way, though, the men are here for pretty much the same reason a lot of women knit or crochet. They don't do it because they really need the garment or whatever it is they're making; they knit because they find the process relaxing. Do you feel that way about your flies? You seem to have a lot more in that case than you'll ever use in a lifetime. At least it seems like it to me."

Vic pictured his well-stocked fly bin. "I never thought of it that way. I always thought I'd have a good variety and be prepared for whatever the day and conditions and seasons are like. But I guess it's true that there are quite a few flies in my collection that I'll probably never use. I just made them because I thought they would either be fun or a challenge to construct."

Together they kicked the legs of the folding tables down, then carried them into the storage room. They set them against the back wall, talking while they worked.

"I wonder what's going to happen tomorrow," Nicole said as she nudged the third table into place with her knee. "Saturday is usually my busiest day, but up until this week, it's been only women shopping. I have a feeling that for the first time I'm going to have a mixed crowd."

"Could be." Vic paused and sucked in a deep breath for courage. "What do you think you'll be doing after you close tomorrow?"

"The same thing I do every Saturday night. Count my stock and make my order for the next week. I do it online now, so if I get it in on the weekend, they deliver it on Tuesday."

"You work on Saturday night?"

"It's the best time to do it. Saturday is my busiest day for sales, so I need to replenish everything quickly. I used to do my order on Sunday, but then it was like I never got a break, and I was getting too tired. I do my order on Saturday nights now so that I can get one day off."

"You know, the Bible says exactly that. To take one day

off as a Sabbath, a day of rest. God gave us His example of that in the book of Genesis, and He says that we should follow His example."

"That's not why I take Sunday off, because you say God says so. I take Sunday off because I need to or I'll drive myself to an early grave."

"I know what you're saying, but mankind has found after years of research that a lot of things in the Bible are based on scientific fact, except God established those things long before man had the capability to analyze or prove or disprove them. Think about it. God told the ancient Jews not to eat pork, and they simply obeyed. It wasn't until many centuries later that mankind figured out that pork is the meat that's the fastest to go bad. God just wanted His people to stay healthy. He gave them other instructions that man only came to understand centuries later."

"I never thought about it like that before."

"Most people don't. God is pretty smart, don't you think?"

She stared at him, her eyes wide with wonder. "I think there's a lot more to this God stuff than I realized. I wonder if going to church on Sunday might help me figure some of it out."

Vic gulped. He should have been the one to ask and encourage Nicole to come to church with him, to get to know God better. It made him feel inadequate and very remiss that instead of him inviting her she'd just invited herself.

He cleared his throat. "I think going to church would be a great idea. I probably won't see you tomorrow, but

I can pick you up at nine thirty Sunday morning."

She smiled weakly. "I guess I'll see you then. Good night, Vic."

He looked down at her. Not that this was anything close to a date, but after bidding good night to a woman in the evening, the natural progression of events should have been to kiss her.

But he didn't have that right. He wasn't dating her, and he didn't want to date her.

But he did like her.

It was just that he wasn't supposed to be getting involved with Nicole, for a number of reasons.

But he wanted to kiss her.

The need to kiss her burned him from the inside out.

Before he did something he knew he would regret, Vic spun around on his heel and headed toward the exit. "I'll see you Sunday then," he called over his shoulder as he walked. "I'll let myself out, and don't forget to lock up behind me."

Chapter 9

The last time Nicole had been in church, not including the premarriage seminar that had ended up being the biggest joke in the universe, it hadn't been like this.

Everyone here was happy. Talking. Laughing. Acting like they wanted to be here, not like they were here to prove their morality to their neighbors.

The music was even good.

Most of the couples present were obviously married, many with children, happy and comfortable with each other even after many years. She saw many people who appeared to be single, as well as a number of young couples holding hands who were obviously deeply in love, young enough that they probably weren't married yet but soon would be.

That was the way she probably appeared to the world when she was with Shawn, before he tore her world apart.

When they were together, she thought she'd never been so happy in her life. Now, enough time had passed that she wanted to be that way again; except next time, it would be with a man who deserved her love and loyalty and someone she could trust without doubt.

Beside her, Vic hunkered down while he talked to the child of a couple he apparently knew well. The little girl giggled at something he said, then launched herself at him and wrapped herself around Vic's neck, sticking to him like a fly to flypaper.

All he did was laugh.

The parents weren't embarrassed for their daughter's behavior. In fact, they laughed, too.

A few people turned to look, but no one stared or even appeared to care that someone was behaving in such a manner in church. They acted like such occurrences were normal.

But one thing Nicole did notice was that a number of people had paused and given her a second glance, some with raised eyebrows, when they saw her with Vic.

Once he disengaged himself from his little fan, Vic turned to her. "It's almost time for everything to start. We should find a seat."

She lowered her voice to a whisper. "Can we sit in the back? A bunch of people have been looking at us, and I'm a little nervous."

His smile faltered for a split second. "I should have warned you about this, but it's okay. They'll soon see that we're just friends. It's certainly okay to bring a friend to church, because that's what friends do. And as friends, we can go sit over there, because usually the couples with kids sit on that side, close to the door, and the people who are just friends sit over here."

Nicole tried not to let her mouth hang open. She hadn't heard the word *friends* so many times in a few sentences since the last time she'd seen a kid's television show about a big purple dinosaur whose name she couldn't remember now.

If Vic was trying to make a point, he'd succeeded. It could never be said that she couldn't take a hint.

If that was all they could be was just friends, then that wasn't necessarily a bad thing. Watching Vic interact with his friends, at the barbecue, at his church, and even at the fly-tying classes, was a vivid reminder that she hadn't seen any of her own friends in a very long time. In fact, when Shawn left her high and dry, and broke, she'd distanced herself from all her friends and family and buried herself in her business.

First, she didn't want anyone to feel sorry for her, even though she'd been put in a very precarious position. Between the hurt and the fear of looking stupid, she'd isolated herself. It hadn't been a wise decision. She'd needed her friends, but when they tried to console her, she'd pushed them away.

She'd kept herself buried, and it was only recently that she'd started to rebuild the bridges to her old friends and to reach out to make new ones.

It had all started a couple of weeks ago. One day she'd been feeling particularly despondent, and she didn't know why, but she'd started talking to Joe from Joe's Bait and Tackle. They'd been talking as one business owner to another. She didn't know why she said it, but she mentioned offhandedly that not only could she not afford a holiday, she was also working six days a week from store opening to closing time because she couldn't afford to hire someone, even part-time, to fill the gaps. Joe seldom had women come into his shop outside of town, and he didn't know anything about what women in general liked to do with their time, but she'd bemoaned to him anyway that she needed to think of some new craft ideas for her regular customers because she needed the money.

And suddenly her store became filled with men—men who were ready and willing to buy supplies to make fishing flies, of all things, and with those men came Vic.

She suddenly had a larger target market and an increase to her profit margin. It wasn't a lot, but over time, that difference would add up. She could see that now, because it had made a difference already.

Maybe Vic was right. Maybe small miracles really did happen after all, and those small miracles did indeed add up.

Maybe God really did care.

"Welcome, everyone!" a male voice boomed over the speakers. "Let's all stand and worship God together."

Nicole's knees shook as she rose and continued to shake as she remained standing. It was time to find out more about this God who Vic said cared for her, and maybe it was one more of His small miracles that she just happened to be in church where there were people who could help her when she came to that decision.

After they sang a couple of songs about praising God, the man at the front encouraged everyone to introduce themselves to the people around them.

Nicole quickly shook the hands of the people around her, then shuffled close to Vic.

"I don't have a Bible, and I think that I'd like to get one. Do you have an extra one I can borrow until I can make it to the store?"

"Uh. . . Well. . ." He stared at her, his eyebrows raised; then he shook his head. "What am I thinking? You can borrow mine for as long as you want. I have another one at home, so I won't miss it. Also, I've written notes all over the place in this one that might be of some help to you. If that's not enough, you can ask me anything you want."

Notes. Already made. Another small miracle. "Yes. I'd like that. A lot."

Nicole did her best to take some notes of her own as the pastor talked. By the time the service ended, she had filled not only the back page of her bulletin and every other square inch of empty space, she also had taken Vic's bulletin and written notes on his, too.

"Now that the service is over, how would you like to join me for lunch? My treat."

She opened her mouth, intending to decline, but she snapped it shut to think a bit first. Her first inclination would have been not to accept Vic's invitation, but in this instance, such a reaction was something she'd done too much of lately, which was to be overly defensive. He didn't mean it as charity, and he certainly didn't mean it as a date. It appeared to be a Sunday routine for many of the people from his church to go out for lunch with a friend. Vic had been very clear earlier on the "friend" aspect of their relationship, and this was exactly that. Two friends going out together for lunch.

"Yes. I think I'd like that. Under one condition."

His friendly smile faded. "But I—"

Nicole raised one palm to cut him off before he could agree or disagree. "Only if next week, I can treat you."

"Next week?"

She nodded. "Yes. I think next week I'd like to go to church again."

Chapter 10

Vic applied the single drop of cement to finish off his sample Rubber-Legged Clouser. "See how I did that?"

Nicole nodded. "Yes. This one is a little different from the rest. I think it will make a great addition to everyone's ever-growing collection."

Vic stared into space as he thought of said growing collections, his own included.

Between the fly-tying classes, Bible study night, and going to church together, he'd seen Nicole every day for more than a month. In that time, Nicole had asked so many questions he couldn't count them, not that he was counting. Every answer was a joy, both in helping her learn more about the God who loved her and in being good for him, too. Whatever he didn't know or wasn't completely sure of, finding the answers to her questions forced him to do more reading and research so he would know enough about what he was telling her. Being with Nicole so much had strengthened his own relationship with Jesus.

To him, that was one more of the small miracles

he'd told Nicole about not all that long ago that was under God's control.

"I'll order what we need, and we can make those with the group next week. I just have to write it down."

Vic's hand went to his back pocket. "Wait. One of the ladies at work asked me to ask you if you could order a special embroidery kit for her. I wrote down the name and put the paper in my wallet."

Nicole rolled her eyes. "Ah yes. The duct tape wallet."

He leaned to the side as he pulled his wallet out of his pocket without getting off the chair. "I don't understand your bad attitude. This wallet is a fine work of art, and it took me a long time to get it right. You, of all people, should appreciate the craftsmanship it took to get this so perfect."

"Perfect? I'll reserve judgment."

Vic grumbled under his breath as he reached into one of the slots in his wallet. "Oops. Not that," he mumbled as he pulled out the receipt for a new power screwdriver he'd just picked up at the hardware store. For a great price, too.

The next paper he pulled out was a receipt for parking that he had to turn in to his boss for reimbursement.

"Not that either."

He proceeded to pull out his grocery list, the slip to go pay his phone bill, and his library card.

Nicole walked around the table and peered down at his wallet, her curiosity obvious. "Got any money in there?"

"Some," he muttered as he reached into the slot and pulled out the next item.

A photograph.

Of Elsa.

His heart skipped a beat.

The woman who had broken his heart.

He'd forgotten where he'd put the only picture of her that he had. Now he remembered. He hadn't taken it out of his wallet.

He looked up at Nicole.

Like Elsa, Nicole was coming to church with him. She was reading the Bible and asking questions.

Elsa had done all the same things, although looking back, he knew now that it wasn't because she believed— she was just telling him what he wanted to hear.

As much as he wanted to believe that Nicole was taking everything they talked about to heart, he wasn't sure. He'd thought he was sure about Elsa, but he'd never been so wrong about anything in his entire life.

It was as if pulling out the picture now was a message from God to be careful, to remind him of what had happened when he let his heart overrule his head.

He rammed the picture back into his wallet. "Not that," he said, then pulled out a business card, the last thing in the slot.

"Here it is. Finally. It's on the back of this." He slid the card across the table.

Nicole picked it up. "She's right: I don't have this in stock. I will have to order it. Thanks for doing this. I feel like I should give you a commission or something."

Visions of the overdue invoices he'd seen flashed through his memory. "I don't want your money. I'm just doing Tiff a favor."

Nicole's cheeks turned the cutest shade of pink.

If he wasn't being bombarded with enough confusing feelings, his heart started banging in double time. Her blush was so endearing he wanted to stand up and hold her tight, but he couldn't do that. If he did, he would be crossing a line that was best left untouched.

She shuffled closer. "Then if you won't take the commission, then here's a *something*."

Before he realized what she was going to do, she bent at the waist and Vic felt the warm brush of her lips on his cheek.

He turned his head to face her. "Nicole, I. . ." His words froze in his throat. By moving, he'd put his face exactly in line with hers. Eye to eye, nose to nose, and mouth to mouth.

He swallowed hard. He was less than an inch from kissing her, and not a simple peck on the cheek like she'd just done to him. The right way.

It was something he'd been thinking about for weeks. But he couldn't. Shouldn't. There were too many unknowns, which made a future together too uncertain, and he wasn't going to repeat the same mistake twice. It hurt too much.

He knew he should pull himself away from temptation, but before he could move, Nicole closed the gap and kissed him. No hands, no touching. Just a kiss.

Vic's eyes drifted shut.

His heart pounded, and his blood ran hot at the soft pressure of her lips on his. Without breaking contact, he raised his hands to cup her chin and kissed her more intently. Love surged through him, empowering him, bringing him to the top of his universe.

The bell above the door tinkled.

He dropped his hands, and the separation was so abrupt it was almost painful to breathe.

Nicole straightened and backed up a step.

Still seated, Vic looked up at her. "That shouldn't have happened," he said, trying not to pant as he spoke.

"I've got to get back to the counter," Nicole stammered, then turned and disappeared around the corner of the aisle as fast as if she'd run. Her voice was faint, but he could still hear her from the back corner of the store where the drop-in session tables were set up. "Good evening, Mrs. McCurdy. I've got that kit you wanted in the back. I'll go get it for you."

Vic stood, but otherwise, he couldn't move. Nicole had kissed him. And he'd kissed her back.

Oh yes, he'd kissed her back.

Part of him said it was the stupidest thing he ever could have done, and part of him wanted to go kiss her again.

The bell above the door tinkled again, but instead of Mrs. McCurdy exiting, it was Trev entering.

Trev ignored Vic completely, sat at the table, plunked his needle-nose pliers in front of him, and dumped the bag of fly supplies. "I'm getting quite a collection of flies. Pretty soon, I'm going to have more than you."

Vic didn't want to think about tying flies right now, but he had to. "You'll never have more than me. I'm here every day, and I've made nearly every fly we've made packages for."

He turned and stared down the aisle, as if by watching for Nicole, she would suddenly appear.

This was a complication neither of them needed right now.

He turned to Trev and sat beside him, ready to help if needed.

Nicole was an intelligent woman. Right when it happened, he'd told her that it shouldn't have happened. That much was obvious to both of them.

But even if it wasn't, he'd said the words. Now, everything would be fine.

Chapter 11

Nicole struggled to keep still as she stood to oversee a group of three men carefully winding their thorax thread. She glanced up to see Vic sitting calmly beside Trev, showing him how to properly bunch up the feathers on the Golden Pheasant Nymph.

That shouldn't have happened.

Vic's words echoed over and over in Nicole's head.

She was a fool.

She'd let herself fall in love again. This time, instead of losing her money, she'd lost her heart.

She thought she'd been in love with Shawn, but now, knowing Vic, what she'd felt for Shawn had only been a well-fueled infatuation. Shawn had flattered her and told her everything she wanted to hear, and she'd fallen for it. In hindsight, everything he did was just an elaborate con to get access to her money, which wasn't much by worldly standards but had apparently been enough to make it worthwhile for Shawn. But then, she'd made herself an easy target by thinking that just because she felt happy, her life was going smoothly, and there were no immediate problems to deal with, she was in love.

Her love for Vic went past surface happiness. Their relationship never started out as dating. If anything, it was more work than fun, yet his cheerful attitude and willingness to go above and beyond the call of duty proved his true character. He had no intent to win her heart, but after spending so much time with him, she couldn't help loving him from the depths of her heart and soul.

But he didn't feel the same. He wanted to be friends, and then when she felt brave and thought he might reciprocate some of her feelings, all he said was that it shouldn't have happened.

"Excuse me, Nicole?" a voice called out from the next table. "Can you help me with this?"

Pastor Larry, who appeared to have dropped his fly-in-progress, sat staring at a mass of feathers, thread, marabou, and twine scattered haphazardly on the table in front of him.

Nicole smiled. "Of course, Pastor."

He smiled. "Please, I'm not Pastor here. I'm just Larry. Tonight I'm just one more guy who likes to fish and has high hopes of winning the prize for this year's tournament. Unless there's something you want to talk to me about."

Vic's laughter in the background almost made her say that there was something she wanted to talk to him about, but in the middle of the drop-in class was neither the time nor the place.

"Let me show you how to wrap this fly. The front section is different from most of the other ones, and it's best to hold it at a slightly different angle to wrap it evenly."

As she picked up the pieces, she hesitated. "This tail piece is folded too much to look nice. Let me go to the back and get a new piece for you." He smiled politely while she hustled into the storage room; except when she got there, she discovered that the box for the gold and black feathers she needed was empty.

She walked to the doorway. "Excuse me, Pas—" She cleared her throat. "Larry? Can you come in here? I need you to pick an alternate color for your tail."

Larry grinned from ear to ear and joined her inside the stockroom.

While they picked through the various boxes and packets, the bell to the door tinkled, followed by a female voice calling a greeting to one of the men at the fly-tying table. Nicole smiled at the concept that hearing a female voice in her craft shop in the evening now sounded a bit odd. However, with a woman who was not participating in the fly-tying drop-in entering the shop, Nicole could only stay in the storage room for a few minutes while the newcomer browsed. Hopefully she would have enough time with Larry to find a good color before she had to run to the front counter.

Just as she found some green feathers the exact same color as the thorax threads at the front of the fly, the woman spoke again. She heard Vic reply, but she couldn't make out exactly what he said.

"I think these are perfect," Nicole said, holding up a sample for Larry. "They're a bit short, but—"

The sound of Vic's laughter made her words catch in her throat. When they first started doing the sessions together, Vic laughed at her jokes like that. But lately he didn't laugh at much she said. In fact, the last few days he'd been spending what felt like as little time as possible with her—devoting most of his attention to other things and other people. She didn't want to feel jealous, but listening to him laugh so freely with another woman made the memory of his latest rejection stab her so hard she felt a physical pain in her stomach.

One of Larry's eyebrows quirked. "Aah," he murmured. "I had a feeling this was happening."

Nicole swallowed hard to bite back the sting of tears. "Is it that obvious?"

"Yes. Probably to everyone except Vic, I would hazard a guess."

"Why doesn't he like me? I thought he did, but today, he all but pushed me away."

Larry reached forward and wrapped his fingers around hers. "I think he does, but I know Vic, and there's something else he has to deal with. You have to leave this in God's hands."

Nicole nibbled her bottom lip. She'd done all she could to show Vic how she felt. Today, she'd kissed him with very little provocation. At first he'd responded, but the second he thought about what had happened, there was no doubt that it wasn't what he wanted.

She wasn't what he wanted. She wondered if Larry was trying to tell her that there was another woman in Vic's heart, even if she wasn't in his life right now.

Again, she'd let her heart lead her in the wrong direction. This time, though, she wasn't alone. She truly believed that God was in charge, and she had to do what God wanted her to do, whether it was what she wanted or not.

"You're right, Larry. It is time to leave this in God's hands. Everything is starting to fall into place for the first time in a long time. My business seems to be on the road to recovery, and I've started to make amends with my friends after pushing them out of my life. I think I'm even ready to talk to Shawn, my ex-fiancé, if I ever see him again. I don't know if I could quite forgive him yet, but I don't feel like hurting him anymore, so that's a start. The first thing Vic said to me was that God is a God of miracles, big ones and small ones, and I see now that he's right. I haven't seen any big ones yet, but God really has performed a bunch of small ones."

Larry smiled. "Yes, that's true."

She cleared her throat. "I thought one of those miracles was that God was going to give me someone to love, someone who could love me the same way as I love him. I thought that person was Vic." At the mention of his name, her eyes burned and her throat tightened. Nicole blinked hard and waited until she could compose herself before continuing. "But maybe I was wrong. Maybe the miracle here is that I'm finally moving forward with my life again. I've prayed that God would show me what He wanted me to do, and I thought I was doing my best to follow Him. But if that means Vic isn't interested in me, then I just have to accept that."

"Would you like to pray about it?"

She nodded, unable to speak with the pain of the loss, but if this was the way God wanted it, then she would accept it.

Larry began to pray, but he'd barely gotten started when a thump sounded from behind her.

"I think I'm needed out there," she said, still keeping her eyes closed.

"Then we'll make this quick," Larry said. He finished a short prayer of thanks and prayed for strength, then let go of her hands.

"Will I see you on Sunday?"

Nicole swiped the back of her hand over her eyes. "Yes. I'll be there—even if I have to come alone, I'll be there."

She hurried out of the stockroom and to the front counter, where Vic was standing and talking to Theresa, one of the women from church with whom Nicole was becoming friends.

"Hi, Theresa. Is that everything for you today?"

Theresa nodded and slid a cross-stitch kit across the counter. "Yes. Actually it's not for me. My mother liked the one I started last week so much that she wanted to make one, too. I don't want her to make the same one, so I'm going to give her this one as a gift."

Vic grinned, emphasizing the attractive crow's-feet at the corners of his enchanting baby blue eyes. Nicole nearly swooned, except his charm wasn't aimed at her. It was aimed at Theresa. "That's a great idea," he said. "If your dad wants to do something, too, Nicole has a whole section of supplies that he can use to landscape his miniature train set."

Nicole forced herself to smile. A few weeks ago, Vic's reference would have been "we," but now it was back to being "hers."

She chatted with Theresa as she rang up the sale, but

even though it didn't take long to complete the transaction, by the time Theresa walked out, Nicole couldn't remember a thing she'd said.

Instead of returning to the craft tables, Vic leaned over the counter toward her. "We need to talk," he said softly. "Because I—"

She held up her hands to silence him. She'd heard it already and didn't need it repeated. It could never be said that she couldn't take a hint. "It's okay. I know what you're going to say, and it's okay. I understand. Now, if you'll excuse me, I have a table to teach."

Chapter 12

Vic's heart thumped in his chest as Nicole turned her back to him and walked away.

He deserved exactly what he was getting.

She'd taken a chance and opened her heart and kissed him. He'd only been thinking of himself. His words to send her away had been cruel, and he deserved the same treatment as he'd given out.

He hadn't realized what was going on in the stockroom when he'd walked in. He'd only meant to tell Nicole that her friend was there, thinking she hadn't heard the bell. The second he walked in on Nicole and Larry's private conversation, he froze, afraid if she saw him standing there, knowing that he'd heard, everything would become even worse than it already was. Although now, he didn't think that was possible. He'd managed to sneak back out, but not before he'd heard a few things that hadn't been meant for him to hear.

But since he hadn't been meant to hear, he knew what she'd said was completely honest and without ulterior motives.

Nicole wasn't like Elsa at all, and he had been a distrustful jerk to even think she could be like that. She was truly being honest and sincere, and every question she'd asked him was legitimate and from her heart. She'd come to her decision to trust in the Lord by herself. She didn't have any hidden motives or plans. She had always been completely honest with him in all her feelings and questions, which was more than he could say for himself. She'd told him all about Shawn and how much damage he'd done to her life. Long-lasting, permanent damage.

He'd never told her about Elsa because he was too afraid Nicole would do the same thing. He didn't know when his ego had become so big that he thought he would be worth the effort. Nicole's noble response certainly put him in his place, and he deserved it.

He hadn't given her a chance. Instead, all his thoughts were clouded by distrust, and that was wrong. Hopefully it wasn't too late to make it right.

Nicole had some new techniques to teach the men, and with every passing minute, he could feel the gap between them widening.

He didn't know what to do, so instead of participating in the demonstration, Vic stood back as Nicole showed all the men the proper way to wrap the thorax on the Golden Pheasant Nymph.

As Nicole talked about forming the fly, she commented on the shape and size of bugs in general and expressed her disbelief in herself, that she was now actively promoting ugly insects willingly.

All the men laughed, and some added their own

comments about some of the bigger bugs they'd come in contact with over the years. Nicole pretended to shudder, comparing their stories to some of the flies they'd already made, and the class continued.

The woman had style and grace and a sense of humor. Everything about Nicole was perfect for him, including her silly little laugh. It was his lack of trust that jeopardized their future.

He couldn't lose her now.

"Oh, Trev, you've ruined your tail feathers. I happen to know we don't have any more of the gold and brown spotted ones, but I have a few more left that are the same green as the thorax section. I'll be right back."

The second she left the room, all the men turned and stared at him. Vic suspected that they expected him to continue the lesson, but he could only think of one thing.

Nicole had gone back into the storage room—the only place in the building that could offer any privacy for the next hour.

If he walked out the door tonight without talking to her, by Sunday the wall that was going up between them would be too high to break down.

If he didn't talk to her now, she probably wouldn't ever talk to him again.

"Excuse me," he mumbled as he pushed his way between the empty chairs. "Consider tonight a test. Figure it out yourselves."

The room became completely silent except for the scraping of the chairs on the tile floor as Vic hurriedly pushed them out of his way. It wouldn't take Nicole long to pick a few feathers out of a box, so he had to move quickly.

He entered the room just as she stepped away from the box, feathers in hand.

Her face paled the second she saw him.

"I know I only have a few seconds, but I have to say this before I make it even worse. Nicole, I know I was a jerk a few minutes ago, and I want to tell you that I'm sorry and that I love you and will you forgive me and will you marry me?"

Her mouth dropped open, and she stared at him without replying.

"That may have been a little abrupt, but I promise I can do better later if you'll give me another chance."

"I. . ." Her voice trailed off. An uneasy silence hung between them.

Vic swiped his hands through his hair. He'd hoped against good sense that she would at least be receptive to his sincere if not very romantic proposal.

"Let me try this. We belong together. Just like all this stuff we've been making the fishing flies out of."

Her eyebrows arched, and her eyes opened wider than he'd ever seen.

But she wasn't asking him to leave, so that meant he was making progress.

"You are the yarn, and I am the marabou. No. Wait. It's the marabou that's soft and pretty. I got it backward. You're the marabou, and I'm the yarn. And God is like the hook, the center and the solid anchor that supports everything tied on it. That would be you and me."

"What are you talking about?"

"It's like this: 'Though one may be overpowered, two can defend themselves. A cord of three strands is not quickly broken.' That's Ecclesiastes 4:12. We've become just as intricately tied together, just like the fishing flies we've been making together, as long as God is tied in there with us."

"Nicole? Vic?" a male voice called out from the group. "Are you two coming back?"

Vic lowered himself to one knee. "You don't have to answer me right away. In fact, you shouldn't. This is too important to make a snap decision. Because when I get married, I don't do catch and release. It's going to be for keeps. And you're definitely a keeper."

"I. . ." Words failed her a second time, which Vic expected.

"If you want, you can stay in here for a while. Just give me the feathers, and I'll go back and finish off the class." He held out his palm, but she didn't give him the feathers.

"I can't. Excuse me."

She walked past him and out of the storage room.

Slowly Vic rose and followed her out.

He had his answer.

He didn't want to walk out on her in the middle of the class, but at this point there was nothing he could do except leave gracefully after the class was over. He hadn't trusted her, and he got what he deserved.

When Nicole asked how everyone was doing, a number of the men proudly held up slightly crooked but perfectly usable Golden Pheasant Nymphs. Nicole gave Trev his new green tail feathers, then left him to help someone else finish up winding the thorax threads.

Rather than standing and doing nothing, and because he wanted to keep busy, Vic settled in beside Trev and guided him through the process of catching up with the rest of the class.

He felt more than saw movement at his side. He turned his head to see Nicole standing beside him.

"Yes," she said, her voice low and husky.

Vic's head swam, and his heart pounded. "Is that your answer? Really?"

"Really. Because I think you're a keeper, too."

"Yee haw!" Vic shouted as he sprang out of the chair. He threw the yarn and thread from Trev's fly in the air and twirled around on his toes.

He didn't care that everyone was watching. He grabbed Nicole, threw his arms around her, and spun her around in the air, laughing as he did so.

She wrapped her arms around his neck and squealed, so he spun her around one more time. When her feet were back on the floor, he didn't give her more than a second to regain her balance. He bent her slightly backward and kissed her, right in front of everyone.

"And that *should* have happened," he whispered against her lips. "And it's going to happen a lot more."

Nicole grinned. "It had better."

Vic's grin widened. "I just got an idea. Instead of the usual boring bride and groom statues on our wedding cake, we should have a pair of fishing flies. Custom designed flies, of course."

"As long as mine can be pink and cute."

"And I want mine to be blue. Not skytone. Blue."

Nicole grinned and gave him a quick peck on the cheek. "Deal. Now, if you'll let me go, we have a class to run."

GAIL SATTLER

Gail Sattler lives in Vancouver, British Columbia (where you don't have to shovel rain), with her husband of twenty-seven years, three sons, two dogs, five lizards, two toads, and a degu named Bess. Gail loves to read stories with a happy ending, which is why she writes them that way. Gail has written many novels for Heartsong Presents, Barbour Publishing, and Steeple Hill. After being voted by the readership of the Heartsong Presents line as Favorite Heartsong Author three years in a row, she was inducted to the Heartsong Presents Authors Hall of Fame with a lifetime achievement award. To see more, you're invited to visit Gail's Web site at www.gailsattler.com.

Idle
Hours

by Kathleen Y'Barbo

Dedication

To Mary Beth and Carla Patton,
Rocky Mountain relatives and precious kinfolk.

*Now faith is being sure of what we hope for
and certain of what we do not see.*

HEBREWS 11:1

Home is where the heart is and hence a movable feast.

ANGELA CARTER

Chapter 1

Joe Corbin never did get over turning in his traveling shoes and hanging up his long-haul trucker's license. Like his opinions, however, Joe kept the truth to himself.

Buying his daddy's bait shop so his mama wouldn't have to run the place alone—now that's something he could take pride in. After all, a man's job was to see to his family. But with Mama gone six years now, he toyed with the idea of buying himself an RV and a new map that would take him out of Verde Point, Kentucky, for good.

Casting his line into the depths of Canyon Lake, Joe could not care less whether he caught a fish. It was a beautiful April morning, and he had nothing to do but sit back and enjoy the hour before the bait shop opened with his buddy Vic Thompson, while Skipper, his year-old black Lab, snoozed at his feet.

Life just didn't get any better than this.

Too bad the man had his mind set on talking about the Lord again. Joe could tell it as surely as he knew the sun would rise again tomorrow. When Vic got that look in his eye, well, a sly comment was sure to follow.

Joe was as aware as the next guy that there was a heavenly Father looking down from some mysterious place in the sky. It's just that his buddy seemed to think that somehow that Guy had an interest in the daily activities of folks here on earth.

It was a nice idea, but nice ideas were better kept in fairy tales. Neither had much basis in reality. Oh, he sat in church as regularly as clockwork, but that was because it made him feel good and not because the Man Upstairs might be listening.

"Penny for your thoughts, Joe," Vic said as he opened the cooler and reached for a bottle of water.

Skipper roused at the sound of a voice. Joe gave him a scratch behind the ears.

"You sound like a woman." Joe leaned forward to accept the bottle and took a long swig. Wiping his mouth with the back of his hand, he set the bottle down and shook his head. " 'Sides, you don't want to know what I'm thinkin'. It might rile you."

"Go ahead. I dare you." Vic chuckled. "Wouldn't be the first time."

"I don't know." Joe pretended to study the bobber at the end of his line. "I'm not the sharpest tool in the shed, but even I know not to irritate a man when you're sittin' in his boat."

Vic chuckled as he pulled one of his fancy hand-tied lures out of his tackle box and fixed it to his line. "The Lord been after you again?" he asked as he sent the lure flying in a perfect arc.

A moment of silence passed while Joe pretended to be absorbed reeling in a line that had nothing on it but a worm. Once he had the bobber floating again, Joe decided to speak his mind.

"Don't you think I'm a little old for the good Lord to fool with?"

Another chuckle. Oh, but that man was irritating.

"What are you, fifty?"

"I'll be sixty soon enough," Joe said. The truth was, he'd turned fifty-two the day after Easter, but he hadn't told a soul. Birthdays meant fuss, and he hated fuss.

That was why he and Skipper got along so well. All the dog needed was a full belly, a nice nap, and an occasional game of fetch. If only his own life were so simple.

"Well," Vic said, "then you've lived long enough to know a few things for sure, haven't you?"

Joe leveled a stare at Vic. "Yeah, I suppose I have."

"And it's not that you don't believe in God. It's more like you don't believe God wants a relationship with you. Am I right?"

"I s'pose that's right." Joe let out the line a bit and watched the bobber float due east with the current. "I guess what I'm sayin' is, if He's so interested in being my buddy, why hasn't He said somethin' Himself?" He paused to let the question sink in. "I mean, like you said, I've lived long enough to know a few things for sure, and I know for sure the Lord hasn't exactly been hangin' around the bait shop beggin' me to sit and chat."

"I wouldn't be so sure," Vic said under his breath.

"What was that?" Oh, he heard him, but Joe wanted

to see if Vic would repeat himself.

"I said. . ." He laid down his rod and stuck his foot on it to keep it in the boat, then looked directly at Joe. "I said I wouldn't be so sure. I'd be willing to bet my best lure that the Lord's been right there in Joe's Bait and Tackle just waiting for you to sit still long enough to listen to Him."

What a card. Joe chuckled. "Oh, would you now?"

Vic's eyes glinted steel, and his look was all business. "Yes, I would."

"Well, you're in there more than most. Maybe you seen Him when I wasn't looking."

"Maybe I have." Vic shrugged. "Or maybe I was looking for Him and you weren't."

Now wasn't that an odd statement? Joe tipped his feed-store cap up to peer down his nose at Vic. "What're you getting at, buddy?"

"I am not a betting man, but I believe the Lord won't mind if I make you an offer." He paused to open his tackle box. "Pick any one of those lures, Joe."

"Now I know you're off your rocker." He shook his head. "Close that thing and stop your jawin' so we can get back to fishin'."

"No, I'm serious. Pick a lure. Which one do you like? How about this one?" He held up a Silver Thorn Dressed, the prize lure of the box.

"Well now, that's a fine lure, but—"

"But nothing. I'm willing to stake this lure that once you ask Him, the Lord will make Himself known to you."

"Oh, come on. Put your lure back and get to fishin'." Vic's line tightened, and the bobber disappeared for a moment. "See there, you got somethin'. Now get to fishin'."

"I'm fishing, all right," he said without giving the rod a second look. "Right now, I'm fishing for men. Why don't you just go on and admit you've never tried to see if God will show you how much He wants to be a real part of your life?"

The line went slack, and the bobber popped into sight. Whatever was on Vic's hook was gone.

Joe threw down his rod in disgust and reached for the oars. "That's it. If you're not going to fish, I'm headin' back to shore."

Vic picked up his rod and studied the reel for a minute before making eye contact. "I'm willing to lose my best lure to prove that the Lord thinks you're a keeper. Just ask Him to make Himself real to you, and He will. If I'm wrong, the lure's yours."

"That's it? Just say, 'Lord, show Yourself,' and if He ignores me, the lure is mine?" Joe shook his head and took another swig from the water bottle. "Come on."

"No, that's not it. Our heavenly Father's not some genie in a bottle. What He is, Joe, is a God who desperately wants His children to know and love Him. I've been praying you would seek Him for a long time now, and I believe it's going to happen soon. You got to promise me that once He does make Himself plain to you, you'll come and tell me."

"That's all you want for that Silver Thorn Dressed? What if I don't but say I do? Then what?"

"Oh, I'm not worried about that." Vic grinned. "You're a terrible liar. Of all the fish stories I've heard, yours are the worst. Besides, once you've met the Lord, you're never the same. It's not something a man can hide."

"So you're saying all I have to do is call and the Lord'll hear me?" He paused to take it in. "You're serious."

"That's right. God's waiting. Just call." He lifted the Silver Thorn Dressed to let it catch the light. "Now let me tell you one thing. Our Lord isn't some pie-in-the-sky being that'll jump when we tell Him to. He does what He will because He is God. I don't fully get that, but if we humans completely understood Him, He wouldn't be much of a God."

"I'll grant you that much," Joe said. "And I'll give the rest some serious thought. I've always wanted that lure of yours."

Vic smiled. "I do believe the Lord's gonna get Himself another keeper real soon."

Chapter 2

Lia Stephanos gripped the wheel of her SUV as she left the city of Verde Point proper and headed for the hills, literally. Five minutes later, at half past four in the afternoon on the second day of May, she negotiated the tight turn at Benders Fork and exhaled a long breath.

Today was a big day. This drive was one she wouldn't soon forget.

The few times she'd traveled this road in the past year, she'd done so in the roomy confines of her friend Ruby Wells's well-appointed "mommy van" or, more recently, in the passenger seat of her Realtor's luxury sedan. Somehow the beauty of the Kentucky countryside seemed much more appealing when the road led to the enjoyment of visiting Ruby and her family or the adventure of hunting for the perfect house.

Now that the road led home, well, the familiar butterflies rose. The choice had been made, and the deal was final.

Final. Oh, how I hate that word.

"Stop it," she said aloud as she pried her fingers off the wheel to punch the button on her CD player. "You know the Lord led you to Verde Point. You're going to be happy here, and that's all there is to it."

The soft strains of smooth jazz filled the car, and she reached to turn up the volume. As the music wound its way around her raw nerves and settled in her heart, Lia relaxed a notch and guided the vehicle past thickets of pine, lush fields, and an empty fruit and vegetable stand.

Spring had touched this part of Kentucky with a brush of brilliant green. Soon there would be fresh produce and—most likely—good conversation with the farmer who grew them, a luxury unheard of in her former abode.

Honestly, who wouldn't be happy in Verde Point, Kentucky? Between the quaint town nestled on the edge of Canyon Lake and the green hills where she'd found her dream hideaway, the area had much to offer. Oh yes, this place was practically right out of an ad from a retirement brochure.

Retirement.

At the thought of her own forced exile, Lia let out a long breath. Who would have thought she'd be a washed-up senior editor before she turned forty? Well, not exactly washed up, but definitely forced to pull over while the rest of the publishing rat race skidded past with the next best-seller.

Too bad about that heart of yours.

She'd heard it first from the most respected and expensive cardiologist in Manhattan, then again from her boss, the CEO of Winston Books. Along the way, the message came from others in phone calls and e-mails and even the occasional cheery get-well card.

Just when she figured she'd heard the last comment about her faulty ventricle, she heard the same words from the guy who ran the newsstand on the corner by her third-floor walk-up in Red Hook, Brooklyn. It seemed as though the only person other than Ruby who didn't think life as she knew it was over was Lia's mother.

No, to the contrary, her dear mother had practically giggled at the thought of Lia turning in the key to her corner office at the largest publishing house in New York. Ever the Southern belle, even though she'd dwelled in Manhattan's Upper East Side since she married into Papa's large Greek family four decades ago, Cordelia Stephanos never quite gave up the idea that women were for making dinner and grandbabies.

More important, Mother never lent any credence to a doctor's diagnosis, at least not when she'd heard from the Lord that all was well with her only daughter. And Mama claimed to have it on good authority that the Lord still had many years of living planned for Lia.

One look at the white cottage by the lake and Mother pronounced it the perfect home for her grandbabies. A reminder that her only child was closer to menopause than the maternity ward had no effect.

A few moments later, Lia signaled to turn left at Barker Point, then began the quarter-mile bounce along a rutted road, gritting her teeth so as not to bite her tongue. Up ahead, she caught sight of the dented blue mailbox on a peeled pine post, its red flag at half-staff. Someone had stenciled a sailboat on either side, but only the barest outline of the vessel could be seen against the pitted rust marks and peeling paint.

Pulling up next to it, Lia climbed out to check her mail, only to find the thing rusted shut. "One more item to add to the list," she muttered as she returned to her SUV.

The infamous list of to-dos had grown to cover two sheets of notepaper in her ever-present portfolio. With this addition and the one regarding the room for younger guests, a third page would probably have to be added.

Some of the items—like switching her cellular phone service to a local carrier and ordering checks with her new address—were low priority. Others, like finding help with her overgrown yard, establishing a new Internet connection, sending a change of address out to family and friends, and stocking her kitchen would come first.

Then there was the issue of the sagging front porch.

Lia brought the SUV to a stop in front of the house, then eyed the angle of the boards on the eastern corner of the porch. Thankfully, Ruby's husband, Travis, had already scheduled one of his construction crews to do the repair in a few weeks. In the meantime, she'd just have to be careful when she replenished the hummingbird nectar in the feeder that hung from the eastern rafter.

Shouldering her overnight bag, Lia climbed from the SUV, then cradled her portfolio and slammed the car door. The sound, echoing in the silence, was quickly followed by the rustling sound of several dozen birds evacuating the trees above her.

She inhaled deeply of the crisp, clean air and noted

the distinct lack of bus fumes and cooking odors. "Lia, honey," she said under her breath as she palmed her keys, "you're *definitely* not in Brooklyn anymore."

With a grin, Lia turned to cross the lawn—her lawn— and smiled. Where weeds choked out any desirable foliage, she soon hoped to plant climbing roses and colorful perennials. In that shady spot under the trees, she planned a bed of hostas, ferns, and pink begonias. Out back, she hoped to have her own garden in the works come next spring.

All of this would have to wait until she completed the massive cleanup and painting job that would have to begin immediately. Her cardiologist would probably have a fit, but she intended to do the work herself. Paint and pine-scented cleaner would replace aerobics and walking in her exercise routine for the next few weeks, maybe months.

She cast a longing glance at the lake shimmering beneath startling blue skies in the distance and the narrow dirt road that led from her place to the small boat dock below. Perhaps she should find time to take a walk after all.

Later, she decided, after the house was aired out and her meager provisions unloaded. The moving van wouldn't arrive with her things from Brooklyn for another three days—plenty of time to steal a moment or two for a stroll to the lake.

Not enough time, though, to make a dent in the list she carried under her arm.

"It's not perfect, but it's mine," she said as she climbed the steps and fitted her key into the front lock.

Chapter 3

The glass-paned front door complained loudly, and Lia paused to open her portfolio and add a note to oil the hinges. Clutching her portfolio to her chest, Lia stepped over the threshold and dropped her overnight bag and purse on the blue rag rug.

The rocker beckoned, and Lia moved to stand beside it. The thought of sitting in this rocker made her smile. The deep windowsill looked to be a perfect spot to place a steaming cup of tea on a winter morning when it was too chilly to sit on the porch, and the side table she'd once placed next to her bed would fit nicely here. A new lamp for reading by and a little footstool for her tired toes and she'd be set.

Maybe I did make the right choice in coming here.

She took a deep breath, and to her surprise, the first thing she smelled was the pine-scented cleaner, quickly followed by a tangy-sweet apple fragrance. Her eyes flew open. The reason for the cleanser smell was evident once her eyes adjusted to the dimness of the interior. Someone had scrubbed the large combination living area and kitchen from top to bottom.

Gone was the grime from the white cabinets and countertops, and the walls gleamed beneath last year's calendar from Joe's Bait and Tackle shop. As she stepped forward, she noted that the picture above the store's logo was of a view that could have been taken from her front porch.

She touched the glossy page and smiled. Thick green foliage dipped down the hillside to reach a lake that glistened with the last rays of the evening sun. Orange sparkles danced across a surface dotted with dozens of boats. The caption beneath the picture read: FIRST DAY OF THE FISHING TOURNAMENT. An August date from two summers ago appeared next to the caption.

Lia turned from the calendar to find the source of the apple pie smell. A red candle in a Blue Willow teacup sat beside a folded slip of yellow notepaper. Next to it on the countertop was a foil-wrapped pie pan, no doubt holding an apple pie.

Note in hand, she made short order of raising the blue toile shades and opening the windows. A fresh breeze danced past, carrying with it the scent of more pine.

"Welcome home to Verde Point, Lia," she read in her friend Ruby's familiar handwriting. "The pie is sugar free, and there's a chicken casserole in the fridge. It's heart-healthy."

Dropping the note onto the countertop, she lifted the edge of the foil and sampled a taste of the perfectly browned crust. "Ruby, sweetheart, you've outdone yourself."

"Thank you."

Whirling around, she found the object of her thoughts smiling back at her from the door. "Ruby! I didn't hear you drive up."

Her friend met her halfway and embraced her. "I'm sure your mind was on other things." She shrugged. "Be glad the kids are napping in their car seats. Otherwise, you might have heard me all the way from town."

She linked arms with her friend and stepped outside. "Lead me to those babies," she said. "I can't wait to see how much little Tyler's grown."

"Auntie Wia!"

Two-year-old Samantha grinned back at her through the open door of Ruby's dark green minivan. Dubbed the "mommy van" during Lia's last visit, a collection of stuffed animals, as well as a pink backpack and matching sweater, decorated the space around the curly-headed girl's seat.

"She looks more like you every day," Lia said as she lifted the dark-haired darling from her car seat and kissed her sticky cheek. Something cool trickled down Lia's back, and she heard Ruby gasp.

"Samantha Wells, where did you get that drink box?"

"I dunno." Samantha leaned away from Lia's shoulder to look her in the eyes. "I wub you, Auntie Wia."

She touched the little girl's freckled nose with the tip of her forefinger. "Oh, I wub you, too, Sam-Sam."

"Don't let her daddy hear you call her Sam. He's determined she will be a girlie girl, you know." Ruby reached past them to pull a towel from the van and dab the back of Lia's sweatshirt. "Sorry about that."

Lia gave the precious child a hug, then set her wriggling

feet on the grass. "No apology necessary. Now let me at that darling son of yours." She shrugged off the towel and went around to the other side of the van to slide the door open and stand over the car seat of the most precious baby she'd seen since Samantha. "Come here to Auntie Lia," she said as she lifted three-month-old Tyler Wells from the cushy, blue-plaid comfort of his travel seat and settled him against her shoulder. "Where's Bryce?"

Ruby snagged a navy diaper bag, then clicked a button on her key to close the van door. "School, then basketball practice until five, Auntie Lia," she said with a chuckle.

"School?"

"Yes, dear. Have you forgotten it's a Tuesday?"

Lia snuggled the blanket around the sleeping baby. "My days have run together lately. I couldn't tell you with any certainty what month it is, actually."

"It's May already. Has been for the past two days," Ruby said as she cast a glance over her shoulder to check on Samantha. "Don't go outside the fence, you hear?" she called.

Rather than answer, the toddler reached for the gate, then turned back to see if her mother was watching. When Ruby shook her head, Samantha turned to amuse herself by rolling in clover, curls bouncing.

"Wonderful. It took me half an hour to get her into that outfit and two seconds for her to get it covered in grass stains." Ruby held the screen door open for Lia. "Guess we're heading back to have a bath and a change of clothes before we pick up Bryce, instead of running errands." She ran her hand through short-cropped hair and offered a weak smile. "Of course, I could take her messy. It wouldn't be the first time. Or, better yet, I wait until Thursday when Samantha is in Mother's Day Out at the church to do my errands."

"I vote for the latter. I'll even offer to go with you. Maybe I can knock a few items off my to-do list." She paused to plant a kiss atop Tyler's soft brown fuzz. "That is, if we can fit a lunch in there somewhere."

"Sure, but don't count on gourmet food. There's a reason I always cook when you come to visit. Verde Point's a great place to live, but the choices in dining are a bit, shall we say, limited." She glanced past Lia to stare out the door. "Samantha, get away from the van. The doors are locked."

"Mrs. Bunny," she demanded.

"Go play. I'll get Mrs. Bunny in a minute." Ruby leaned against the counter and shook her head. "Honestly, I don't remember Bryce being anywhere near as active as that one. Not that I'm complaining, you understand, but I've had to cut way back on my writing time. I'm sure your replacement isn't happy with me."

Lia knew she must have grimaced, for Ruby's expression turned to horror.

"Oh, honey, I'm sorry. I didn't mean to talk business today of all days."

Lisa shifted Tyler to the crook of her arm and blinked back the tears that threatened. Eventually the idea of her forced unemployment wouldn't sting so much. In the meantime, she refused to allow her silly feelings to ruin a perfectly lovely day, especially since Ruby went to so much trouble to welcome her.

"Hey," Lia said, "have I told you how very much I appreciate all you've done here?"

"Done?" She shrugged. "I just spruced it up a bit. Didn't take but a couple of hours."

"Spruced up? Are you kidding me? You managed to accomplish what I couldn't have done in a week."

"Still. . ."

Ruby grinned. "Believe me, when you are the mother of one preteen, one toddler, and a baby, an afternoon appointment with cleanser and a dust rag is pure heaven. Besides, Travis needed the time with the kids."

"Travis baby-sits?"

"Of course he does, although I prefer to call it parenting rather than baby-sitting. Besides, all jokes against males multitasking aside, he does a good job of watching them," Ruby said. "Well, for a few hours anyway. Anything beyond that, we're still working on. For all his many good qualities, the man does not do multitasking well."

Tyler opened his eyes and began to rub his cheek against Lia's arm. When she shifted him back to her shoulder, he began to squirm. "Looks like someone's hungry," she said.

Ruby checked her watch, then nodded. "Yep, it's about that time." Looking around the empty room, she nodded toward the front porch. "The porch swing?"

"Sure," Lia said as she handed the blue-clad bundle back to her friend.

Once settled on the swing with the baby happily nursing beneath his blanket, Ruby turned to regard Lia with a solemn look. "Tell me the truth. What does the doctor say about, well, you know—your health?"

How much to tell? The lab results said what her doctor did not. Still, she had to go with Mama on this one. Unless the Lord said otherwise, she had a long life ahead of her.

"Very little, actually." Lia leaned against the back of the swing and closed her eyes. "I think the man's a bit overprotective."

"How so?"

Lia opened her eyes and focused on Samantha, who seemed to be having an animated conversation with a squirrel perched safely out of her reach on the roof. "Well, he insisted I have three months of meds on hand, and he made me promise I would call him if I needed him." She paused. "I won't, you know."

Ruby's brows furrowed. "Won't need him or won't call?"

"Mommy, come quick. Look what I found." Samantha squatted in the tall grass, then lifted a slithering ribbon of golden brown, twice the length of her arm. "See, look how pretty."

"What do you have, honey?" Ruby called as she adjusted her clothing and lifted Tyler to her shoulder to burp him.

Lia rose. A second later, she froze. "Oh no," she whispered. "It's a—"

"Copperhead," a male voice said firmly.

Chapter 4

Joe eased toward Samantha Wells with a forced grin on his face. "That's a real pretty plaything you got there, honey," he said gently. "How about I put it in a safe place for you?"

"No, it *my* pwetty wibbon."

Great. The kid thinks a poisonous snake is a hair ribbon.

The little one stared at him, oblivious to the fact her chubby fist held a copperhead by the middle. Unless he came up with a plan, the little darling who generally rode on her daddy's shoulders into the bait shop on Saturday mornings, bunny in one hand and a hank of Travis Wells's hair in the other, would end up bitten by a snake.

Think, Corbin. What was the name of that rabbit she always dragged around with her? Ah!

"Hey, Samantha, where's Mrs. Bunny?"

The girl looked past him toward her mama's van, then pointed with the hand that held the snake. "She in the van," she said as the copperhead wove from side to side.

Out of the corner of his eye, he saw Samantha's mama and another lady standing on the corner of the porch. So far, neither had panicked. At least he didn't have *that* to deal with.

"All right now," he said as he took a step toward Samantha. "Why don't you just let that little ole snake go now, and we'll fetch Mrs. Bunny from the van?"

Samantha shook her head. "You not got keys."

"Don't need 'em," he said as he inched forward. "All Mama's got to do is click that beeper of hers, and those doors'll slide right open." Another step, then another. He could almost reach her. Just another couple of steps. "Ruby, is that you over there on the porch?"

"Yes, it's me, Joe."

He could tell from her shaky voice that Travis's wife was about at the end of her rope. "Well then, you think you could hit that clicker on your key chain and open the door so Samantha and I can go get Mrs. Bunny?"

The woman at her side jumped into motion, disappearing inside to come right back out with the keys. From where he stood, he could see her fumble with the key chain; then, an eternity later, the van chirped.

"All right now, let's go get Mrs. Bunny." Another step toward her and this time he dared to reach out to try to grab the snake. To his horror, the girl clutched the squirming snake to her chest, its pink tongue a perfect match for the flowers on her dress.

In the desperation of the moment, a voice, Vic's voice, floated across his mind. *"God's waiting. Just call."*

Please, Lord. Right now, I want to believe You're hearing me.

"Look, honey," he somehow managed, "that little ole

snake is gettin' lonesome for his mama. And I bet Mrs. Bunny's gettin' lonesome for you. How about we go and see her?"

Samantha seemed to consider the question for a moment as she held the snake out at arm's length. Meanwhile, the snake looked poised to strike. It swayed rhythmically from side to side, bobbing and weaving far too close to the girl's face.

She leaned down to pick a flower just as the creature jabbed toward her and attempted to strike. "*Not* a snake. It a *wibbon*."

"All right, honey," he somehow managed. "It's a ribbon."

Please, come down here and fix this. An eerie calm came over him. *Show Yourself. Please, God, I'm asking. No, I'm begging. If You're listening and You're of a mind to help, please come on down here and show Yourself like Vic said You would.*

Joe paused to watch the snake, which had turned its attention on him. Swaying slowly, the pink tongue pointed in his direction. The thing seemed to be challenging him, daring him to do something.

He was about to make a grab for the critter when the strangest sensation came over him. Like a wave off one of those jet skis, something washed over him. While he couldn't say for sure, it felt like he wasn't alone out there with Samantha Wells. It was as if. . .

No, it couldn't be.

Joe looked around, then stared back into the beady eyes of that copperhead. *I believe, Lord,* he added. *I really believe.*

To Joe's surprise, the snake went slack in Samantha's hand, and she tossed it aside to race toward the van. Before Joe could form a coherent thought, the toddler had the purple stuffed rabbit in her hand.

"Me beep the van door," she called to her mother.

Joe landed on his knees, barely missing the copperhead. It took him a full minute before he realized the creature was stone-cold dead.

Lia swayed twice before she fell against the rail. The man, whoever he was, disappeared beneath the cover of thick grass. So, it seemed, did the snake.

Ruby said something in a voice that begged immediate action. The words were lost among the pounding of Lia's heart and the urgent need to run.

Somehow she sailed off the porch and crossed the rutted driveway to reach the tall grass on the western slope. Pinpoints of light appeared at the corners of her vision. She ignored them to sail over a downed fence post. Landing hard on one knee, she righted herself and kept running toward the place where she last saw the stranger.

"Joe," she heard Ruby call.

"Joe?" Lia echoed as she nearly stumbled over the still-kneeling sandy-haired man.

He rose on unsteady legs to brush off his khaki trousers, then thrust his hand in her direction. "Pleased to meet you, ma'am," he said in a slow-as-molasses Kentucky drawl.

Lia shook his hand, noting the firm grip despite the fact the man seemed to sway a bit. "Are you all right?" She quickly studied his hands, then the tanned skin of his arms. "Did the snake bite you?"

"Well, it's the strangest thing." He pointed to a spot beside his feet. "Looks that ole snake never knew what hit him."

She glanced down to watch him pick up the lifeless snake and nearly fainted dead away. Though her heart had been declared nearly useless, it certainly seemed to be pumping with vigor at the moment.

"Please put that down," she said through teeth that were determined to chatter. "I appreciate that you killed it, but I really—"

"Well now, that's what's odd about all this." He gave the offending creature a toss, landing it squarely in the dented silver can beside the garden shed. "See, I didn't do a thing. Never touched it."

Lia shook her head. "But it's dead. Are you telling me Samantha killed the snake?"

The stranger looked down at her from his superior height and grinned. And he did have the prettiest eyes. The color of the Kentucky sky, they were, framed in lashes that belonged on a woman.

Stop it. What is wrong with you? These are not the appropriate thoughts of a woman who's just seen a dead snake tossed about.

Out of the corner of her eye, she saw Ruby tuck the baby into his car seat, then gather Samantha into her arms. While Lia's friend was in tears, little Samantha seemed more worried about her stuffed rabbit than her crying mother.

"I don't rightly understand it, either," he said, oblivious to the direction her thoughts had turned, "but I'm here to tell you I believe I might know who is responsible."

"Who?"

A look crossed his face. "Never mind. It's dead, and that's all that matters."

Lia clutched her throat as a wave of lightheadedness gripped her. "Yes," she said, "that is what matters. I don't suppose you might know someone who could rid me of this tall grass and whatever inhabitants it has."

"Ma'am," he said as his face began to swim before her, "I believe we ought to talk about this later. Looks like you're about to. . ."

Lia swayed, then sank. The lights went out, then blinked on again. A haze of swirling colors formed into a man's face. He wore a worried look.

"Lia." Ruby knelt down to grasp her hand. "When I couldn't get Doc Warren on the phone, I called your mother to get your doctor's name. I'm on hold."

"My mother?"

"No," Ruby said. "This is your doctor's office."

Lia reached for the phone and punched the button ending the call. "I'm fine." She rose and dusted off the back of her jeans. "I just got a little light-headed. Must have been. . ." She paused to look past Ruby to focus on the man still staring at her.

"You don't look so good," he said.

"Must be the grass in my hair," she said as she shook

her head and watched bits of greenery litter her clothing. "I promise I clean up just fine." A realization hit her hard. Lia leveled a stare at her friend. "Ruby, you called my *mother*?"

Chapter 5

Ruby turned three shades of pink, then studied her nails. "I guess I panicked." She met Lia's gaze. "I just thought, well. . ." She cast an embarrassed glance at Joe, then swung her attention back to Lia. "You *know.*"

The lone male of the trio seemed more preoccupied than concerned. He stared past her to where the lake shimmered beyond the trees. A lone boat with a fisherman casting a line seemed the object of his attention. *Typical man.*

"Mama, baby's stinky," Samantha called from the van.

Ruby gave Lia one more imploring look, eyes narrowed. "You call him back, you hear?"

"Right after I call my mother to tell her that your overactive imagination got the better of you." She paused. "And I am *fine*, you hear?"

"Mama! Baby yucky!"

"Coming, sweetheart," she called. "Joe, would you see that she gets back to the house and gets something cold to drink? It wouldn't hurt if you put that casserole in the oven for her, too. Just turn the oven to—"

"Oh, come on," Lia said. "I love you, Ruby, but you are treating me like one of your children."

"You fainted."

"I was just a little light-headed. It wasn't an official faint." She paused. "Nothing like—well. . .*that*. Really, I would tell you."

For a moment, she thought Ruby might protest. Rather, her friend gathered her in an embrace, then whispered, "You're not alone in this, Lia. God and I are here."

"I know, and I am so grateful," Lia said softly. She held her friend at arm's length and smiled. "I am, really, and I honestly would tell you if I needed more than a good friend and a great casserole and pie." Pausing for effect, she added, "I promise."

Her friend's relief was visible. "All right then," she said. "But put the casserole in, light the candle, and relax until your supper's ready."

"Sure," she said as her friend sauntered toward the van.

Relax? She had a list that grew by the minute, and in light of the snake incident, she would be shifting priorities in order to get this field cleared of high grass and objectionable inhabitants.

Lia had already turned to head to the house when she realized her visitor still stood in the knee-high grass, his gaze still affixed to the lake and the bobbing boat. *What an odd man.*

By the time Lia reached the porch, she'd begun to wonder if *he* might need a doctor. She decided to do as Ruby asked and put the casserole in the oven. If the fellow was still knee-deep in her field when the timer went off, she'd just ask him inside for dinner.

As it turned out, she didn't have to. When she walked back out onto the porch after slipping the casserole in the still-warming oven, the man was gone.

"Strange," she said as she stepped back inside. "He never said why he was here."

I never even said why I went there.

A jingle for the local used-car lot played on the radio as Joe pulled his truck over to the side of the road and yanked down the visor. A slip of paper fluttered onto the seat beside him.

Worst part of getting old was the reminders he had posted everywhere. Without them, he'd forget his own name.

Picking up the folded paper, he studied the note he'd written to himself, then set it aside. He had something else on his mind besides asking the new owner of the cottage if he could use her boat dock for this year's fishing tournament pictures.

In fact, the tournament was the least of Joe's worries. He had half a mind not to bother with the overblown event anyway. Sure, it brought in a good amount of money to fund scholarships for a couple of deserving Verde Point High students, but he was just plumb tired of the fuss.

Maybe he ought to suggest to the town council that they hold a bake sale and a couple of car washes instead.

He'd be the first one to buy a cake or get his truck cleaned for sure.

The car commercial on the radio gave way to a tune by the Bluegrass Boys. Any other day, he would have turned up the volume and tapped the steering wheel in time with the music. Today, however, the familiar banjo and fiddle sound jarred at his frazzled nerves and jangled his addled brain. What he needed to think on, he had to do in silence.

And what he needed to ponder had nothing to do with fishing and everything to do with a God who, for some reason, seemed to be listening when he called. Any other time, he'd ask Vic or one of the others who were in the know about the Lord.

This time, though, a prize lure was on the line.

"Lord, if You're up there, would You show Yourself just once more? I'm sorry to be so dense, but I just need to know for sure."

The truck pulled to a stop beside Lia's SUV, and a man dressed in jeans and a green T-shirt jumped out. A fringe of sandy hair showed at the back of his feed-store ball cap.

Lia quickly recognized him as the man who'd killed the snake in her field. What was his name? Ruby told her he ran the bait shop, the one on the pretty calendar that she hadn't managed to part with. Ah yes, Joe. As in Joe's Bait and Tackle.

She'd driven past the shop on her way to Ruby's home just yesterday and noted its prime location on the lake. Papa, ever on the lookout for a spot to open a new restaurant until the Lord took him home, would have claimed that place as perfect for another fancy Stephanos eating establishment.

Lia, on the other hand, could easily see a casual but elegant place for locals and visitors to the area to dine on the fresh seafood and bountiful vegetables. She even had a name for her first-ever foray into the restaurant business. It would be called Idle Hours, after her favorite William Merritt Chase painting of Victorian ladies lounging on the shore.

What a pity a bait shop stood where tourists ought to be enjoying the view. And how odd that the bait store owner had come to put up her mailbox for Travis. Still, it was three o'clock, the time Travis said he would be sending the fellow.

"Hello there," Joe said as he bounded up the steps. "I'm Joe Corbin."

"Yes." Lia shook his outstretched hand. "Lia Stephanos. I remember you. You're the snake killer."

He looked as if he were about to contradict her. Finally he smiled. "I suppose you could say I had a hand in the critter's demise."

She studied him a second longer, then nodded. "Yes, well, if you'll just hang on a second, I'll go get it."

"It?" She thought she heard him say as she slipped into the spare bedroom to retrieve the mailbox.

"Yes." Lia stepped onto the porch with the mailbox. "Will you need any help with this?"

Chapter 6

For a full five seconds, Joe considered setting the pretty lady straight. Then he made an executive decision. The idiot who showed up late for the mailbox raising would be plumb out of luck.

Joe Corbin had just become a carpenter. At least as far as Lia Stephanos knew, that is.

"Let me make a quick call to the boss man," Joe said with a grin. "Soon's I finish talkin' to Travis, why don't you and me head up to the road and see if we can't get that nice mailbox of yours set up on a post?"

"Fine," she said as she set the mailbox on the porch rail and backed away from it to toy with the little gold cross she wore around her neck. "Would you like some coffee?"

"I'd love some, thanks." Truthfully, he wasn't much of a coffee drinker, but he would have happily sipped swamp water if she'd served it with one of those smiles.

Joe stared at the empty doorway; then, when his wits caught up with his feet, bounded to the truck and climbed inside to reach for his cell phone. He punched in Travis

Wells's number, then waited while the connection was made.

Lord, what's come over me? I'm acting as goofy as a school kid chasing the prom queen.

"Wells here."

Taking a deep breath, Joe affected a casual tone. "Yeah, hey, it's Joe."

"Hey, Joe," Travis said. "Something wrong?"

"Wrong, uh, no."

He paused to watch Lia emerge onto the porch with a tray that held a silver coffeepot and two blue mugs. She placed the tray on a small table, then balanced on the edge of the swing and began to pour. Crossing one long leg over the other, Lia sat back in the swing and took a sip.

Never had he seen denim and a plain white T-shirt look so good. And that ponytail of hers, well, on any other gal, it might look like she'd forgotten to fix her hair, but on Lia, it looked like she'd spent all morning making it—and herself—look good.

She caught him looking and smiled. Joe upped the wattage on his grin and waved.

"Joe, you there?"

"Oh, yeah." He swallowed hard and forced his attention away from the porch. "Um, see, I was out here looking to get permission for pictures for the fishing tournament and ran into the owner of the property."

"Are you at Lia Stephanos's place?"

"Lia Stephanos?" He tried to sound casual. "Yeah, I think that's her name. Anyway, I figured since I was here and she had a mailbox to put up and all, I'd just help her out."

Silence.

"Travis, you there? I said I thought I'd save your man some trouble and go ahead and help the little lady with her mailbox."

Was Travis laughing? "Yeah, um, okay, Joe." He paused. There went those muffled sounds again.

Joe stared past the hood of his truck to the trees and the lake beyond, noting the Stephanos woman had cleared out a little patch for gardening. "Somethin' wrong, Trav?"

"Wrong, um, no," Travis said. "Nothing's wrong. I'll just call Bob and tell him he can drop off the new post and cement but he doesn't have to stay."

"That'll be fine." A thought occurred. "Now I insist on going ahead and payin' you whatever Miss Stephanos agreed to. Wouldn't want to be the cause of you losing business."

"Lia's like family, Joe," Travis said. "I don't charge family."

"Good enough, then." Joe removed his cap and brushed his hair back with his hand. "I guess she and I'll be looking for Bob to bring the supplies. Any idea when he'll be here?"

"Should be anytime. He called awhile back and said he was down at the lumberyard changing a flat on the truck." Travis paused. "I'd say you've got just enough time to have a cup of coffee and get to know Lia a bit."

"Well now, I suppose I could do that." He swung his gaze back to the frilly front porch where the object of his thoughts was studying the lacy pillow beside her. " 'Preciate you understanding, Trav."

"Oh, I understand, Joe. Believe me."

"It's hazelnut decaf." Lia filled his mug, then replaced the coffeepot on the tray. "I hope you don't mind, Joe."

"Nope, don't mind a'tall."

A gentle breeze floated past, carrying the now familiar scent of pine and fresh earth as Lia studied her guest. He was rather broad through the shoulders and thick through the arms, giving him the look of a man who lived a life that included hard work and sunshine. The deep lines at the corners of his eyes told her he was a few years older than she, and his square jaw gave him an air of distinction.

He smiled as he took a sip, and Lia noticed the deep dimple on his left cheek did not have a match on the right. This only served to add interest to what was already quite an interesting face.

The tanned skin on the backs of his hands was criss-crossed with tiny white scars and dotted with a light scattering of cinnamon-colored freckles. Sandy hair covered thick arms that disappeared under the rolled-up sleeves of a red-plaid flannel shirt. Jeans, a feed-store ball cap, and work boots completed the picture.

In all, he looked 100 percent male and completely out of place in the feminine haven of blue pillows, white wicker, and red potted flowers that she'd created on her porch. And yet Lia had the strangest feeling that Joe Corbin belonged here.

The bait-shop owner leaned against the back of the settee and rested his hand on his knee while he brought the mug to his lips. "It's delicious," he said, although the sentiment didn't quite match the look on his face when he swallowed.

"Would you like some sweetener?" She pushed the container of pink, blue, and yellow packets in his direction.

Joe took one of each and poured their contents into his mug, then stirred. Another taste and his smile seemed genuine. "That's good stuff."

"It is?" She regarded him with what she hoped would be a casual look. "So, how long have you worked for Travis?" When he seemed puzzled, she clarified. "I mean, Ruby told me you own the bait shop in town."

"Yes, I do," he said slowly. "Why do you ask?"

Lia formed her words carefully. "Well, it's just that your shop is in such a beautiful location, and if. . ." Pausing, she tried again. "What I'm saying is, if you're working for Travis, that must mean the bait shop isn't doing well. I wonder if you've ever thought of selling the place."

As soon as she said the words, she wanted to reel them in. Closing her eyes, she felt the heat rise in her cheeks. How awful of her to bring up a man's misfortune in such a crass way.

She opened her eyes and was about to apologize when she saw the strangest thing. Joe Corbin was grinning. Not just a weak smile or even one of those expressions you put on when a camera is aimed at you. No, the man was positively beaming.

"Oh, the shop's doing just fine. More business than I know what to do with most days." He leveled her an even gaze. "Why?"

The temptation to share her dream gave way to logic.

She could never manage the pressures of a restaurant, not now. "No reason."

Lia set her mug on the table with a loud clatter. She looked down to see that she'd upended the container of sweetener packets. Busying herself with containing the mess, Lia felt her heart begin to pound.

No, Lord, please. Not now.

Chapter 7

Lia reached for a yellow packet, and so did Joe. His fingertips brushed the top of her hand as he retrieved the sweetener and set it atop the tray.

"You're not gonna faint again, are you?"

"Faint?" Lia took a deep breath and let it out slowly. "No, of course not. That was terribly embarrassing. I rarely do that, you know. Unlike what my friend, Ruby, would have you believe, I am perfectly fine."

"I like the way you talk."

Lia shook her head at the abrupt change of topic. "What?"

"You've got a real businesslike voice," he said. "Every word you say comes out just right. I can't place the accent, though. Where are you from?"

"New York, sort of, by way of Greece and Texas." At his confused look, she chuckled. "Our home was in New York where Papa had his restaurants. He was Greek." When Joe nodded, she continued. "And my mother, well, she was born and raised in Texas, a real Southern belle. I spent time with both sets of grandparents, so I guess I ended up with a hodgepodge of accents."

"How did they meet? Your parents, I mean."

"Mama was a stewardess back in the days when they wore hot pants and go-go boots. Papa spied Mama boarding a flight for Houston and raced over to trade his ticket to Athens for one to Texas. He ended up in a cramped seat on the back row of the plane, but the rest, as they say, is history. Papa used to say he'd fallen for Mama because she had nice gams."

"Gams?"

"Legs." She shifted positions and reached for her mug. "But that was their own private joke. They both loved the Lord very much and knew He had brought them together. Theirs was no chance meeting in that airport. God put them there so they would find one another."

Lia looked away, embarrassed that she'd rattled on with a complete stranger. Well, not a complete stranger, but still. She really didn't know this man.

"That's a nice story," he said.

"So." A gust of north wind blew past, and she pushed a strand of hair from her face. "What about your parents?"

"Not much to tell really." He stretched his legs out and crossed them at the knee, then rested his hands in his lap. "Mama's family ran a produce stand out on the highway to Groveton, and Daddy worked for the county on the paving crew. One day, Daddy's crew put a coat of fresh asphalt on the highway in front of the produce stand. Mama offered Daddy an apple, and the rest is history. His pet name for her used to be Eve."

"And she would call him Adam?" Lia asked with a chuckle.

Joe gave her a confused look. "Well, that *was* his name. How did you know?"

Teasing Lia sure was fun. "I'm just jokin'," he finally said. "His name was Henry."

Her laughter made him smile, not an easy feat considering his right flank was under attack by a shifting mound of lacy pillows and his left side was being gored by a particularly sharp piece of wicker. No, this lady's front porch was way out of his comfort zone.

And yet he could have sat here all afternoon with a goofy grin and a cup of girlie coffee.

Too bad he spied a vehicle coming up the road.

"That must be the supplies." Joe rose to head for the steps. "I do thank you for the coffee," he said over his shoulder. A thought occurred, and he stopped short. "Hey, I was wondering somethin'. The Terros always let us use the boat dock during the fishin' tournament. Now that you own the property, I wonder if you might be of a mind to continue the tradition. It's mostly for pictures and such."

"Like the one on the calendar?"

Joe nodded as he stepped onto the freshly cut grass. Travis's man waved from the gate, then climbed out of his truck.

"Be right there, Bob," Joe called. "So anyway, we mostly use the dock for pictures, but the occasional fisherman may need to tie up there dependin' on the weather. I promise to keep the intrusion to a minimum."

"I'm sure it will be fine." Lia stood and picked up the tray. "When is this tournament?"

"End of July."

She wore an expression that troubled him. One of those "I've-got-a-great-idea" looks that women got when they were planning trouble.

"Do they let women enter?"

There it was. Trouble.

"Well, sure," he said. "We've had a woman or two join us." *But none as pretty as you*, he wanted to add.

A moment passed, and he realized Lia had nothing more to say. With a shake of his head and a smile, he tucked the flowery mailbox under his arm and strolled to the gate to converse with Bob. By the time the cement and post were unloaded, Lia had joined him with a hammer, shovel, and screwdriver.

"I thought we might need these."

"We?" he asked as he tipped his hat back.

"Yes, *we*," she stated in a matter-of-fact way. "The way I see it, two can work better than one."

"I believe the Bible does say something about that," he replied as he accepted the shovel from her outstretched hand.

"Yes, Joe, I believe it does."

Lia stared at him a moment too long for his comfort. Well, actually it didn't make him feel bad, the way she looked at him. Rather, it made him feel good.

Which he didn't much like.

A confirmed bachelor thinking of setting off to see the world didn't need to be entertaining ideas of sipping sweet coffee and teasing pretty women on a regular basis. It was a hazard to his plans, even if it did promise to be a balm to his soul.

"Well now," he said as he pushed any thoughts besides those directly related to setting a mailbox post out of his mind. "How about I dig the hole while you fetch the water hose and a bucket? Once I get the spot set up, we'll mix and pour, then set the post."

And with any luck, you'll get tired and go back inside. That way, I won't be so distracted.

Not only did Lia fetch the hose, but she also mixed the quick-set concrete like a pro. "Granddaddy had a ranch where I spent most of my summers. This is just like setting fence posts," she said by way of explanation.

He couldn't resist teasing the city girl once more. "And you say you're from New York?"

His joke was rewarded with a laugh that set his heart to thumping.

"Yes, I am, Joe, but I can milk a cow or run a trotline, if need be."

Now that did beat all. "You know about trotlines?"

Lia nodded. "The lazy woman's way to fish a stream."

Run for the hills, Joe Corbin. You've just found a pretty woman who fishes and sets fence posts.

Chapter 8

You going to stand there all day, Joe, or are you going to help me stir this concrete?"

"Well, finally." He nudged her out of the way and took up the shovel. "Something Lia Stephanos can't do."

Between the two of them, they managed to get the old mailbox out and the new one in place before the sun dipped behind the trees. While Joe held the box's wooden post in the wet concrete, Lia helped him position it straight.

"That's it," he said as he tucked the level into his back pocket and took a step back. "Looks pretty good, I'd say."

"It certainly does," Lia said. "Can I offer you a glass of water or some iced tea?"

Joe thought seriously about accepting her offer, until he considered how much business he might have lost to this little side trip up the hill. He'd left a sign on the bait shop's front door saying he'd return in an hour.

Checking his watch, he groaned. A quarter past four. The sign had been up for the better part of three hours.

Good thing it was a Wednesday. Wednesdays were generally his slow days.

"I'm sorry, but I'm going to have to pass," he said. "I need to get back to the bait shop."

"About that." Lia leaned against the shovel and met his gaze with eyes the same color as the freshly polished copper pipes down at the hardware store. "I *might* be interested in. . ."

Interested in what? Him?

Joe set his cap back into place and tried not to puff his chest out too much. He was old but evidently not *that* old.

Just about the time he decided to ask her if she wanted to talk about her interest over supper at the steak house, Lia's expression turned sour. "What's wrong?"

He swiveled to follow the direction where she stared and saw a taxicab swerve to avoid a rut. "I don't believe I've ever seen a taxi 'round these parts. Why, the nearest airport's—"

"Oh, it can't be. She wouldn't." Lia stabbed the shovel into the loose dirt, then brushed past him as if he weren't even there.

Joe fell in step beside her. "What's up?" When she didn't respond, he gestured to the cab. "Someone you know?"

Lia stopped long enough to give him a look that told him she wasn't pleased in the least. "You could say so. It's my mother."

Before Joe could blink twice, the driver had jumped from the cab to unload two large suitcases and stack them next to the mailbox. That job complete, he opened the back door.

A tall woman with silver hair stepped out of the taxi and handed the driver a wad of cash, then gave him a hug. "You are an absolute dear. I don't know what I would have done without you." She held the man out at arm's length, then hugged him again. "I declare I'd be sitting by the side of the terminal back in Atlanta waiting for a connection."

"Atlanta? Mother, that's three hundred miles from here."

Joe glanced over at Lia. "More actually," he said, "it's right at three hundred miles from Atlanta to Lexington and another—"

"Darling!" The silver-haired woman headed their direction to engulf Lia in a hug. Joe couldn't help noticing that Lia's mother treated her like she might break, gently patting her back before holding her at arm's length. The contrast to the healthy hug the taxi driver got was striking.

Then the woman aimed her attention at Joe. "And who is this handsome man, Lia?"

"I'm Joe." He stuck his hand out to avoid the hug he figured was on the way. "Joe Corbin."

"He put in the mailbox today." Lia touched Joe's sleeve. "I'm sorry. Joe, meet my mother, Cordelia Stephanos."

"Pleased to make your acquaintance," she said. "Thank you for seeing to the mailbox."

Her expression told Joe he was dismissed. Then he caught the look on Lia's face. Unless he missed his guess, she was practically begging him to stay.

"How about I haul these suitcases up to the house for you, Mrs. Stephanos?"

A few minutes later, the ladies were headed for the house, leaving Joe to try to figure out how to keep from looking like a fool. The bags were much heavier than he'd expected, and by the time he'd accomplished the task of getting both items from the road to the porch, his back was complaining and his knees had set to wobbling.

He was more than a little happy to bid the Stephanos women good-bye and head his truck back to town. Too bad thoughts of those copper-colored eyes and the way Lia flirted with him chased him all the way home.

So did something else: continued thoughts of that snake and how it seemed to be struck dead right in little Samantha's hand.

Joe clicked the radio off and closed his eyes. "Lord," he whispered, "You heard me at the old Terro place, didn't You? You listened when I begged You to do something, and You went and did it."

No answer came, but Joe felt fairly sure of the answer. Just like his buddy said, the Lord had been waiting for him to sit still long enough to listen.

If only he could know for sure.

Chapter 9

There were two things Lia knew for sure about Cordelia Stephanos. First, her mother loved her almost as much as she loved the Lord, and second, the woman could cook. Unfortunately that's all she seemed to want to do during her visit, until she slipped on that low spot on the porch and ended up in the emergency room with a broken ankle.

"I'll just have to extend my visit for another few months. It's a good thing I planned ahead."

"Right." Lia plumped the pillows around Mother and handed her the remote.

"I don't need that," her mother said. "But could you hand me my notebook? It's over there in my tote."

Lia reached for the brown leather journal. "Is this it?"

"It is." She smiled. "My collection of recipes."

For the next half hour, Lia listened to her mother's reminiscences of days spent at the first Stephanos restaurant, each memory tied to a particular restaurant or a special recipe. Stories from her childhood came tumbling back in the honeyed tones of her mother's Texas accent.

Lia smiled. Even after all these years in New York, Cordelia still sounded like she'd only recently made the trip north from San Antonio.

"Would you do it all again, Mama?" Lia tucked her feet under her and snuggled into the comfort of the sofa pillows. "Build a restaurant from the bottom up again, I mean."

Her mother looked thoughtful, and then a smile dawned. "In a heartbeat." She punctuated the statement with a wink. "Your papa taught you a thing or two about the business. I always wondered why you chose that English degree instead."

Why indeed? Lia pondered a moment. "I suppose I wanted to do something on my own. Not be known as someone's daughter." She shrugged. "Besides, I love books."

"Well, so do I," her mother said as she folded up her notebook and put it away. "Wasn't Ruby coming by to bring us copies of her new book?"

"Oh, I forgot." Lia rose and plumped the pillows. "The baby's got the sniffles, so I told her I would stop by and get them." She checked the grandfather clock in the corner. "It's still early. If I leave now, I can see Samantha before she goes down for a nap. Would you like to go?"

"Thank you, dear," Mother said, "but I think I might just watch that movie after all. Which button is it that I push to start that thing?"

"Are you okay?" She knelt down and placed her hands atop her mother's. "What's wrong?"

Mother's eyes were shimmering with unshed tears when she lifted her gaze. "I'm a silly fool, Lia," she said as the remote slipped from her fingers. "I'm sorry. I came here to take care of you, not the other way around."

"You don't have to apologize." Lia swiped at her mother's eyes with her shirttail. "I love you. I know it's hard without Papa."

"It's just that I miss him so." She ran her hand over the smooth leather of the notebook. "And the cooking, oh, honey, the only time I feel like I haven't lost that part of my life is when I'm standing in front of a stove. If only I could do that again."

All the way to Ruby's house, a thought nagged at Lia. By the time she'd visited with Ruby, read Samantha a nap-time story, and cuddled with the baby, the thought had blossomed into a full-blown idea, which she handed to the Lord as she drove.

Lia pulled into the parking lot of Joe's Bait and Tackle with a prayer and a plan. This time, the lot was empty and the door was locked. Beneath the CLOSED sign was a piece of cardboard attached with silver duct tape.

GONE FISHING, she read as her heart sank. So much for speaking to Joe while the plan was fresh and her good sense hadn't yet kicked in.

Chapter 10

The water was fine, and so was the new boat he'd been testing. Oh, Joe could've taken the thing for a spin around the cove after the shop closed, but anyone who needed bait or tackle before he got back knew where the key was. Leastwise, the ones he would trust to mark down what they bought and leave him the money on the till.

A flash of white caught his attention, and he glanced over to see a fancy SUV come to a stop inches from his front door. He patted Skipper and woke the hound up.

"Well, now, Skip, looks like we've got company."

The dog roused, ears perked. A moment later, he sniffed at the air. Pulling hard on the right oar, Joe pointed the boat toward his dock. Although he was still a good fifty yards from shore, he recognized the vehicle.

Joe also recognized the woman who stepped out of it. He watched Lia walk the length of the back of the shop. She seemed to be measuring something, taking long strides like a man without a ruler. Finally she went back to her vehicle and rummaged around inside.

Joe reached for the oars and set the boat on a path for the dock. Lia slammed the door and walked around to disappear on the other side of the SUV.

Before he realized he'd done it, Joe let out a whistle that probably stopped traffic three blocks away—if there was any traffic, that is. Skipper barked a protest at the sound. A ponytailed head popped up over the roof of the SUV, and Joe let himself imagine he'd seen a smile on Lia's face.

As he rowed toward the dock, he realized she *was* smiling.

"Well, hello there," he called, waving his hand in greeting. "Lookin' for a fishing lesson?"

Skipper added a yelp, his tail thumping a furious rhythm.

"Funny, but that does hold some appeal," she said. "However, I'm here to talk business."

"Are you now?" Joe slowed the canoe and allowed it to drift sideways toward the dock. "I conduct a good part of my business out on the lake, you know. Why don't you come on aboard?" He paused to gauge Lia's reaction, then decided his cruise was over. "I'll talk business with you on dry land if you'll promise to go fishing with me."

She waited a second, then nodded. "Deal."

He stuck the oar in the water and slowed the boat's progress. "When?"

"When what?"

"When will you go fishing with me?"

"Honestly, Joe, I don't know." She paused. "See, my mother's here, and I—"

"Sorry to hear about your mama's broke ankle," Joe

said, fighting the tide to keep the canoe from reaching land. "I was gonna ask if she wanted to go, but I guess we'll have to go by ourselves."

"I guess so."

Joe couldn't tell for sure, but she seemed pleased with the invitation. "Wednesday afternoon?" he asked. "Say two o'clock?"

The canoe sat less than five feet from Lia with the tide inching him forward. Skipper stood at the ready, poised to land on the dock as soon as it was within reach.

If Lia didn't answer him in about half a second, he'd have to push off and row backward. Skipper would probably jump in and swim the short distance. He probably ought to warn her.

She shifted positions. "Make it three, and I'm all yours."

"All mine?" Joe lifted the oars, and the vessel began to drift back toward the dock. "I like the sound of that."

The dog hit the dock running, greeting their guest by circling twice, then nudging her hand. Lia knelt to offer the dog a belly rub.

"What's your name, sweetie?" she asked the big lug.

"That's Skipper," Joe said. "He runs things around here. I'm just the guy who fills the food bowl and tends the shop."

Lia gave the dog one last pat on the head, then rose. "Maybe I ought to take up my business with him then."

The dog jumped to his feet and sniffed the air. When he caught sight of a squirrel over near the oaks, his ears perked up and his tail wagged double time.

"Don't worry," Joe said. "I run everything by him for his opinion. How 'bout we go inside? I think we're interrupting the chairman of the board's hunting."

With Skipper in the lead, Joe climbed out to secure the boat, then escorted Lia to the door. Pausing, he tipped back a brick to retrieve the key. The door swung inward on silent hinges, attesting to the fact he had nothing better to do this afternoon. Meanwhile, Skipper broke ranks to race for the trees.

Lia watched the dog for a moment, then swung her attention to Joe. "You keep the key to your business under a brick?"

"Sure. Never can tell when there'll be a fishin' emergency." He stepped back to let her pass. "After you."

Her smile faded to serious. "I'll be brief."

He set down the key, then leaned against the counter and looked past her to watch Skipper tree a squirrel. "Take your time," he said over the sound of the dog barking.

Lia cast a slow glance around the room, then fixed a stare on him. "I would like to make you an offer."

"An offer?" Joe drummed his fingers on the counter and affected a broad grin. Outside, the dog barked twice. "Just what kind of offer are you talking about? And before you tell me, don't think I entertain offers from just anyone."

Lia ignored his jibe to pull her checkbook from her purse. With a flourish, she wrote a check that would significantly drain her savings account. Adding a prayer that the Lord would stop her should she be misunderstanding His will, Lia slid the check across the wooden counter, all the while trying to keep from looking at the live bait swimming around in the tank behind the register.

There would definitely be some changes around here once she owned the place. Gone would be the rods and reels, except possibly for a few artfully placed antique ones. And the slicker suits and bait buckets would be history, as would the shelves of tackle boxes and bobbers and sinkers.

She forced her mind off the redecorating and onto the negotiations. Joe's fingers stopped their motion. He looked down, then quickly back up at her, his face pale.

"What's behind this? And give me the short version."

"I'll skip the formalities and go right to the point. You have the perfect spot in town for a restaurant. I want to purchase this bait shop and make my mother happy. How's that for the short version?"

"Well, now, that is a mite short." His jaw went slack, and he rubbed it with his right hand. For a moment, he seemed to be at a loss for words. Finally he added, "That's a lot of money, Lia. How come?"

"Excuse me?"

Joe leaned forward, eyes narrowed. "How come you want to do this for your mama?"

Good question. Where to begin?

"I'm thirty-eight years old, Joe, and all my mother has left, and I'm not getting any younger. At this rate, there will be no grandchildren to dote over, no son-in-law to handle her affairs, and no knight in shining armor to sweep her away and fill the empty spot my papa left in her life. I'm it, and if I can do this one thing for her, I'm going to do it."

The man barely blinked.

"Do we have a deal or what? I've already made a call to my real estate agent. Once I let her know you are in agreement, she'll draw up a sales contract for that amount."

His posture stiffened. "You didn't tell her I was sellin', did you? 'Cause I haven't agreed to nothin'."

"Relax, Joe. She won't say a word."

He seemed to think about it for a moment. "A man doesn't just walk away from his life's work because a pretty lady writes him a check."

A pretty lady? He thinks I'm pretty. Get your mind back on the business at hand.

"Are you angling for more money, Joe? Because if you are, you ought to know that this is all there is." She touched the check with her index finger. "I've researched the price of commercial lakeside real estate, and though this is the top of the price range, I figure with that view it's worth every penny."

"Well, yeah, that is quite a view." He placed his finger beside hers, his gaze capturing hers. "But why, really, are you here? Who sent you?"

Odd, but in that moment, Lia knew exactly how to answer that.

"I believe the Lord sent me, Joe."

Chapter 11

I s that a yes?"

"Well," Joe said slowly, "it's not a no, Lia."

The door opened, and the bell jangled. A nice-looking fellow walked in with Skipper on his heels. "Hey there, Joe. I'm fresh out of— Say, hello there. I'm Vic Thompson. A friend of Joe's."

Lia heard the cash drawer close. She turned to see that the check was gone.

"Vic, this here is Lia Stephanos. Friend of Ruby's," Joe said. "She bought the Terro place."

"Pleased to make your acquaintance, Lia," Vic said.

Pleasantries aside, the men soon became deeply embroiled in a technical discussion regarding the different weights of test lines that might be used in the upcoming fishing tournament. Skipper edged close and offered her his snout while Joe said something to Vic about a silver something or other that he'd lost.

Lia scratched the Lab's ears, then stepped back when the dog fell at her feet and offered his belly. "Not this time, Skipper, but I'll owe you one."

While the men talked, Lia slipped outside and headed for her vehicle, her heart racing. *What have I done?*

"You've just made your mother very happy," she whispered as she climbed into her SUV and cranked over the engine.

Just as she shifted into reverse, her cell phone rang. Her mother had found another recipe and needed ingredients purchased. Lia rummaged for paper and a pen, lifting her head in time to see Vic drive away.

The extras added to the list, Lia hung up the phone and tossed it into her purse. Before she could grab the wheel, she saw Joe coming out of the bait shop and heading her way. A press of the button and the window rolled down.

"I'm glad you're still here," he said. "I need to talk to you."

"Sure." She unlocked the passenger door, and he climbed in.

Joe studied her a moment, barely blinking. "I agree to your terms as long as you'll do one thing for me."

"What's that?"

"Don't tell a soul that I'm selling out until after the fishing tournament."

"Why?"

"This here's a small town, Lia. I'd rather keep my peace as long as I can." He paused to release a long breath. "I'd rather this be between you and me until then. I feel strong enough about this to give you back the check if you're not willing to abide by it."

His expression told her he was serious.

She gave the matter some thought. "All right, I suppose I can do that, but I will need to do some renovating, and it would help if I could bring in someone ahead of time just to give me some estimates. I promise the actual work won't be done until after the tournament."

"No."

"But no one will know they were here. I promise."

"Then it's no deal." He fished out the check from his shirt pocket, set it on the console between them, then opened the door and stepped into the parking lot. "I'll still be by to pick you up Wednesday for that fishin' lesson, though."

Lia watched him disappear into the bait shop. Now what?

Suppressing a groan, she turned off the engine and stuffed the keys in her purse. "What a stubborn man." She marched back into the bait shop and laid the check on the counter in front of him. "Have it your way."

The irritating bait-shop owner took an eternity to respond. First he seemed to study her; then he looked to be studying the check. Finally he met her gaze and thrust his hand in her direction.

"How come you never married?"

"What?" She felt a flush rising in her cheeks. How dare the impertinent man ask such a question. "Mr. Corbin—"

"Joe."

"All right, Joe, I fail to see how the answer to that question is any of your business."

He shrugged. "Probably isn't, but I'm askin' all the same."

Lia studied the man a moment, then looked past his red-plaid shirtsleeve to the stack of fishing magazines on the counter. A headline emblazoned on the cover gave her the words to answer the arrogant man.

"Well, Joe," she said slowly, "I guess I just haven't found a keeper yet. So do we have a deal, or do I go make an offer on the craft shop?"

Joe stared at her with what had to be admiration; then slowly a grin grew into a full-blown smile. "Deal."

Chapter 12

Just like Vic said, the Lord had been waiting for him to sit still long enough to listen. Now Joe had to go tell Vic about it just as he promised he would.

"Well, it looks like I lost that fancy lure." He chuckled. "But I have a feelin' I just gained something much better." Joe exhaled a long breath. "Who would have figured the good Lord thought I was a keeper?"

That evening, Vic sent him home with more than just a slap on the back and a handshake. He had a Bible. Not one of those fancy ones like you keep on the shelf, but an honest-to-goodness Bible written in words he could read and understand.

Vic must have been pretty sure this day would come, because he had already seen to it that Joe's name was written across the bottom of that Bible's front cover in neat silver letters. The best part was the envelope Vic had tucked inside at the place where the book of John started.

"Don't open that until you get home," Vic said.

So he waited until he reached the back stairs of the

bait shop before he pulled the envelope out of the Bible and gave it a shake. Something other than a letter was in there, for the lump in the middle of the thing was as plain as the nose on his face.

Joe settled on his coffee-drinking step—the third one from the bottom—and held the envelope up to the fading light of the evening sun. A dark blob of a familiar size and shape was visible beneath the white paper.

Skipper nudged his leg with his favorite chew toy. Joe took the bait and wrestled the plastic bone from the Lab's jaws, then threw it in the direction of the lake. The dog's oversized feet threw up chunks of sod as he headed toward the toy at high speed.

Smiling, Joe ripped off the end of the envelope and tipped the contents into his hand. Out tumbled a Silver Thorn Dressed lure and a folded piece of paper.

On it, Vic had written, "Joe, if you are reading this, God thinks you are a keeper. Start with John and see why."

He wrapped his fingers around the lure, careful not to stab himself on the hook. A few yards away, Skipper danced around the toy, yipping and nudging until he settled in a shady spot to chew happily.

That dog looked like he felt: content. Well, almost content. He and the Lord still had some unfinished business.

"Lord, I sure am sorry I waited fifty-two years to get around to understanding that You're right here and not up floatin' around on some cloud not caring what's goin' on down here."

Saying the words should have made him feel silly. The knowledge that they were being heard made him feel good.

Real good.

Climbing to his feet, Joe tucked the lure back into the Bible and headed for his apartment over the bait shop with Skipper at his heels. Tomorrow he would begin planning this summer's fishing tournament. Tonight, however, he had some questions that had been pestering him, and there seemed no better place to turn for an answer than to the Lord.

Skipper nudged him once more, then headed for the kitchen, returning with his supper dish in his teeth. Setting the red plastic bowl at Joe's feet, the dog looked up at him with woeful eyes.

"All right then, let's find us some supper. Guess you go first."

Joe took the bowl to the kitchen and scooped out a measure full of food, then set it on the floor. The dog went at the familiar kibble with the gusto of a starving man at an all-you-can-eat buffet.

"Enjoy yourself with that now. Once you and me get to travelin' light, you might not be so well fed."

Chapter 13

Their fishing trip had been postponed twice, so it was nearly two weeks later when Joe finally set off toward Lia's place with a grin and a gift. He doubted she had a fishing pole of her own that would be up to standard, so he decided he would bring one.

The boat went in the back along with a pair of oars and two life vests. He also threw in a cooler filled with water, bait, and a roll of garbage bags in case Lia wanted a dry place to sit. The last thing he did was throw in his lucky fishing hat for good measure.

Perfect.

And so was she when she stepped outside to join him. *Lord, thank You for spending a little extra time putting that one together.*

"What's that smile for, Joe?"

"Just giving thanks to the Lord."

He threw the truck into gear and headed for the lake, soon turning his attention to easing the truck over the rutted road without jostling the canoe. In no time, they'd reached the dock and unloaded their supplies. As Lia adjusted her life jacket, Joe put in the boat, then set the cooler in the center.

Time could have stood still right then, and Joe wouldn't have complained a bit. Instead, Lia spied a fish jumping in the shallows.

"Wow, that's a big one." She turned to Joe. "When do we get these lessons started?"

He chuckled. "First things first. I brought you a little something." Joe lifted the rod and reel up to hand it to Lia. "Thought you might want one of your own if you're gonna learn to fish."

She looked up at him as if he'd just given her the Hope Diamond. "Thank you. Now let's see if I can catch anything with this."

He helped her get the line cast, then settled to his spot. A glint of gold caught his eye, and he looked up. "Say, that's a pretty cross you got there."

She met his gaze. "Thank you. It was my grandmother's."

"So do you go to church around here?" It was a bold question but one that mattered to him a great deal. While he was learning what it was to give one's life to Jesus and walk His way, he knew enough to realize anyone he was interested in ought to at least be treading the same path.

And to his surprise, he was definitely interested.

"Actually I do."

Pretty as a picture and a Christian to boot. Well, how about that?

When Lia said the name of the church, he frowned. "Well now, that's where I go. How come I haven't seen you there?"

"I'm somewhat of a morning person," she said. "Mother and I have been attending the contemporary sunrise service. What time do you go?"

Well, he did feel sheepish admitting he liked to sleep as long as he could on Sunday mornings, that being his only real day off. "Eleven," he said slowly.

"The traditional service." Her grin broadened as she curled her index finger around the little gold chain. "I've been thinking of trying that one."

"You let me know, and I'll save you a seat."

Lia looked away with the cutest pink color in her cheeks. "I just might do that."

"See that you do," he said as her bobber disappeared beneath the water. "But first, let's see if you can land that trout you got on the line."

Lia did catch that trout along with a few other things: four good-sized catfish, a perch, and Joe's heart.

Taking her home was the hardest part of the trip. When she declined his offer to clean the fish, he knew it was time to go.

"Thank you." She offered him a sly smile. "Same time next Wednesday?"

"Sure." Joe took three steps toward the truck, then jogged back. "Lia, I don't believe I've met anyone like you before."

"Likewise, Joe."

"Well, good night then." For a minute, he thought she might respond, but instead, she ducked her head and disappeared inside, leaving the screen door to close behind her.

The next week and the week after, Joe felt like he'd

rather pull his eyeteeth than walk her to the door after their fishing trips. Still, he held back and played the gentleman. Something about Lia Stephanos had him thinking he needed to watch his ways and move slow.

After all, the Lord had mentioned to him that He might think she was just the kind of fish Joe ought to land, that she might be the one for him. And that kind of news set a man back a few paces.

It also made him a might curious as to how the heavenly Father was going to pull off such an improbable feat.

Chapter 14

Lia returned home from her meeting with her Realtor to find her mother sound asleep, the remote in her hand. Lia clicked off the television and gently shook her mother.

"Hey there, sweetie," Mother said as she roused. "Ready to start cooking?"

"In more ways than one." In response to Mother's raised eyebrow, Lia knelt beside her. "Mother, how would you like to stay awhile after your cast comes off? I haven't gotten around to fixing up the guest room in any fashion other than functional, so you'd have free rein to do with it as you saw fit."

"Well, now, I don't know." She sat up and patted her hair into submission. "What did you have in mind?"

Lia told her, then waited for Mother to comment. To Lia's surprise, her mother began to cry. "Are you serious, honey?"

"I am." Lia climbed onto the sofa to settle beside her mother. "What do you think?"

Mother swiped at her eyes with the backs of her hands,

then jumped to her feet. "I think I'd better get busy. If we're going to open a restaurant by the end of the year, we can't be sitting on our duffs."

"Remember you can't say a word until after the fishing tournament at the end of July. I promised Joe Corbin."

She waved away the warning with a sweep of her hand. "You don't have to worry about me. No one will know a thing about this." She settled at the table and opened her notebook.

"What are you doing? I thought you'd decided what we were having for dinner."

"Oh," she said with a grin. "I have. No time like the present to begin planning dishes for. . ." She shook her head. "What are we going to call it, dear?"

Lia looked up at the print of Victorian ladies idling on the beach that now hung over the mantel. "I was thinking about naming it Idle Hours."

"Perfect." She rose to hobble over to reach for the phone book.

"What are you doing?"

"Never you mind. Why don't you check the mail? I'll start assembling ingredients for the cake, then we can start on supper."

By the time Lia returned from the mailbox, her mother had begun to sift out the dry ingredients. They fell into a preparation rhythm based on years of culinary practice, and the cake, as well as dinner, was soon done.

Mother looked up from the platter of pork chops. "Set the table, would you, dear?"

Lia stacked up two sets of plates, then opened the silver-ware drawer.

"One more, Lia. We've got company coming."

"Company?"

She glanced out the window over the sink. "Oh, look. There he is now."

"He?" Lia joined her mother at the window in time to see a familiar vehicle approaching. "Did you call him while I was at the mailbox?"

Her mother affected an innocent expression. "Lia Stephanos, I don't know what you are accusing me of, but have you ever considered that I might have forgotten to mention Mr. Corbin would be dining with us?"

She stared her mother down, then tossed the dish towel into the sink. "No," she said as she scooted into her room to change out of her flour-dusted clothing. "I think you called him while I was outside."

Frantically digging in her poorly organized bathroom for the brush, Lia paused. "What am I doing? It's just Joe from the bait shop."

"The Idle Hours," she corrected. If only she could tell the world about their new project.

The front door opened and closed amid the sound of voices. Joe was here.

Lia stepped into her closet to throw on an I LOVE NY T-shirt, then thought better of it and settled for a tailored shirt in soft blue. She checked her reflection and spotted flour on her jeans. Those were added to the laundry pile, and she donned a slim-fitting pair of pink jeans and changed into a matching top.

Businesslike loafers were tried on, then cast aside. Finally she slipped into a pair of pink sneakers and stepped out of the closet.

She almost made it to the door before noticing the stray hairs escaping her ponytail. "Ponytails aren't for women your age anyway," she said as she removed the clasp and began brushing out her hair.

"Lia, dear, are you all right?" her mother called.

"I'm fine. Be right out."

She jammed her hair back into some semblance of a ponytail and dropped the brush into the drawer. A touch of clear lip gloss and the slightest dash of after-bath cologne and she dashed out into the hall.

Slowing to a more casual pace, Lia rounded the corner into the living area with what she hoped would be a welcoming smile. She spied Mother perched on the edge of the wicker rocker engaged in conversation with Joe.

Rather than a bait-shop owner, Joe looked more like a cowboy fresh off the range—except for the facts that his boots seemed to have a fresh shine on them and his jeans wore a crease down the front that could only be attributed to a woman's attention to detail or heavy starch from the dry cleaner's.

Funny how she had the odd thought that she hoped she might run into him at the dry cleaner's.

"Well now, there you are," Mother said. "Come and entertain our guest, Lia. I need to check the pork chops."

"Smells good, ma'am," Joe said.

"Thank you, young man," Mother called.

Lia pasted on a smile and tugged at the hem of her

shirt as she settled on the opposite end of the sofa. "Hello, Joe."

He leaned toward her. "You didn't know I was coming, did you?"

"Honestly?" When he nodded, she continued. "I didn't." She paused. "But truthfully, I am glad you're here. Mother's a wonderful cook. When you taste her pork chops, you'll see why I. . ."

She caught a whiff of something and wrinkled her nose. That didn't smell like well-cooked pork chops. It smelled more like burned pork chops.

"Would you excuse me?" Lia dashed to the oven and threw open the door. Inside, the pork chops were black on top and bright pink underneath. She looked up at the oven setting. "Mother, since when do you broil your pork chops?"

"Oh my," her mother said. "Looks like I've ruined our dinner party."

Something in the way Mother seemed so calm didn't set right. While no cook made a perfect meal every time, Lia was hard-pressed to remember when Cordelia Stephanos had burned anything, least of all the oven-baked pork chops she'd been making practically since girlhood.

Lia gave her a sideways stare. "Mother, what's going on?"

Chapter 15

Joe had fallen victim to his share of matchmaking, but never had a decent pork chop been sacrificed in his honor. At least he had his answer about whether the younger of the Stephanos women was in on the setup.

Lia Stephanos obviously didn't know what her mother had in mind, but the fact she seemed so unhappy about it once she'd figured it out didn't set well. Still, she did seem at a loss for words.

He decided to put the poor woman out of her misery. " 'Scuse me, ladies. What say we all hit the trail for the Saddle Up Steak House? I'm sure the cookin' can't hold a candle to what Miz Stephanos could whip up, but I sure hate to see two pretty women go hungry."

"Oh no," Lia said. "I'll just pull three steaks out of the freezer and—"

"Don't be silly, dear," her mama said. "The steak house sounds lovely. I'll just go fetch my purse." The older Stephanos woman brushed past, pausing long enough to squeeze his hand and offer an apology for her kitchen mishap.

He watched her disappear into a back bedroom, then turned his attention to the younger of the pair. The one who set his heart to racing every time he thought of her.

"You coming with us, Lia?"

Her eyes narrowed, and she got the cutest wrinkle between her eyebrows.

"You don't have to, you know. I'm sure your mama and I'd have just as much fun without you." He added a wink lest she think he was serious.

Well, that must have got her, because off she went, leaving him with a smile and a thought that tonight just might be more interesting than he expected. He'd be willing to wager his truck and new boat that Mrs. Stephanos would be sending the two of them off without her.

"I'll just grab my purse and meet you outside." As she passed by her mother's room, she noticed Mother sitting in the chair by the window, book in hand. "Mother? Something wrong?"

To her credit, Cordelia Stephanos always told the truth. Sometimes the full truth with all the details didn't appear until much later, but that was Mother. Eventually you'd get the whole story.

Tonight, however, that story was written all over her guilty face.

"Well, you see, I came in here for my purse, and what did I find but that book I was looking for." Blue eyes looked up with too much sparkle not to be plotting something. "Darling, would you make my excuses to Mr. Corbin? I was just getting to the good part when I lost this book. Now that I've found it, I would really like to finish it." She paused to offer a smile. "You understand, don't you?"

"Oh, believe me, I understand completely." Lia stood at the door a moment longer, then took a step backward. "However, it won't work."

"Sure it will," Joe called. "Come on out here, Lia. This man's gettin' hungry. 'Sides, you and me got a business deal to celebrate. Let your mama alone so she can read." He paused. "Miz Stephanos, can we bring you something back?"

"No thank you, young man. Don't worry about me. I put a Greek salad away for my supper."

Lia gave her mother a look that said she'd be hearing more discussion later; then she stepped into her room to gather her purse and a light sweater. Returning to the hallway, Lia paused to look in on her mother. Cordelia Stephanos sat at her writing desk studying paint and fabric samples. Obviously her novel wasn't nearly as interesting as her plans for redecorating the bedroom to reflect her taste.

"Have a nice time, dear," her mother said.

Lia sagged against the door frame. "Mother, you are *impossible*."

She turned to offer a broad smile. "Yes, I am, but you love me anyway, don't you, darling?"

"Of course I do, but it amazes me that you knew all along you were going to burn those pork chops."

Mother merely shrugged and went back to her decorating. "A mother does what she must," she said. "Someday you'll understand."

"If you'd told me, I wouldn't have splurged on the good ones." Lia walked back into the living area expecting to see her escort for the evening lounging on the sofa. Instead, he stood at the door.

"I'm sorry, Joe. You don't have to go through with this. My mother—"

"Is a wonderful lady who recognizes she has a wonderful daughter." Joe stepped out onto the porch and held the door open. "Now how 'bout we do our talkin' in the truck? I'm hungry."

She allowed him to lead her to the truck, then he helped her in and jogged around to climb into the driver's seat.

"I told you I was hungry," he said as he stabbed the key into the ignition. "And that's part of the reason I was in a hurry to leave."

"Part of the reason?" Lia shook her head. "Dare I ask what the rest of it is?"

"Sure." He cranked over the engine and threw the truck into gear. "The rest of it's simple. I wanted to get out of there before your mama changed her mind and came with us."

Mama would have been proud. Joe remembered all his manners, including the right way to eat soup and the fact that a gentleman stood when a lady excused herself to leave the table. While he would never lay claim to the title of gentleman, Lia Stephanos made him want to try.

Joe tugged at the napkin he had stuck into the neck of his shirt, then glanced to his left. A fancy-dressed couple held hands and made eyes at one another while their steaks got cold. For the first time in his life, Joe understood.

Spending time with a good woman was worth letting your prime rib turn to ice.

He glanced around the room and noticed two things: Those who were eating didn't seem to be making eyes at one another, and none of the men wore napkins in their collars. Joe jerked at his napkin and let it drop to his lap just as Lia came around the corner.

"I'm sorry," she said. "I just wanted to check on Mother to be sure she's fine."

"And is she?"

"Of course." Lia met his gaze, then looked away. "Joe, I'm really sorry about this."

"Sorry about coming here with me?"

"No." She shook her head. "My mother, she's just—"

"She's just helping nature along." He reached for her hand and patted it. "I, for one, am glad. I don't know if I'd have found the courage to ask you on a date. I owe her a debt of thanks for doing that for me."

Was she blushing?

"Lia, I'm no kid," he said. "And I know what I like." He paused. "I like you. A lot." He waited, barely breathing, until she smiled.

"I like you a lot, too, Joe."

"I believe I'd like to court you right and proper." Joe narrowed his eyes to study the woman who held his heart. "You okay with that, Lia Stephanos?"

Her smile could have lit the sky. "I believe I'm fine with that, Joe Corbin."

He reached over to hug her, and she fit just right in his arms. Intending to break the embrace, he ended up nose to nose with her.

So he kissed her.

Afterward he tried to decide whether to apologize or do it again. He decided to do it again.

"That you, Lia?"

"Yes, Mother."

"I'll be back tomorrow," Joe said. "No more waiting until Wednesday to see you." He placed his finger beneath her chin and tilted it up. "For the record, I think you're a keeper."

Lia looked away with the cutest pink color in her cheeks. For a minute he thought she might respond, but instead she ducked her head and disappeared inside, leaving the screen door to close behind her.

The next Sunday, he did save a seat at church, and the Sunday after that. Pretty soon, preparations for the fishing tournament took almost all his time, that is, except for his Wednesday fishing trips with Lia.

They enjoyed the next Saturday together and the next, until the corner booth at the steak house became their regular spot for dinner. At least once a week, they would share a meal and some good conversation. Sometimes Lia would even get him to talking about his dreams. While she'd coax him out of just about anything in the way of future plans, there was one thing he hadn't found the courage to admit.

There was no future without her in it. He'd figured that out weeks ago. The only problem was deciding how to tell her.

Chapter 16

Whistling the theme from *High Noon*, Joe rolled out of the parking lot and came to a stop at the light. In the rearview mirror, he caught a glance of the bait shop, the place he'd spent his entire adult life and a good part of his teen years.

"Wonder what it will be like. . ."

A horn honked behind him, and he shifted his attention to the flashy pickup and the kid who seemed to have more impatience than time to spare. His irritation edged up a notch as he aimed his truck toward Lia's place, but by the time she climbed into the seat beside him, he felt as happy as a rooster in a henhouse.

She wore pink again—from her ball cap to her sneakers—and it looked to Joe like the Lord had created that color just for her. Something in his heart jumped to life when she looked his direction.

"What's that smile for, Joe?"

"You."

He turned his attention to easing the truck over the rutted road without jostling the boat. In no time they'd reached the dock and unloaded their supplies. As Lia adjusted her life jacket, Joe put in the boat, then set the cooler in the center. Five minutes later, they were headed for Joe's special fishing spot.

Today Lia was quiet. Like something was wrong. While he cast his line, Joe tried to think of a way to ask her what he'd done.

Finally he leaned over and stole a kiss. She smiled, barely.

"Something bothering you?" he asked.

Lia seemed to give the question some thought before nodding. "Actually, there is," she said. "I need to tell you something."

Joe scooted near to Lia and wrapped his arm around her. "Long as it's not good-bye, I can take just about anything."

She nodded. "I hope you're right. See, I want to be completely honest with you about my. . .well, my health."

Joe's smile gave her courage, as did the way he held her close. "I've got a defective heart," she said. "I could give you the technical diagnosis, but suffice it to say, I'm damaged goods. That's why I had to leave the publishing industry."

"I wondered if there might be something like that going on the day I first met you." He nudged her shoulder with his. "You may find it hard to believe, but not every woman swoons when I show up."

Despite the butterflies in her stomach, Lia giggled. "That is hard to believe." She paused to collect her thoughts. "Joe, be serious a minute. This could be bad."

"It might." He grasped her hand and squeezed it. "But I'm willing to take that chance."

For a moment, Lia allowed her hopes to soar. Then reality crashed in. "I don't think you understand what could happen."

"No, Lia, I don't think you understand. I don't care what happens." Joe shifted to the seat across from her. "What I mean is, none of us get any guarantees. I figure I'd rather risk something I don't like if it means I might have something I do like. Besides, the Lord can heal a broken heart in a lot of ways. If He chooses, that is. Our part is to call on Him, then wait and see what He will do. Make sense?"

She looked up into his eyes. "Yes," she said, "it makes perfect sense."

"Know what else makes sense, Lia?"

"What's that?"

He lifted her fingers to his lips. "You and me," he said. "We make sense."

Lia smiled. "We do, don't we?"

"After this fishing tournament's finished. . ." Joe looked away. "Maybe I ought not talk about this. I reckon you've got plans that might not fit with mine."

Plans. Yes, she had plans to settle into the life of a restaurant owner, and Joe, well, it seemed as though he intended to take his life on the road. Maybe they didn't make sense after all.

"Lia, did you hear me?"

She focused on Joe, who now held both her hands. "No, I'm sorry. What did you say?"

"Will you be patient with me until after the fishing tournament? After that, I promise I'll go back to courtin' you proper."

Lia had made good on her promise not to tell about buying the bait shop, but she was chomping at the bit to get her hands on the inside of the place so she could fix it up. Joe could tell by looking at her. Oh, she was still the prettiest thing he'd ever laid eyes on, but she looked plumb tired of waiting.

Yesterday, the two of them had exchanged words over that very subject. While he wanted no one to know, Lia wondered if she could tell Travis. Her reason—that Trav could get started on the drawings for the changes—was a good one, but Joe had said no all the same. At the moment, Lia wasn't too happy with him.

Actually he wasn't real happy with her either. He also wasn't happy without her.

With the fishing tournament just days away, things had begun to get complicated. Every time the bell jangled above the shop door, he grumbled. Finally he'd had it.

Taping a note across the door, he stormed to the truck and headed it for Lia's place. He found her in her garden.

"Woman, you and me need to settle this."

She rose and dusted off her legs. "All right. Coffee?"

"Not if all you've got is that sissy stuff." He shook his head. "I came here to see you, not to be sociable."

"If it's about Travis, I—"

Joe crossed the distance between them and embraced her. "No, it's not about Travis. It's about you. And about me. And, oh, Lia, I love you. Go ahead and do whatever you want to the bait shop. I don't mind. Just let's get back to how it was."

Lia just stood there.

"Say somethin', Lia."

She offered a weak smile as she shook her head. "Did you say you loved me?"

"Yeah," he said slowly, "I did."

Falling into his embrace, Lia buried her face in his shoulder. "I love you, too, Joe."

"Then we can get through this."

Lia lifted her head to meet his gaze. "But you're leaving," she said, tears shimmering at the corners of her eyes. "How can I love you if you're in an RV somewhere on the other side of the country?"

Joe held her at arm's length. "Will you trust me?"

Nodding, she gave in to her tears. "Yes, I'll trust you," she managed.

Chapter 17

The day of the fishing tournament dawned bright and beautiful, with the temperature in a blessedly moderate zone. Joe started the fishermen off, then went to sit under the umbrella on the dock. In another hour, Lia would be back from her first round of fishing. While in his official capacity as tournament sponsor, Joe couldn't play favorites, but right now he was just plain Joe.

And plain Joe wanted his woman to win.

His woman. That did have a ring to it, although Lia had no idea what kind of ring.

Skipper's tail thumped against the wooden deck. Someone was coming. Joe swiveled to smile at a familiar face.

Travis crossed the dock to clap Joe on the shoulder. "You sure about this, Joe?"

Joe winked and reached out to accept a small paper sack from his buddy. "Positive. And, hey, thanks for the help."

"No problem, man," Travis said. "Just don't let my wife know I was involved." He shrugged. "Unless Lia's happy. In that case, you can go ahead and give me all the credit."

Lia set her rod down on the boat and picked up the oars. The fish were biting, but Lia had no tolerance for fishing today. She owed Joe an apology, and she'd failed to deliver it this morning. The tournament would end soon—no time like the present to right the wrong.

Ten minutes later, she tied up her boat at the dock and crossed the distance to where the tournament sponsor sat with his dog, Skipper. "I just want to say—"

"No, Lia, I need to tell you something." He rose to grasp her hand. "Come with me. I've got something to show you."

She followed Joe to the bait shop and ducked beneath the promotional banner that covered the door. "Where are we going?"

"Close your eyes." Joe wrapped his arm around her waist and nudged her forward. "Okay, now open them."

Lia gasped as she took in the transformation. While she knew she stood inside Joe's Bait and Tackle, she might have been anywhere else. Any reminder of the building's former purpose had been removed in favor of pristine white walls and gleaming white rafters. The old wood floor had been buffed to a gentle shine, and the windows were framed in shutters that had no trace of cobwebs or dust.

She caught sight of the framed print between the big windows on the lakeside wall. "Oh, Joe, it's the Chase print *Idle Hours*."

"Your mama helped me with that. She also told me that you'd probably prefer an empty room that needed furnishing to anything I might pick out." He paused. "You're not saying anything. Did I do okay?"

"Did you?" She leaped into his embrace. "Yes, you did great, Joe, but—"

"But what?"

Lia lifted her face to look up at him. "I love this place, but I love you more. As beautiful as it is, I don't want it if you're not here."

He smiled as he touched her nose. "I'm glad you think that, because I've decided to put off buying that RV."

"You have?"

Joe nodded. "Yeah, you know that empty lot next door to the shop?"

"That one?" She pointed out the side window. "It's tiny."

"Sure, but a man doesn't need much space to set up a proper bait shop."

She gave him a skeptical look. "You're not intending to open a bait shop next to the Idle Hours, are you?"

Joe chuckled and gave Lia a hug. "No, of course not, but the money I made from selling that lot to Bill Jenson ought to pay for a new shop down closer to that special fishing spot I like."

Lia walked to the window to look out at the lot in question. "What's Bill Jenson going to put on that lot?"

"He mentioned something about a little farmer's market. You know, a place where farmers can bring their produce for sale."

"Joe, that's absolutely perfect." She returned to kiss him soundly. "And so are you."

The door opened, and Vic stuck his head inside. "Excuse me, but, Joe, they're ready for you to announce the winners."

"Be right there." He stole a quick kiss from Lia. "So I'm on a roll?"

She smiled. "Yes, you're on a roll."

"Good." He linked arms with Lia and led her outside. "Let's go get this tournament finished."

Depositing Lia in the deck chair, Joe climbed the platform to test the microphone. Most of the town of Verde Point stood assembled on the grounds behind what would soon be formerly known as Joe's Bait and Tackle.

He quickly went through the names of the winners, handing out each prize and trophy until the table beside the speaker's platform held only one item. Joe picked up the small gold plaque and smiled.

"This one's for our newest resident, Miss Lia Stephanos. Come on up and get your prize, Lia."

Heart pounding, Lia made her way through the crowd with Skipper following close behind. When she reached the platform, she looked up at Joe. "What's this for?"

"Just read it, Lia."

She accepted the plaque, then held it to her chest. "Thank you, Joe, but I didn't do anything to deserve a plaque."

"Read it out loud," someone in the crowd said.

Lia looked up to see that the source of the female voice was Ruby Wells. Beside her stood Mother. Joe grabbed her hand and gave it a squeeze. "Go ahead, hon," he said.

"All right." Lia held the plaque up and cleared her throat. "To Lia Stephanos, a real keeper. Will you marry me?"

Epilogue

One year later

I brought the paint chips, Joe. Are you sure you want to do this yourself?"

Joe looked up at his wife, then pulled her down into the recliner beside him, mindful of her advanced stage of pregnancy. "Yes, I'm sure. Are you sure you're feeling all right? What did the doctor say about, well, you know?"

"My heart?" Lia smiled. "Healthy as a horse. The cardiologist wants to see me next week to confirm, but everything seems fine."

"And the baby?"

Lia smiled. "Well, that's interesting." She glanced around to see if her mother was in the kitchen.

"Cordelia's at the restaurant. Travis finished the last of the flooring this morning, and the movers came this afternoon. She will sleep in her own apartment over the Idle Hours tonight."

"That fast?"

Joe nodded. "I promised her I'd take you over later so she can show it off." He paused to turn her face toward him. "Now, about the doctor's report. You've got me worried. I mean, it's not every day a man of my age becomes a father for the first time."

She nudged his ribs with her elbow. "Well, Joe, I'm no young kid, either."

"You're only thirty-nine, honey."

"And you're only fifty-three."

He kissed the tip of her nose. "All right. Now, about the baby."

"The baby is just fine." She paused to look up into his eyes. "Did I say 'baby'?"

"Yes," he said, "I believe you did. Why?"

"Because the proper term would be babies. Two babies. A boy and a girl." She kissed her shocked husband. "No more idle hours for us, Joe Corbin. Looks like we will land two keepers."

KATHLEEN Y'BARBO

Kathleen Y'Barbo is a tenth-generation Texan and mother of three grown sons and a teenage daughter. She is a graduate of Texas A&M University and an award winning novelist of Christian fiction whose first published work jumped onto the Christian Booksellers Association bestseller list in its first month of release. Kathleen is a former treasurer for the American Christian Fiction Writers and is a member of Inspirational Writers Alive, Words for the Journey, and The Writers Guild. In addition, she speaks on the craft of writing to schools and writing groups and teaches an online creative writing course through Lamar University in Beaumont, Texas. Find out more about Kathleen at www.kathleenybarbo.com.

A Letter to Our Readers

Dear Readers:

In order that we might better contribute to your reading enjoyment, we would appreciate your taking a few minutes to respond to the following questions. When completed, please return to the following: Fiction Editor, Barbour Publishing, Inc., P.O. Box 719, Uhrichsville, OH 44683.

1. Did you enjoy reading *Kentucky Keepers*?
   ❑ Very much—I would like to see more books like this.
   ❑ Moderately—I would have enjoyed it more if _____

   _____

   _____

2. What influenced your decision to purchase this book?
   (Check those that apply.)
   ❑ Cover   ❑ Back cover copy   ❑ Title   ❑ Price
   ❑ Friends   ❑ Publicity   ❑ Other

3. Which story was your favorite?
   ❑ *Hook, Line, and Sinker*   ❑ *Lured by Love*
   ❑ *Reeling Her In*   ❑ *Idle Hours*

4. Please check your age range:
   ❑ Under 18   ❑ 18–24   ❑ 25–34
   ❑ 35–45   ❑ 46–55   ❑ Over 55

5. How many hours per week do you read? _____

Name _____

Occupation _____

Address _____

City_____ State _____ Zip _____

E-mail_____

HEARTSONG
PRESENTS

If you love Christian
romance…

$10.⁹⁹

You'll love Heartsong Presents' inspiring and faith-filled romances by today's very best Christian authors. . .DiAnn Mills, Wanda E. Brunstetter, and Yvonne Lehman, to mention a few!

When you join Heartsong Presents, you'll enjoy four brand-new, mass market, 176-page books—two contemporary and two historical—that will build you up in your faith when you discover God's role in every relationship you read about!

Imagine. . .four new romances every four weeks—with men and women like you who long to meet the one God has chosen as the love of their lives—all for the low price of $10.99 postpaid.

To join, simply visit www.heartsongpresents.com or complete the coupon below and mail it to the address provided.

Mass Market, 176 Pages

- -

YES! Sign me up for Hearts♥ng!

NEW MEMBERSHIPS WILL BE SHIPPED IMMEDIATELY!
Send no money now. We'll bill you only $10.99 postpaid with your first shipment of four books. Or for faster action, call 1-740-922-7280.

NAME _____

ADDRESS_____

CITY_____ STATE _____ ZIP _____

**MAIL TO: HEARTSONG PRESENTS, P.O. Box 721, Uhrichsville, Ohio 44683
or sign up at WWW.HEARTSONGPRESENTS.COM**

ADPG05